"Darn it, Serena, what's got under your butt?"

Instantly he called back the words, but too late. She'd goaded him beyond reason, and now she needed a lesson in…something.

"You!" She shouted the word in his face. "*You're* what's gotten under my—" She broke off with a gasp. "Oh! I mean under my…whatever."

Carleton bit back an irrational urge to laugh. "Okay, Sis, have it your way. What's gotten under your *'whatever'?*"

She puffed herself up again. Toe-to-toe with him, she jabbed her forefinger at his chest. "Not 'Sis'! Serena! You can't even remember my name! You don't know who I am!"

"I sure as hell know who you are, Serena," he insisted. "You're that spunky little thorn in my side makin' my life miserable!"

He didn't know where those words came from either, but they sure felt good clearing his throat….

Dear Reader,

This month we've covered all the bases. You'll laugh, you'll cry, *you'll find romance*. And if you're interested in tall, dark and handsome cowboys, look no further than *Lost Acres Bride* by rising talent Lynna Banning. In this fun and frolicking Western, a rugged, by-the-book rancher must contend with the female spitfire who inherits a piece of his land—and gets a piece of his heart! Don't miss it!

The illustrious Tori Phillips returns this month with the final book in the CAVENDISH CHRONICLES, *Three Dog Knight*. This "prequel" to *Midsummer's Knight* is about a painfully shy earl whose marriage of convenience must survive the machinations of an evil sister-in-law. In *Blackthorne,* a medieval novel by Ruth Langan, a nursemaid shows the lord of Blackthorne how to love again and helps him unravel the mystery that has haunted his estate for years.

Rounding out the month is *Apache Fire* by longtime author Elizabeth Lane. In this emotional Western, a Native American army scout on the run from vigilantes finds shelter in the arms of a beautiful young widow.

Whatever your tastes in reading, you'll be sure to find a romantic journey back to the past between the covers of a Harlequin Historicals® novel.

Sincerely,
Tracy Farrell, Senior Editor

Please address questions and book requests to:
Harlequin Reader Service
U.S.: 3010 Walden Ave., P.O. Box 1325, Buffalo, NY 14269
Canadian: P.O. Box 609, Fort Erie, Ont. L2A 5X3

LOST ACRES
BRIDE

LYNNA BANNING

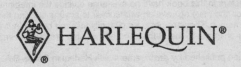

HARLEQUIN®

TORONTO • NEW YORK • LONDON
AMSTERDAM • PARIS • SYDNEY • HAMBURG
STOCKHOLM • ATHENS • TOKYO • MILAN • MADRID
PRAGUE • WARSAW • BUDAPEST • AUCKLAND

ISBN 0-373-29037-3

LOST ACRES BRIDE

Copyright © 1998 by Carolyn Woolston

Books by Lynna Banning

Harlequin Historicals

Western Rose #310
Wildwood #374
Lost Acres Bride #437

LYNNA BANNING

has combined a lifelong love of history and literature into a satisfying new career as a writer. Born in Oregon, she has lived in Northern California most of her life, graduating from Scripps College and embarking on her career as an editor and technical writer, and later as a high school English teacher.

An amateur pianist and harpsichordist, Lynna performs on psaltery and recorders with two Renaissance ensembles and teaches music in her spare time. Currently she is learning to play the harp.

She enjoys hearing from her readers. You may write to her directly at P.O. Box 324, Felton, CA 95018.

For Dad

Acknowledgments

With grateful appreciation to Robert Banning,
Jean Banning Strickland and Floyd Strickland.

Chapter One

Douglas County, Oregon, 1887

Serena bowed her head until her chin grazed the collar of her dusty red gingham shirt and gripped the mare's saddle horn with both hands. *Lord, if You're listening, I need Your help!*

The journey from Ohio had been harder than she'd expected. Much harder. Her backside ached from the hours in the saddle, and she wondered if she could dismount without stumbling.

Please, God, I'm tired and now that I'm finally here, I'm scared. Don't let me make a fool of myself out here. At least not until I've got what I came for.

She clicked her tongue at the mare and moved to the crest of the hill. In the wide valley below, fields of green alfalfa undulated like an emerald sea, whipped by the hot July wind. Serena caught her breath. How beautiful it was! So unbelievably beautiful.

And it was hers! Part of it, anyway. She urged her mount along the trail skirting the meadow toward the white-painted ranch house at the end of the rutted road. Dismounting unsteadily, she removed her hat and flapped it against the trail dust clinging to her riding skirt. Then, with a twist of her head, she tossed back the single thick braid that fell over her shoulder.

At her knock, the front door swung open and a young woman in a blue-striped work dress peered out. The thin face was flushed, and she balanced a squalling baby on one hip.

"What do you want?" the impatient voice queried.

Serena blinked. "I'm sorry to bother you, ma'am. I'm looking for Mr. Carleton Kearney."

The sharp hazel eyes narrowed. "What for?"

Taken aback, Serena hesitated. "I—I have some business to discuss with him." She watched the woman's flat bosom expand and then deflate as she shifted the child to the other hip and pursed her unsmiling lips.

"What kind of business?"

"It's a legal matter, Mrs. Kearney. If you could just tell him I'm—"

"I expect he's in the corral, next to the barn." The woman jerked her narrow chin to indicate the direction.

Serena's gaze traveled past the wide porch to the trim, russet-stained outbuilding beyond. A split rail fence encircled a large open space, inside which a man was working with a horse. "Yes, I see. Thank you, Mrs.—"

The door slammed before she could finish. Serena flinched. What was the matter with the woman? Was it so obvious, then, that she was part Indian, despite the way Mama had raised her? Even Mama had dressed in print dresses with petticoats and proper drawers; she'd done it to please Pa, and so that her daughters would fit into the white community. Now Serena wondered if her normally fair skin was so tanned she looked...foreign.

Well, no matter. She'd encountered such rudeness before. She was here, and she'd come to stay. Drawing a quick gulp of air into her lungs, she stepped off the porch and headed for the corral. Pa had said folks out in Oregon were generally friendly. But then Pa hadn't spoken to anyone in Wildwood Valley for more than twenty years. She hoped Mr. Kearney would at least be polite.

She studied the tall, well-built figure in the corral yard. Close to forty, she guessed from the silver in his dark sideburns, but he moved like a much younger man, his motions quick, his body relaxed. He walked with an unstudied loose-limbed grace that made her breath catch.

He held the restive roan mustang with a short length of rope in one hand while he advanced toward it, talking softly. "Whoa, boy, that's it. Easy, now. Easy." Keeping the rope taut, he reached his free hand to stroke the animal's nose. "Easy, boy," he repeated, his voice gentle. "You're a good old boy. Easy, now."

The horse backed away, but the man kept on talking, soft and low. Little by little, the roan settled down, then took a hesitant step forward. Serena knew just how the animal felt. It was hard to trust.

"Easy, now. Come on, boy." The man smoothed one hand over the roan's neck. "That's right, eas—"

"Mr. Kearney?"

The horse jerked away.

Eyes the color of a summer sky pinned her right where she stood. Under his dark mustache, the well-shaped lips pressed together into a grim line. "Just who the hell are you and what are you doing out here?"

Serena blanched at his tone. Hard and cold as steel, the sound was so unlike the low, gentle murmur of a moment ago she wasn't sure they came from the same person.

"I— Oh, I'm sorry!"

He swung away from the horse and planted his dusty leather boots in front of her. "Sorry," he repeated, his tone skeptical.

Serena gathered her courage and lifted her gaze from

the hip-hugging denim trousers to the buttons of his shirt, then moved up to the bronzed, regular features and the unkempt dark hair visible under the wide-brimmed hat. She avoided the penetrating blue eyes, concentrated instead on his forehead, now creased into a frown.

"Sorry," he repeated in a low drawl, "is a word overused by the blundering fools of the world. Don't you know better than to interrupt a man working with a horse?"

Serena raised her chin a notch. "Under the circumstances, 'sorry' is the best I can do. The animal is already spooked."

One dark eyebrow quirked. "Would you mind telling me—"

"My name is Serena Hull," she said quickly. "Jeremiah Hull was my father."

Carleton Kearney rocked back on his boot heels and stared at her. "Jeremiah Hull," he echoed. "Well, what do you know. We always wondered..." His voice trailed off. He nodded slowly, studying her. "And Walks Dancing is your mother. I should have known," he said in a gravelly voice. "You've got her eyes."

Serena gaped at him. "You knew my mother?"

"No, I didn't. I saw a photograph of her once. Jeremiah sent it to my brother's wife, Jessamyn Kearney. Some years back it was. There were three little girls in the picture, too. You've grown a good bit since then."

With an effort, Serena jerked her thoughts away from her mother. "Mr. Kearney, I've come out from Ohio, where my mother and father lived, because...because..." Her throat closed over the words.

"Alone?" he said, his tone disbelieving. "From Ohio? How in the hell—?"

"From Stark County, yes." She hesitated. "I came part of the way with a wagon train. When they turned south at the Platte River junction, an army cavalry unit let me travel with them. I rode the rest of the way on horseback.''

"Jehosaphat," he breathed. "How old are you, anyway?''

Serena struggled to appear unruffled. "Mr. Kearney, is my age of concern here?''

"You mean is it any of my business? Can't say that it is, no.''

She flicked a glance at him. The steady blue eyes were calculating. He had guessed how difficult it had been. Could he also see through the facade of calm she maintained to mask her unease? She worked to keep her voice steady.

"I'll be twenty-five next month. Old enough to travel two thousand miles to claim what's mine.''

She saw him come instantly to attention, like a hawk protecting its kill.

"The ranch, is that it? That run-down spread my brother and I sold to Jeremiah years ago? Hell, I never thought he'd—''

"It's mine, now, Mr. Kearney. In his will, Pa named me and my sisters to inherit, and I've got legal papers to prove ownership. We never knew he even *had* a ranch until he—''

"How'd he die?'' Carleton interrupted.

Serena swallowed hard and stared down at the tips of her riding boots. "Mama went into a white woman's dress store in Canton City one day,'' she said dully. "When she came out a man called her a name and when she didn't respond, another man shot her. Pa went to help her, and they...they shot him, too.''

"Bastards,'' Carleton breathed. "Damn Yankee bastards.''

"About the ranch, Mr. Kearney,'' she reminded him.

He looked at her sharply, his eyes blazing fire. As she

watched, they cooled into two icy blue pools. "Well, now, Miss Hull. I don't mind telling you it goes hard on me to give up that land. It's near a thousand acres of winter grazing pasture. After Jeremiah up and left, I never expected—"

"Pa always said you were an honest man, Mr. Kearney. I wouldn't have come all the way out here if I thought—"

His voice hardened. "Don't push me, Sis."

Serena waited, gathering her thoughts and her courage. "I don't like this any more than you do, Mr. Kearney. Or Mrs. Kearney either, with a new baby and all."

"*Mrs.* Kearney?" A flicker of pain crossed his face.

"The woman at the house," Serena reminded.

"Mrs. Kearney is dead," he said in a flat voice. "That's my daughter, Alice. Stepdaughter," he corrected. "Nowadays, she looks older than her years. The baby is my daughter, Sarah. My wife..." He paused to draw in a long breath. "My wife died when she was born."

Aghast, Serena stared into tired eyes that seemed to look right through her. "Oh, I'm so sorry," she whispered. "So awfully sorry."

He said nothing. He turned away, working the horse rope between his two hands. "Can't be helped."

Unable to think of one sensible thing to say, Serena stared at his back. The broad shoulders drooped for an instant, then he slapped one end of the rope hard against his thigh. "Not likely you're gonna ranch out here on your own." He uttered it as a statement, not a question.

"Yes, I am. I came to take possession. I plan to raise cattle."

"Alone?"

Serena hesitated. "If I have to, yes. I left my two younger sisters with Pa's maiden aunt back in Ohio. We sold everything we had to finance this trip. You see, I intend to make a new home out here for us—Jessie and

Mary Irene, and myself. I—we can't get far enough away from Stark County."

The rancher studied her with assessing blue eyes, and her heart lurched.

After a moment, he shook his head and coiled the rope in his hands, muttering something under his breath.

"I beg your pardon?"

"Just some country words I reserve for green city folks who come out here thinking ranching's like raising turnips in their backyard."

"I think no such thing, Mr. Kearney. I'm prepared to work, and work hard. In fact, I—"

Carleton tossed the rope onto a post in the fence and pivoted away from her. "Come on, Miss Hull. This is a ranch, not a vegetable garden. You'd best let me show you what you're up against."

Without looking at her, Carleton tramped toward the gate at the far end of the corral yard. "Hurry it up," he snapped. "My horse needs working."

He moved to the barn door. "Thad," he shouted through the opening. "Take over out here."

His lips set, Carleton tramped off in the direction of Hull's Lost Acres. The hands at the Double K had fancy names for everything; Lost Acres was their designation for the sections of land he and his brother, Ben, had sold off to Ben's deputy over two decades ago. The name didn't make him smile this morning.

Balls of fire, nobody'd heard a peep from Jeremiah for twenty-five years, and now this chit of a girl rides out plain as you please, claims she's his daughter and says she's gonna ranch it? Not unless hell froze over. He'd bet money she didn't know beans about cows.

Besides, for years he'd used that land as winter pasture for his own stock, filled his watering pond from the spring at the bottom of the draw, even put up a makeshift barn to house the bales of alfalfa hay his crew harvested each summer. He wasn't going to give up one square inch if he didn't have to.

On purpose, he did not alter his long-legged gait as he strode past his own neat, outsize barn—"big as a chautauqua tent," his foreman joked. He took the shortcut, heading across the lush field of rye to the far meadow where Hull's Gate marked the entrance to the adjacent ranch.

The girl waded into the waist-high grainfield after him. It surprised him that she could keep up, considering that newfangled garment she was wearing—some back East kind of skirt split up the middle so she could ride, he guessed. It was neither a pair of trousers nor a proper dress, but some kind of outlandish cross between the two.

A town woman, he fumed. A *northern* town woman. Probably used to ladies' quilting socials and polite talk over tea. One look at the sprawling odd-shaped spread her daddy had called a ranch and she'd turn tail and scuttle back to Ohio. Or melt in the searing late-summer heat, rent a room in town and forget all about ranching. Either way, he'd bet she wouldn't last the day. About five minutes on Jeremiah's ramshackle acres ought to do the trick.

He reached the first of the gentle hills between his ranch house and the gate to Jeremiah's place and cast a covert glance back at the figure laboring at his heels. Somehow she'd managed to flail her way through the hip-deep rye and still keep her head up. She was breathing hard, though. The material of her red-checked shirt rose and fell as her chest heaved. Her hat had slipped off. Held by the chin thong around her neck, the brim bounced against the single thick braid that hung down her slim back. He noted her black Stetson was well creased and had small feathers and shells decorating the sweatband. It looked like a Klamath Indian chief's ceremonial neck piece.

That figured. Her mother had been a Modoc. The girl

was half Indian and half Scots. A half-breed. It couldn't have been easy for her back in Ohio. That might explain her unnerving air of quiet stoicism.

And it also might explain why she was savvy enough not to ride her horse through his winter grainfield. Didn't explain why she spooked the mustang, though. On second thought, maybe it did. Ohio had more farms than green horses.

"Mr. Kearney," she panted behind him.

He raised one hand in acknowledgement, but did not slow down or turn his head. The quicker he got this over with, the quicker she'd leave and he could get back to that mustang.

"Mr. Kearney, is—" She stopped to catch her breath. "Is this a hay field?"

"Rye."

"When— When do you cut it?"

"Summer." He sighted the Lost Acres gate and lengthened his stride. "Crew comes next week," he called over his shoulder.

She floundered in the thick grass behind him, her split riding skirt slapping against the nodding grain heads. She had to take two steps to his one. He noticed she was careful to put her right foot in the depression his own boot had made to trample a minimum of grain.

Maybe he should have taken a horse. Riding double would have been faster, but it would cause more damage to the rye. Besides, he didn't want her behind him on a horse. He didn't want to get that close to her. He hadn't been anywhere near a woman since Ella died.

The familiar rush of anger and black despair settled in his gut at the thought of his wife. He clenched his jaw against the choking ache in his throat and lengthened his stride. *Why did she have to die?*

In mindless fury, he strode on through the gray-green

field and at last came up to the wide gate marking the entry to Jeremiah's property. He rammed both palms hard against the wood. *Why?*

He lowered his head and shut his eyes while the girl caught up to him. The swish of her skirt stopped at his elbow.

"Mr. Kearney?"

He didn't trust himself to answer.

"Mr. Kearney, is this…?" Her voice trailed off as she scanned the barren expanse of earth on the other side of the fenced rye field. "Is this it?"

"Yep. All one thousand acres." He found great satisfaction in the words, even more from the look on her face as she stared out across the sparse vegetation. She had no right to be here, to be young and alive when Ella was dead. He wanted to punish her for that.

He watched her dark eyes widen, the thick black eyebrows arch upward. "Just a—a barn? No house?" Her voice sounded pinched.

"Not even a barn," Carleton corrected. "Can't tell from here, but that's a hay shelter—open on the backside."

She thought a moment. "Is there a source of water?"

Carleton hesitated. He'd have to tell her about the spring. It was the one valuable asset Lost Acres Ranch had, and the only one he couldn't do without. His stock needed that water.

"In the draw. Can't see it from here. Serves both spreads—the Double K and Lost Acres."

"Lost Acres," she breathed. She turned away from him, gazing out over the land. "Oh, I see. I thought surely there would be a house of some sort. My sisters can't join me until I have a place for them to live."

"Yeah, well. Might be smarter to live in town, give up this idea about ranching."

Serena looked him full in the face. "You don't like me, do you?"

Carleton opened his mouth, then shut it with a snap. "To be frank, ma'am, I haven't got an opinion. I'm just stating what's obvious. You're a single female with no ranching know-how, a city-bred lady with two sisters—not one man among the lot of you. If you don't mind my saying so, ranching isn't a refined pastime like quilting or playing whist on Sunday. You're not going to make it out here on your own."

Her slight frame stiffened, and she looked directly at him with fire blazing in her chocolate brown eyes. "Mr. Kearney, must I contact my attorney in Canton City to prove this ranch is mine?"

"I grant it's yours, Miss Hull. Don't see what that's got to do with the problem. A bill of sale doesn't make a person a rancher."

"And it isn't pretty words that make a man a gentleman, either," she observed quietly. "The least you could do is shake my hand and wish me luck."

Carleton's jaw dropped. Since when did he get ordered around on his own land? Well, maybe not his own land in this case, but—dammit, it was pepper pots like her that gave modern women a bad name. Next thing you know they'll be voting! Still, that remark about being a gentleman stung.

Firming his lips together, he thrust out his hand. "Good luck," he growled.

She laid her small, warm hand in his and pressed his fingers. "Thank you, Mr. Kearney." She sent him a shy smile that lit up stars in the depths of her dark eyes. "I'm sure you're right. I'll need lots of luck."

He dropped her hand as if it burned him. "Damn right."

Again, her startlingly direct gaze met his. "You think

I'm going to give up, don't you, Mr. Kearney? Before I've even got started?''

"I do. Only sensible thing, the way I see it.'' He'd give her a day—maybe two—tramping over the hard ground she'd inherited before she'd figure out this was no place for a lady and hightail it back to Stark County. Hell, she had no house to live in, no stock, no feed. It'd be kind of fun watching her wrestle with reality.

She nodded. "Sensible, Mr. Kearney, would have been to remain in Ohio. But that would mean staying in a community where my sisters and I were not accepted because our mother was an Indian. My younger sister, Jessie, wants to teach school. She's sixteen. Mary Irene—she's only twelve—can't understand why she has no friends in town. And I— Well, never mind about me. We thought it would be better to start over in some other place. I intend to make a home out here for myself and my sisters, Mr. Kearney. And that's all there is to it.''

She pushed open the gate and spoke over her shoulder as she marched through it onto her land. "I'll want to buy some cows. And I'll need some lumber to make that structure over there into a temporary shelter.''

Dumbfounded, Carleton stared after the slim figure in the swinging skirt as she headed toward the run-down three-sided barn. Great balls of— She planned to live in his hay barn?

"Hold on a minute, Sis.'' He caught up to her. "What am I gonna do with my winter rye and alfalfa? I've got a crew coming in—''

"Yes,'' she interrupted. "Next week, you said.''

"It's winter feed for my stock. It's got to be kept dry.''

"I know that, too,'' she said evenly. "I'll make you a bargain, Mr. Kearney. If you'll advise me how to convert this barn into a house of sorts, I'll share my roof with your hay bales. And,'' she continued with a quick glance at his expression, "you can continue to water your stock from my spring."

His head spun. Before he could recover, she took a step toward him and stuck out her hand. "Is it a deal?"

Carleton blinked. She might not have the best judgment, but her brain worked pretty good. She was sharper than he'd thought. In fact, he'd swear he'd just been blown over by nothing stronger than a soft, warm wind.

Balls of fire, a woman in his hay barn. She'd maneuvered him into it, but if he lived to be a hundred, he'd never understand how. And he knew he didn't have a choice. The land was hers—any court in Oregon would rule that the spring and his hay barn belonged to her.

He took her small, firm hand. "Deal," he growled. He released her fingers at once, turned away and stomped off into his rye field.

Chapter Two

The freight wagon driven by mercantile owner Otto Frieder rattled down the road past the Double K corral. Carleton and his nephew, Thad Kearney, turned together to watch the rickety vehicle—loaded to the top slat with lumber, rolls of tar paper, a keg of nails and various lumpy gunnysacks—disappear over the rise. Behind the wagon, dressed in a blue denim shirt and brown riding skirt, Serena Hull stepped her mount at a pace sedate enough to avoid the dust kicked up by the horses ahead.

Thad shoved his hat back on his unruly black curls. "That her?"

Carleton scowled at his nephew. "Hell yes, that's her." At nineteen, his brother's older son exhibited the same forthright manner and playful sense of humor Ben had at the same age. Still, Thad was a top hand. Carleton valued the boy almost as much as he did his ranch foreman, Lyle Bartel.

"Helluva good-lookin'—" Thad shot a twinkly-eyed look at his uncle "—horse," he finished.

Carleton expelled a breath. "You're blinder than I thought, Thad. Maybe you should stick to raising chickens and forget about breeding cow ponies. Give me a hand here."

Thad lifted the bridle from Carleton's hand and slipped the bit between the roan's teeth. "Easy, boy. Easy now."

When the saddle cinch was tight, Carleton mounted and stepped the horse around the perimeter of the corral.

"She looks good, boss."

Carleton snorted. He knew Thad meant Serena, not the mustang he'd saddle-broken. "Too much spirit, if you ask me," he quipped, assessing the roan's uneven gait. "Needs more work with the rope."

Thad grinned. "And maybe a good rubdown."

"Hell's fire, kid, don't you think of anything but women?"

"Nope. Nuthin' better to think about."

Carleton snorted again and dismounted in a jerky motion. The truth was, Thad's perfectly normal male instincts nettled him. Ever since Ella died, his own body had felt dried up as an old piece of leather. The fact that his nephew's male drive perked like boiling coffee at the mere sight of a female set his teeth on edge. He didn't blame Thad; he blamed Ella. A part of him had died with her.

"Come on, you randy young pup. Time to muck out the barn."

Thad draped an arm around Carleton's shoulders. "You know, Uncle Carl, this barn gets cleaned so often it squeaks when I walk past it! It's been a year since Aunt Ella passed on—isn't it about time to stop all this scrubbing and start—"

He ducked the cuff Carleton directed at him.

"Mind your own business, Thad."

"I'm trying, Carl," Thad replied, his tone serious. "Trouble is, you're part of my business, seein' as how I work for you. Now, the way I see it—" he danced out of

Carleton's reach "—we oughta leave cleaning out the barn 'til later...."

He took refuge behind the still-saddled roan. "And go see what Miss Serena's up to."

Carleton stopped short. "She's turning my hay barn into a house," he grumbled. "Damn pigheaded woman."

"Pigheaded, huh? Seems to me, any man dumb enough to build a barn on property he doesn't own deserves—"

"Thad?" Carleton interjected, his voice low and quiet.

"Yeah?"

"Shut up. Just shut the hell up."

The young man's grin widened, revealing even, white teeth. "I will if we can go see Serena."

"Oh, hell's bells, saddle up, then." Carleton stuffed his booted toe in the stirrup and swung himself up on the roan. "I'd better go with you. I wouldn't trust you within a mile of a decent woman."

Serena wiped her dirty hands on her bandanna and watched Otto Frieder lift down the last of her wagonload of supplies. Instead of two-by-sixes and nails, in her mind's eye she saw a little house with four complete walls and clean plank flooring. Inside, she envisioned the dry sink, washtub and tiny potbellied stove she'd bought in town. The new wall would have two glass windows and a front door wide enough to get her trunk through. The remainder of the lumber Otto unloaded would be used to build a privacy wall between her living area and the hay bales she knew would be stacked within the enclosure after the haying crew finished.

Her makeshift quarters would be barely livable with the winter wind whistling through the chinks in the walls, but it would do for the time being. It would have to. She'd dipped so deep into the savings, she didn't have money enough to buy even a small herd of cattle and build a proper house, too. The house would have to wait until next spring, after she sold off her first crop of beef cattle at market price. Then she could send train fare for Jessie and Mary Irene and build a real home for them.

Oh, how she missed them! Her sisters were so close they could almost read each others' minds. Mary Irene, particularly. Her youngest sister had known something was wrong the minute Serena had walked into the yard that awful night, had begged Serena to tell her what had happened down at the river. She couldn't tell her—Mary Irene had been only three years old at the time. She couldn't tell anyone, not even Mama. Especially not Mama. She'd been afraid of what her mother might do. But she'd held on to her youngest sister's thin frame and cried and cried until the hurt had eased.

Oh, she longed to have them here with her. Jessie could continue her education, maybe even have a school of her own when she was a few years older. And Mary Irene…she was so alone. Now all she had was Aunt Letty, and Aunt Letty was old and confused and a little mean.

But she couldn't ask them to come and live in a hay barn—half a hay barn—where the air was thick with dust and chaff and the only place to sleep was the tiny loft, accessible by climbing up the ladder propped against the opening in the ceiling. Jessie's lungs were weak enough as it was.

But, oh my, she ached to see them! She'd never again scold Mary Irene for scorching a pan of cookies, and Jessie could read by lantern light until all hours and Serena vowed she'd never say a word. *Oh, God, just let me get money enough for a house and the train fare. Please, God. In the spring.*

"That's all of it, Miss Serena," Otto Frieder called from the wagon seat. "I go back to town now. Anna-Marie, she makes strudel for supper tonight. You are welcome to come, too.''

"Thank you again, Mr. Frieder, but no. Now that I have a sink and a stove, I'm going to set up housekeeping this very afternoon.''

She waved goodbye and turned toward the barn. The nights were still warm enough to sleep outside in comfort, but last night she'd eaten cold beans from a can before she rolled herself up in the blanket and laid her head on her saddle like that nice cavalry sergeant had shown her. Tonight she'd eat a hot supper, then heat water and sponge off in the tin washtub before she made up her pallet in the loft.

And tomorrow, she'd figure out how to build a wall to enclose her tiny space.

At the sound of hoofbeats, she pivoted toward the road. Mr. Kearney, she guessed. She recognized the roan he'd been working yesterday. The other rider looked younger and not as muscular. He clattered up first.

"Miss Serena?" He leaned down and smiled. "I'm Thaddeus Kearney, Carl's nephew. Everybody calls me Thad.''

Serena acknowledged them both with a nod. "Thad. Mr. Kearney."

"I was named after my grandfather," Thad volunteered with a grin. "He ran the newspaper before Ma came out from Boston. Guess that's why I'm so smart.''

Serena bit back a smile and studied the young man. A little younger than she was, but taller, with soft green eyes and black hair.

"I look like my Ma," Thad ventured, evidently noting her perusal. "Leastways my eyes do. The rest of me—" he puffed out his chest and grinned down at her. "—is pretty much like my dad, right down to my—"

"That's enough," Carleton cautioned.

"Toes," the younger man finished with a wicked grin.

"Congratulations," Serena offered.

Thad's cheeks turned rosy and Carleton chuckled. He slapped his nephew across the shoulders. "He's a good boy, Miss Hull. Just gets a little rambunctious around females. Too much mash in his feed, I guess."

She couldn't help laughing. Mash, she knew, was for laying hens.

Carleton gestured at the lumber Otto Frieder had stacked against the barn wall. "Going to hire a crew?"

Serena started. "A crew? Oh, no. I mean I don't think it will be necessary." She couldn't afford to hire labor and still have enough cash to buy the cows she needed to start a herd of her own.

Carleton stroked his mustache. "You build many houses back in Stark County?"

Damn him! He was baiting her. "I— Well, no. But I'm sure I could learn."

Thad sobered all of a sudden. "You mean you're gonna make this old barn into a house all by—" He closed his mouth and the green eyes widened.

"Yes, I am."

"Huh! I bet you don't even own a hammer."

Serena bridled. "Oh, yes I do. I bought one in town today."

The two men stared at her.

"It's here, somewhere. Over there—on that nail keg!"

"You hear that, Uncle Carl? She's got a brand-new hammer!"

For the first time in over a year, Carleton felt a smile tug at his mouth. "Yep," he said in a dry voice. "A hammer's good. A saw'd be better, but a hammer's good."

"I've got a saw!" Serena blurted. "I bought—"

"One in town today," both men finished in unison.

Thad pushed his hat back with his forefinger. "Balls of fire, ma'am, you're a regular one-man building crew!"

"Thad." Carleton's voice took on a warning tone.

An uneasy silence descended as Serena looked from the younger to the older man. Carleton's dark blue eyes and Thad's now-smouldering green ones stared back at her and she found herself momentarily at a loss for words. Finally, she straightened her spine and raised her chin.

"I bought a washtub, too. And a stove and a dry sink and a kitchen table and two chairs." She paused to draw breath. "And I see nothing funny about any of it."

Carleton noticed the faint rose stain grow under her skin, and a dart pricked his conscience. It was no laughing matter, a young woman alone on a hardscrabble ranch, trying to build a new life for herself and her orphaned sisters. As much as he questioned her good sense in deciding to stay, he had to admire her courage. She wasn't going to give up without a fight. She stood before him, her hands on her hips, her dark eyes flashing. Yesterday he thought he'd enjoy watching her wrestle with the problems she'd encounter. Wrestle and lose. Today an unexpected part of him wanted her to succeed.

Thad got down off his horse and faced her. "Miss Serena, I'd like to offer my services. I'll build your place, make it good and snug before winter. That is, if you'll hire me as your foreman when you get your herd started."

Her mouth dropped open.

"Hey," Carleton interjected. "You work for me! Or can you remember that far back?"

Thad flashed the older man an unfathomable look. "Maybe not, Uncle Carl. Whaddya say, Miss Serena?"

"I can't pay you," she said simply.

"Don't have to, at least not right now," he answered. "You can pay me my back wages when I—we—sell off your first beeves."

Serena bit her lip. Her mother's words echoed in her mind. *The white man takes what he wants, and the Indian suffers. Even though you live in the white man's world, remember the teaching of my people. Accept no gifts and trust no one.*

"Why are you offering this?"

Thad's moss-colored eyes held hers. "You want the truth?"

She nodded.

Thad flashed a quick look at Carleton. "For one thing, I'd like to get experience as a foreman. Carl, here, already has a good foreman, Lyle Bartel, so there's no chance for me at the Double K. Second, I'm a top hand. Carl can verify that when his brain's not so addled his tongue's knotted up. Third, I like helping folks. My dad's the sheriff around these parts, and I guess I sort of inherited the tendency. And fourth—"

He paused to send his uncle a wide grin. "You're a helluva lot prettier than my current boss."

Flabbergasted, Serena stared at the irrepressible young man who stood before her, his dusty hat in one hand. He seemed too young to be a ranch foreman—even a ranch as small as hers. Too fun-loving, like a frisky colt—all high spirits in the beginning, but would he have enough depth for the long haul?

Still, he worked for Carleton Kearney, and she could imagine no more businesslike and demanding a taskmaster than the owner of the Double K. Part owner, she amended. She'd learned that from Mr. Frieder in town. Carleton's older brother, Ben, owned half the ranch, but Carleton ran the entire operation. She could understand why Thad wanted additional experience and responsibility; as Ben Kearney's oldest son, he would someday inherit half of the Double K. Perhaps all of it, if the Kearney girls—Carleton's stepdaughter, Alice, and the infant Sarah—married eventually and moved away.

Thad took a step closer. "Come on, Miss Serena," he urged, his voice low and earnest. "Give me a chance. Don't let my uncle bluff you. He's a crusty old codger, but he's a good man. He doesn't mind losin' me. He's well-known and respected—he's got his pick of the best cowhands in the state."

Serena blinked. Crusty old codger? Blunt-spoken, maybe. Taciturn and unsmiling. Of course the man had recently lost his wife. But old? She didn't think of Carleton Kearney as old. Quite the contrary. He was unwelcoming—formidable, even. But he'd been the only man she'd allowed within touching distance since...since that day ten years ago. His nephew seemed nice enough—straightforward and friendly. But as a man he seemed a pale shadow compared to his quiet, more experienced uncle.

"Miss Serena?"

Thad's youthful tenor pulled her thoughts away from the tall, intriguing man atop the roan horse which stepped restively in what she now considered her front yard. The animal's hooves were trampling her future flower bed. She'd need to put up a fence. And...

Carleton's hard blue eyes met hers. "Go ahead, Miss Hull. Hire the boy. You two young, addle-brained colts deserve each other."

Serena thought she saw a glimmer of a smile touch his mouth, but she couldn't be sure.

The older man turned his steady gaze on his nephew. "Listen up, son. This tongue's not so knotted it can't tell you to stop at the ranch house and draw your pay."

Thad clapped his hat on his head and brushed a two-fingered salute across the brim.

Carleton sent Serena an incomprehensible look and turned his horse toward the rutted road separating their two ranches. Plain as apple pie she didn't know hay from horsefeathers. What in blazes did she know about ranching? About life out here in the West?

Oh, what the hell. The emptiness he'd felt ever since Ella died yawned even larger. He groaned inwardly. Let her learn. He knew of no better teacher than hard, unforgiving work and bitter experience. He'd seen enough heartache and pain out here to know it wasn't going to be easy for a snip of a girl from Ohio, even if she did seem mature for her age.

Time would tell. Thad would survive. He didn't know about Serena. Part of him didn't want to live to see it.

Chapter Three

Serena watched Thad Kearney drive nails into the last plank separating her tiny living space from the aromatic bales of green-gold alfalfa on the other side of the wall. Alfalfa, Thad told her, was baled and stored indoors. The rye field adjoining her property would be cut, bound in bundles and left in the field for winter feed.

Above her on the ladder she held steady, her new ranch foreman sang under his breath as he enthusiastically pounded away.

"Buffalo gals, won'tcha come out— Ow!"

Serena laughed so hard the ladder shuddered.

"Watch what you're doing!" her foreman yelped. "The ladder's shakin' so bad I hit my thumb again instead of the nail!"

Serena fought to quell her amusement. She mustn't laugh at him—at least not out loud. His pride would bruise easily now that he was trying hard to prove himself. He'd appeared at sunup, worked steadily until their noon meal of ham sandwiches his mother had sent out with him and cold coffee left over from her meager breakfast of hardtack and one of Otto Frieder's fresh peaches, then insisted on finishing the wall before the sun went down. He'd taken extra time to build framing for a double interior partition, then stacked the twelve hay bales left over from the previous winter between the supporting studs. The hay reached all the way to the ceiling.

"For insulation," Thad explained. "Uncle Carl will never miss those old bales once the haying crew starts in."

Serena felt uneasy about the small deception, but the thought of extra warmth come winter silenced her conscience. And the thought of what the two of them had accomplished in just one day buoyed her spirits even higher. With Serena measuring lumber and feeding him nails from her bulging skirt pocket, together they had completed both the outside wall and the inside partition. Tomorrow, Thad would hang the door and install the windows.

She was exhausted. Her arms and neck ached from holding the heavy boards in place while Thad pounded in nails. And her knees! If she knelt to measure and mark one more plank, she'd never be able to get up. Fortunately, all the flooring pieces were already cut to size. Tomorrow they'd just lay them in place on the joists and nail them down.

"Oh, I almost forgot," Thad began as he pulled his swollen thumb from his mouth. "Uncle Carl invited us up to the house for supper."

Serena stiffened. "You go, Thad. I think I'll stay here and plan out my flower bed."

"Flower bed!" Thad snorted from his perch above her. "You can't plant flowers at night. Besides, you got no seeds. Why don'tcha come up and eat with us instead?"

Serena tipped her face up toward the young man on the ladder above her. "Because your uncle doesn't like me, Thad."

"Well, sure he does," Thad spluttered. "He's just been short with everybody since Aunt Ella died. Aw, Serena, you gotta come! My dad's gonna be there, too. He's ridin' out special just to meet you.''

"Me!" The ladder wobbled again, and Thad grabbed at the wall and swore under his breath.

Serena leaned her shoulder against the splintery wood. "Why on earth would he want to do that?"

Her foreman plunked his boots rhythmically onto the lower rungs as he descended the ladder. "Because of your pa, you goose. He was Dad's deputy for years. And before that, they were in the war together. In a northern prison, too. Jeremiah saved his life twice. I think Dad wants to meet you because he liked your pa. He liked him a lot."

Serena hesitated. She'd heard a lot about Sheriff Ben Kearney over the years. And Jessamyn, Ben's wife, was the newspaper editor who had taught her father how to set type. That's how he had supported them in Stark County, working for the *Ohio Repository*.

"Will your mother be there, too?"

"Nope. It's lockup night for the *Wildwood Times*. Ma's likely to work 'til dawn. Come on, Serena. What are you scared of?"

She shot him a quick look as he stepped off the ladder and began gathering up the tools. She didn't know what frightened her. She'd dealt with the town marshall and her father's lawyer back in Stark County, come out west on her own, slept on the open ground in the company of a bunch of rough cavalry men, ridden through Indian country. Why would supper with an old friend of Pa's frighten her?

She lugged the ladder over and leaned it against the loft opening. Men frightened her, she acknowledged. Even a boy like Thad would frighten her if he got too close. But he didn't. They'd worked side by side all day long and he'd never once even brushed her hand.

Ben Kearney would make her uneasy. He knew she was

half Modoc—was that it? Was she afraid of what he might think of her? Thad must know her heritage, too, but it didn't seem to matter to him. Nothing bothered her young foreman. Often she wondered what it would be like to have a brother like him.

And Carleton Kearney—what about him? She sucked in a quick gulp of air. Did her Indian heritage matter to the owner of the Double K?

"What's the matter, Serena? You look kinda funny."

"Nothing," she said quickly.

Thad laid down the hammer and the saw, then straightened. "You're lying," he said. "You're scared."

"All right, I'm scared." She knew she didn't look like an Indian woman. Even though she had her mother's large, dark eyes, her skin was fair, like her father's. But inside she felt different. Inside she cringed at the fear that was never far from her mind. If people out here knew she was a half-breed, would they still accept her?

Thad gave her a long, thoughtful look, hooked his thumbs in his pants pockets, and in his best adult voice announced, "I'll protect you."

Serena burst out laughing. "You big idiot, they're your family!"

She winced at the crestfallen expression on his face. She'd injured his manly pride.

"Oh, Thad, for Lord's sake, don't be so melodramatic. I'm just a little shy around...strangers."

"Huh! They wouldn't be strangers if you'd just come and meet—"

She cut him off with a gesture. *Serena Hull, you are a fortunate woman.* It had been difficult for her mother to set aside her Indian heritage and live in white society. But despite what Mama always cautioned about a world that might not accept her, Serena knew she should take this offer of goodwill, calm her fears, and do what she intended to do when she came out here. Try!

"Oh, all right. Anything to shut you up." She smiled at him to soften her words, then added, "But remember, you quit the Double K to work for me. Don't go rubbing it in with your uncle."

"Hell, Serena— Sorry, I mean, heck. That'd be half the fun, joshing him about that. Actually, it'd do him good. Take his mind off things."

Serena studied the open, beardless face, the hopeful expression in the guileless green eyes. Thad was a good boy, caring and honest. He'd make a good man someday. And in the meantime, he was her friend—her only friend outside of Otto Frieder and his wife, who had taken her into their hearts ever since her first trip to the mercantile in town.

"What time is supper at the Double K?"

Thad grinned at her. "Right about now. Come on!"

Serena resolutely set her foot on the bottom step of Carleton Kearney's ranch house and turned to wait while Thad tended to his horse in the yard. She had walked over, savoring the fragrant evening air as Thad stepped his mare alongside her. Ranch hands, she was discovering, avoided walking if a horse was available. She preferred to travel on foot—she saw more of fields and wildflowers at a slower pace.

In the dusky July twilight, the building gleamed as if freshly painted. A scraggly patch of black-eyed Susans rambled along the dirt path leading to the two-story structure, and Serena frowned as she studied them. They looked as if they hadn't been tended for months.

"Come on," Thad breathed as he mounted the steps. "I'm starving!"

The front door swung open, and a tall, silver-haired man

with smoke blue eyes stepped out onto the porch. Without a word, he grasped her by the shoulders, turned her completely around and gave a low whistle. "Thank God, honey. You don't look a bit like Jeremiah!"

Thad chuckled. "I told you she was pretty, Dad. Guess you're gettin' hard of hearing!"

Ben Kearney raised one eyebrow at his son. "I still see good, though. Welcome to Wildwood Valley, Serena." He removed his hands from her shoulders. "I'm glad you came."

"Thank you, Mr. Kearney. Pa often spoke of you."

A slow smile creased the older man's lips. "I'll just bet he did. All of it fancy embroidered stories, I'd guess."

"Not all of it," Serena answered. "He thought a great deal of you, Colonel."

Thad strode past them, sniffing the air. "Pot roast!" he chortled. "Come on, Dad. I haven't eaten since noon." He led the way into the house and headed for the kitchen.

"Alice, my Alice," he sang out over the clatter of pots and spoons. "What's for supper?"

The flush-faced young woman poked her head out the kitchen door. "Wash up!" Alice snapped. "We've been waiting."

Serena recognized the woman—Mr. Kearney's stepdaughter, Alice. The voice was as thin and harsh as she'd remembered it. She stepped around the men and spoke to her.

"May I help with the supper?"

No answer but the metallic crash of an iron pot lid.

Serena raised her voice. "Miss Kearney?"

"Your place is next to Ben," Alice announced from the stove. She stood with her back toward Serena, her tall frame bent over the black iron cooktop. A once-crisp apron hung limply over a faded rose percale work dress, the ties looped into a lackluster bow at her undefined waist.

"All of you sit down," Alice ordered.

The men remained standing until Serena sank into the high-backed wooden chair. Ben broke the awkward silence.

"Smells mighty good, Alice." He watched his son snake a hand across the table toward a basket of hot biscuits. "You sure can tame a slice of—" he rapped a table knife across Thad's knuckles "—beef. Remove your hat, son," he concluded in a low voice.

Thad rolled his eyes, then aimed his dusty head covering at the wall hook behind him. The hat sailed over the dinner table and caught.

Alice clunked a steaming bowl down at his elbow. "Help yourself to mashed potatoes. Not much left after the hands and the hay crew finished. Good thing we never run short of beef." She slapped down a huge platter of sliced meat and fanned herself with her apron skirt. "Chores around here never end," she muttered.

"Come and sit down, Alice," her stepfather said quietly.

Alice grabbed a pot holder and the blue graniteware coffeepot and turned back to the table to address Serena. "Drink coffee, do you?"

Serena noticed that Alice's hand shook as she poured the dark liquid into her cup. "Thank you," she murmured.

She lifted the cup to her lips. Good heavens, Alice didn't like her any more than Carleton Kearney did! She cast a covert look at the ranch owner where he sat at the head of the table, and her cup clattered onto her saucer.

A scowl spread over his tanned, regular features. Without raising his voice, he spoke to his stepdaughter. "Sit down, Alice. We'll say grace."

Alice pressed her lips together and plopped into the chair opposite Serena. "Say it, then," she bit out.

Carleton reached his hands to either side, grasped his

stepdaughter's work-roughened fingers in one and Serena's small, brown hand in the other. Alice laced her fingers through Thad's on her left, and Serena accepted Ben Kearney's strong, comforting grip.

"Lord," Carleton began in an unsteady voice. "We open our hearts to you and ask…"

Serena bowed her head as the rich baritone voice washed over her. Carleton's fingers lay warm against her palm, and suddenly she felt dizzy. Seated between the two men, her hands encased in theirs, she felt an irrational bolt of fear tighten her belly. She closed her eyes and concentrated on the sound of Carleton's low, weary voice.

Dear God, would she never get over it? Never forget the thing that had happened to her because of what she was? Even now, she had to force herself not to jerk her hands out of their grip, fight the urge to scream.

Carleton's amen was echoed by Thad and his father. Alice didn't say a word, merely rose and returned to the stove. Serena watched her dish up snap peas and carrots with jerky movements.

Something was wrong. Serena knew instinctively it had to do with her presence in the Kearney household this evening. Alice seemed hostile and angry. Was it because of Serena's Indian heritage? Or was it because of Alice's own mother's death almost a year ago? Alice seemed hostile and angry. Perhaps the girl resented spending her youth taking over her mother's duties, cooking for the hired men and caring for an infant child.

She wondered what Alice wanted. She herself wanted nothing other than to keep house with her two sisters. Did Alice want to marry? Have children of her own or embark on a career—as a teacher, perhaps? Serena sorted through the possibilities in silence until Thad's voice captured her attention.

"Serena's fence needs some fixin', Uncle Carl. 'Bout

another week and we'll be ready to run some beef in there.''

"Another week and you'll be ready for a man's job again," Carleton observed. "I hear you're building outhouses and hen lofts at Lost Acres."

"Hey, there's more to ranchin' than ropin' steers!"

"Not much." Ben stirred cream into his coffee. "Besides, only a greenhorn has to rope a steer. An experienced ranch hand just talks to it real nice, and it follows him home."

"Like a woman," Carleton said with a hint of laughter in his voice.

"Pa!" Alice shot. The thin woman sank onto her chair with an embarrassed smile. "Really, Pa."

"Why, I hear Thad has ladies clear to Nevada pantin' after him," Ben joked. He gulped a mouthful of coffee and replaced his cup on the china saucer. "Can't figure it, myself. Must be that sweet-smelling stuff he's been splashing on ever since…"

"Jehosaphat, Dad—"

Carleton reached out and jabbed his nephew on the fleshy part of his shoulder. "I apologize for this young pup's inappropriate language, Miss Hull. The truth is, with a name like Thaddeus, his mental capacity never progressed much beyond spelling. Makes it hard for him to talk properly."

Thad glowered at his uncle and nursed his shoulder.

With that, the men dug into their heaping plates. The banter continued as they ate.

"A ranch is no place for a dude or a dandy," Carleton observed, his tone unemotional. He held out his plate and Alice shoveled a slab of apple pie onto it. "But one that smells as good as Thad does could herd cows just by walkin' by, don't you think?" He sent Ben a crooked smile.

His brother picked up the bait with practiced ease. "No doubt about it. But, then, what about the neighbors' cows—Miss Serena's, for instance? Since I'm the law in the county, I wouldn't look too kindly on a foreman who collects other ranchers' stock just by riding by in the morning."

Thad picked at his dessert. "Aw, come on, Dad." He squirmed on the wooden chair and the men laughed softly. Even Serena smiled.

"It isn't funny," Alice snapped. "Thad doesn't work for us any longer. He works for her." She shot a hard-eyed glance at Serena.

Thad rose and leaned over his cousin's chair. "Alice, my Alice," he crooned. "I'm glad to hear you miss me." He caught her hand and clutched it dramatically to his chest. "Women everywhere miss me," he said with exaggerated conceit. "But you, fair cousin of mine, you at least don't love me for my smell—" he shushed her protest with a gesture "—but for my advanced and superior…maturity."

Even Serena laughed at that. And then she noticed that Alice stared down at the oak table in silence.

Oh, my Lord. She caught her breath. Alice cared about Thad. And Thad—young, untried, brash boy that he was— Thad Kearney hadn't a clue.

Serena looked at the faces around the table in the Double K kitchen. They were a family. They cared for one another in the easy, warm way families did. But Serena sensed it was more than that for Alice.

And it was much less than that for herself. Again, she was an outsider, a half-breed as she was called back in Stark County, with a Scottish father, a Modoc mother. Carleton Kearney tolerated her company only because his brother, Ben, had welcomed her. Alice resented her.

A sick, lonely feeling washed over her. She didn't belong here. Once more she wondered if she'd ever know where she *did* belong.

Chapter Four

July 7, 1887

Dearest Jessie and Mary Irene,

I hold in my hand your precious letter, which arrived just today. I must admit I laughed and cried over it until I was almost sick.

Jessie, don't let Aunt Letty bully you. She is an old woman and quite far behind the times. Bustles have been out of fashion for years, even here in Oregon, though once in a while you see one bouncing down the street in town. I'll tell you a secret. I tossed my corset on the campfire the first night out with the wagon train, and I'm not sorry a bit! When you come out in the spring, you can burn yours, too.

Last week the haying crew finished cutting and baling Mr. Kearney's alfalfa. Bales and bales of it are stacked floor to ceiling in the other half of my "barn house," and the smell permeates the air day and night. It would be impossible for Jessie, with her asthma, but Mary Irene would love the scent—like a sweet musky rose with a dash of pepper.

I have not forgotten the sunflower seeds you packed in my trunk, but the trunk has not yet arrived. Mr. Frieder says sometimes it takes weeks and weeks. All my clean clothes and dresses are inside, along with the seeds. I admit I do long for a change of attire. I will wash clothes once a week, on Mondays, but I will only scrub half of my garments at one time. While I wait for those to dry, I will wear the other half.

The Frieders, who run the mercantile, have a daughter about my age. Her name is Amanda Jane, and she works in the store. I told her all about you, Jessie, about the books you like to read and your writing journal. And about you, Mary Irene. Amanda says she likes cats, too, and she will save you a kitten for your very own when you come out next spring.

Mr. Kearney is a bit gruff. However, his wife died this past year while having their baby. His manner bothers me some, but I do feel sorry for him. I remember how terrible it was to lose Mama and Pa.

While Mr. Kearney is not terribly polite, he is a fair man. He does not hide the fact that he believes I cannot manage a ranch on my own. I plan to prove him wrong, and now am more grateful than ever to Mama for training us in the ways of her people even though we attended school in Canton City. Mama's wisdom about life is proving invaluable out here. I know I can bargain for what I need to survive, and I am convinced we made the right decision, that we will be happier in Wildwood Valley.

Yesterday, Thad, who is my ranch foreman—doesn't that sound grand?—rode out earlier than usual from town and found me marking off my garden plot in nothing but my drawers and chemise! He was so embarrassed he turned bright red and ran his horse smack into the gate. Today he's fixing it.

Tomorrow I am going to withdraw some of our bank money to buy cows. Mr. Kearney has some he says he will sell me. Thad says they're good stock, a mix of Herefords and animals from Texas with long, pointed horns. If I buy at seven dollars a head and can sell off half the herd in the fall for twenty-five or thirty dollars a head, I can make a tidy profit.

Mary Irene, I already have the chickens you wanted—three red ones and a black-and-white speckled one with a mean look in her eye. I call her Attila the Hen. Thad built a henhouse for them, but none of them are laying yet. I can hardly wait to eat a boiled egg for breakfast instead of my usual hardtack and coffee.

Thad admits he is getting restless without cows to worry over. After the henhouse, we rode fence for one whole day and then he built some shelves next to the stove plus an outdoor privy in the back.

Feeding the chickens will be your chore, Mary Irene. I remember how you love them. We can sell the extra eggs to Mr. Frieder in town. Maybe I'll get a milk cow, too, so I can sell butter as well. Every penny I save, and every dollar I earn, brings us closer to our goal of being a family again. Without Mama and Pa now, we need each other more than ever.

I will bid you good-night, dearest sisters. I cannot tell you how much I miss you both. I have a good cry about it once a week, and then I ask God to watch over you and keep you safe.

I send you all my love.

Your Sissie

P.S. Jessie, don't forget to take your lung medicine. Tell Aunt Letty that Mama always added a bit of molasses to sweeten the taste.

"Here they come!"

Fourteen-year-old Jem Kearney stretched his skinny frame as high as he could, clinging to the corral fence with just the tips of his boots hooked under the wood rail. Serena craned her neck to see past Jem's bobbing head.

"Gee willikers, they're real beauties, aren't they, Serena?" The boy ducked his head. "I mean Miss Hull. Dad said I shouldn't—"

Serena laughed and patted Jem's hand. "Just Serena will do fine, Jem." She smiled into the eager blue eyes of Thad's younger brother. With her hat, she fanned a honeybee away from her face and squinted in the direction of Jem's avid gaze.

"Lookit, Serena—there's so many cows I can't count 'em!"

The lowing herd plodded toward the corral yard, Thad and the Double K foreman on horseback driving them toward the gate. Amid the tumult of shouts and the occasional sharp whack of a hat slapped against a dust-covered thigh, the first of the bunch ambled into the yard. She counted thirty head.

"That's the lot," Lyle Bartel shouted, reining in his sorrel. He shoved his hat back, revealing wavy blond hair down to his ears. "Close the gate!"

How, Serena wondered, had Thad managed to buy so many? Surely Mr. Kearney would object. She shot a surreptitious look at the tall rancher lounging against the fence opposite her. His thumb tipped the dark gray Stetson back, and she saw his sharp gaze seek out his nephew.

Serena blinked. By whatever means, Thad had garnered the best of the Double K stock to seed her own herd. Across the dusty corral yard, the ranch owner's piercing blue eyes met hers.

A shiver of apprehension curled up her spine. He must be furious! First she stole his top hand away from him, and now by some feat of ingenuity Thad had talked him out of thirty of the handsomest animals she'd ever seen. Mr. Kearney would never forgive her.

As she watched, Carleton raised one dark eyebrow and sent her a purposeful two-fingered salute. Then he pulled his hat low enough to hide his eyes and pushed off the fence.

"Thad." He spoke her foreman's name in the same low, deliberate tone he would ask for the salt at supper. Serena wondered if he ever got angry enough to raise his voice.

Thad edged his mount close to the rangy figure. "Uncle Carl?"

"How much?"

"Seven dollars a head, Carl. It's all she's got."

"This all she wants? Fifteen steers and fifteen cows?"

Thad cleared his throat. "Well, as a matter of fact…"

Carleton nodded again. "Thought so." He headed across the yard toward Serena, moving steadily through the milling cattle.

Serena caught her breath. *Here it comes,* she thought. He'd had his fill of her, and now… Well, she didn't know what he'd do. Carleton didn't say much, but when he did open his mouth, she noticed his ranch hands—even the most garrulous one, called Snap, paid attention.

"Jehosaphat, Serena," murmured Jem at her side. "Uncle Carl looks madder'n a bull."

Jem was right. Carleton's eyes looked as hard as two blue stones. She unfolded the hands she'd unconsciously clenched in her lap and forced herself to climb down off the fence.

"Miss Hull."

"Mr. Kearney."

"You want to reconsider something here?"

Out of the corner of her eye, Serena saw the hired man, Marsh, sidle out of the barn and position himself within hearing distance. Then she noticed the Double K hands gathering along the fence. One laboriously rolled a cigarette, but it was clear he was listening more than concentrating on the task; tobacco rained onto the ground at his feet. The other men—Snap, and a handsome, dark-skinned Spaniard—leaned their elbows on the top fence rail and waited.

"Reconsider?" Serena gulped down her unease. "Why would I reconsider? My foreman knew my top price. From the look of the stock you sold me, I'd guess I got a pretty good deal."

The cigarette-smoking cowhand choked on his first drag.

Carleton's gaze didn't waver. "You would," he repeated.

"Why, yes, I would." She worked to keep her voice even. For some reason, it took all of her courage just to talk to the man. Something about him made her heart hammer whenever he looked at her.

"After all, Mr. Kearney, a deal is a—"

"You plan to increase this herd of yours?"

"Yes, I— Cows bear calves in the spring, do they not? These look like fine, healthy animals to me."

Behind her she heard Jem Kearney suck in his breath. "Serena," he hissed.

"Yep," Carleton commented in the same low drawl. "Fine and healthy, all right."

"Serena!" Jem whispered again.

She waved her hand at the boy to shush him. "Well, then? What objection do you have to my taking possession?"

"Miss Hull." Carleton removed his hat and raked his fingers through his unruly dark hair. "I figure that's two hundred ten dollars for my thirty head of what are shortly to be Lazy A branded cattle. But if you don't mind my saying, in all my years as a rancher I've never seen even a fine, healthy female cow make a calf all by itself.''

A snort of laughter erupted from the knot of men leaning against the fence. Serena bristled. She hated the sound of rude laughter, especially when she was the butt of it.

''And why not?'' she said, louder than she intended. ''Is there something wrong with your stock, Mr. Kearney?''

''Serena!'' Jem reached out and tugged her rolled-up shirtsleeve.

Serena shrugged away from the boy's grasp. ''Not now, Jem.''

Carleton's mouth twitched oddly. ''Not a thing wrong with them, Miss Hull. But it's a bull that makes a calf—the cow just goes along for the ride and squeezes it out at the end of the road.''

A bull! That's what Jem was trying to tell her. She'd forgotten about needing a bull! She felt her face flame.

Guffaws rolled over the corral yard as the Double K hands stamped and slapped each other on the back.

''So,'' Carleton continued in his low, lazy drawl, ''unless you want to walk your fifteen cows out to my south pasture to get them bred one at a time, mind you—there's only so much ol' Candy can do in one day—you'd best buy a bull to round out your herd.''

''Oh, but I've already spent—''

Thad reined in his horse and leaned down over the saddle horn toward his uncle. ''I told her you'd let her have Big Red in exchange for the first healthy bull calf he throws. Red goes with the herd now, the yearling later.''

Carleton's face darkened into a scowl. "You said that, did you?"

"Yeah, Carl, I did."

Carleton blew out a heavy breath. "Hell's fire, Thad. That bull alone is worth two hundred dollars."

"No, he ain't, Uncle Carl!" Jem's boyish tenor sang over the noise of bawling cattle and snickering ranch hands. "He ain't worth nuthin' 'less he's got a lady cow! You said so yourself!"

"Hush up, Jem," Thad shot.

Frozen with embarrassment, Serena studied her toes. She knew her face had flushed scarlet; her cheeks burned with heat. Oh, my, a cow and a bull...what a topic of conversation!

Jem plucked at her sleeve. "I tried to tell you," he whispered. "Don't feel bad, Serena. Please don't."

Serena absentmindedly squeezed his thin shoulder. On the other hand, she reflected, this was a stock corral, not someone's front parlor.

"Miss Hull?" Carleton's voice cut through her thoughts.

She raised her head and forced herself to look him in the eye. "Mr. Kearney."

"You'll need a bull," he said quietly. "I can't help but think Thad and my foreman cooked this up between them, but I don't hold you responsible for the antics of two crazy young buckaroos out to impress you. Big Red is yours."

Serena's head reeled. He was giving her the bull? No, she amended immediately. He was just rescuing his nephew and his foreman from making fools of themselves. He could make Thad back down if he wanted to, but she admired his way of handling it so the two young men could save face.

An unusual man, Carleton Kearney. Hard and stern and unpredictable. Still, he hadn't minded making *her* the butt of a joke! She shook his hand and spun away toward the corral fence.

She took no more than three steps when an idea occurred to her, and she stopped short. Pivoting, she marched back to stand toe-to-toe with the owner of the Double K.

"You still think I'm not going to make it out here, don't you? That I'm going to fold up and go back to Ohio."

"Don't put words in my mouth, Sis."

"You'll have your calf, Mr. Kearney. I realize you've been very generous in selling me a start on my own herd at a rock bottom price, so I'm going to offer you a deal. If I can't make enough money ranching by spring to build a house and bring my sisters out, I'll sell out to you and go back to Stark County."

Carleton studied her face for so long she wondered if the few freckles on her nose had turned purple. A glimmer of a smile curved his lips.

"Fair enough," he said at last. He tipped his hat and turned away. "Marsh," he called to the black man leaning against the barn. "You still got that old Lazy A iron around?"

"Yassah," the stocky man replied. "Sho' do. I got mos' ever'thing saved up somewheres."

Carleton strode toward the barn door. "Thad. Lyle. Let's get Miss Hull's stock counter-branded before she changes her mind. And Jem," he called over his shoulder. "If you want to go on roundup this year, you'd best get your butt down off that fence and help out."

Serena turned away as the big, white-faced Hereford thumped to the ground, its neck encircled by Thad's effortlessly tossed lariat. Snubbing the rope to his saddle horn, the cowboy's spirited cutting horse danced this way and that as the animal struggled. Thad held the rope taut, immobilizing the bawling cow while Snap and the Spaniard yanked it sideways.

The horse backed away, dragging the thrashing animal close to the fire. Jem trod up and down on the bellows, sending hot jets of flame to lick the glowing red iron. The quick, dark-skinned cowhand grabbed the handle in his gloved hand, straddled the jerking flank and plunged the brand downward. A sizzling sound, punctuated by the animal's anguished bawl, made Serena stiffen. She breathed in the acrid odor of singed hair.

Her gorge rose. It was horrible—sickening!—for a living thing to be pinned down and assaulted like that. She shut her eyes tight, then gripped the fence rail, bent double, and threw up her breakfast.

Gasping for breath, she did not notice Carleton Kearney striding toward her.

"Miss Hull? Are you unwell?"

His voice seemed to come from far away. "I'm quite all right, thank you." Tears stung into her eyes at the bitter taste in her mouth.

"I'll grant you, branding is no picnic for the cow. It's obvious you've never seen it done." He offered her a dipper of water.

Serena rinsed her mouth and wiped the back of her hand across her lips. Her saliva tasted sour. "I'll get used to it."

Carleton hesitated. "Go on up to the house. Alice keeps hot coffee on the stove."

"Thank you, no, Mr. Kearney. I'll stay. They're my cows now, and I'd better learn this part of the business. If there are calves in the spring, I'll have to help with my own branding."

With a covert gesture, Carleton waved the hands into action, and once more Jem trod the bellows while Thad cut out another fat, white-faced cow. Serena's mouth whitened when the iron burned into the hide, but she said nothing.

Three more cows were roped and branded with the symbol denoting Lost Acres Ranch property. Carleton watched an unflinching Serena observe the proceedings, her dark eyes hugely dilated, her fists clenched at her side. At the sight of her face, a lancet of anguish lodged under his rib. Each time an animal bellowed in pain, her hands twitched. He realized she fought against covering her ears.

He couldn't blame her. A hurt thing had made him a bit queasy when he first came out from Carolina and started ranching after the war. He'd almost forgotten the first time he'd marked a steer twenty-five years ago. And Ella...Ella never could stand to watch them even heat up the iron. His wife had always made sure she had washing to do on branding day.

Castrating the male calves would be even worse. How in blazes was Serena going to be a rancher if she couldn't stomach the bare bones of the business?

Maybe she wouldn't. He should feel elated at the prospect. He'd get back his winter pasture, plus all the cattle he'd sold her this morning—including Big Red and the calves he would sire. He couldn't lose.

But he didn't feel elated. Instead, he felt an odd tightness in his chest that drew around his heart like a lasso. He didn't want her to quit, he realized. For some reason, he wanted her to stay.

Beside him, Serena used her hat to brush the dust off her two-legged skirt, then settled it firmly on her head again. The single dark plait down her back, thick as a man's forearm, switched as she snapped her head toward the branding fire. "Mr. Kearney, I'd like to try it."

Carleton blinked. "What, you mean branding?"

She nodded. He noted that she pressed her lips together until the gentle curve of her mouth narrowed to a thin line.

"Right now?"

"Right now," she said unsteadily.

"Jupiter," Carleton swore under his breath. She'd probably faint or puke her guts out.

"Thad," he called to his nephew. "Let Miss Hull take a turn."

Thad reined his horse up short and frowned. "You crazy?"

Carleton kept his voice noncommittal. "It's her idea, kid."

"Is *she* crazy?"

"Maybe. Let her try one, anyway." He bent toward Serena. "You sure about this?" he intoned near her ear.

"Of course not," she breathed. "What does that matter?"

Chuckling, Carleton led her toward the branding arena just as Thad lassoed another cow and the hands flopped it onto its side. The lithe, dark-haired Spaniard stomped one fancy tooled boot onto the animal's flank.

"Here, *señorita*." He pulled the hot iron from the flames and wrapped her hand around the handle. After a slight hesitation, he took her other hand and closed it around the shaft as well. Then he stepped back and pointed downward. "Right there, next to my boot. I press hard so she not jump."

Serena looked down at the red-brown hair on the animal's hide.

"Now, *señorita*," the man urged.

She straightened her spine, tightened her fingers around the shaft and gradually lowered the glowing tip. The closer the rod came to the quivering hide, the slower its descent. It wavered uncertainly over the intended spot.

"*Señorita*," the Mexican cajoled in a gentle voice. "Do not keep the cow waiting."

"I—" Her throat closed. She scrunched her eyes shut and tried to force the iron downward. She couldn't. *Couldn't.*

She sensed a movement beside her, and then a large, warm hand settled over hers, pressing the hot branding iron onto the animal's flank. For a moment she thought it was the soft-voiced Spanish man's hand, but in the next instant the animal lurched and Carleton spoke into her ear.

"Hold it steady, Serena."

She sucked in her breath at the sharp smell of burning flesh.

"Okay, that's it. Now, take a deep breath," he ordered.

Shuddering, she obeyed as the cow lurched to its feet and trotted off.

"Now another one."

"I'm all right." A wave of dizziness overtook her and she gulped more air. "Really I am."

"Sure you are," he said dryly. "Thad. Ruiz. Take over."

He pried her fingers from the branding iron and handed it to the grinning dark-skinned man.

"Bueno, señorita! Bueno!"

Carleton chuckled deep in his chest. She was white as a sheet on wash day. "Come on, Miss Hull. Time for some coffee. Unless of course you want to try it again, just to be sure you've got the hang of it?"

She sent him a stricken look.

"Don't devil her, Uncle Carl." Thad's voice rose from beyond the branding fire.

"Yeah, Uncle Carl," Jem chimed in. "She done good!"

Grasping her slim elbow, he managed to guide her out of the corral and halfway up to the house without uttering another word. He could feel her tremble under his fingers, hear her jerky breath pull in and out in uneven gasps.

"Alice," he called when they reached the porch steps. "Get some hot coffee."

Serena weakly waved one hand in protest. "Oh, no, I don't need—"

"And pour some brandy in it," Carleton added.

Yes, she did need. She was a damn fool woman with more guts than good sense. What the hell ever made her think she could run a ranch?

On the other hand, considering she'd just bought a herd of prime beef at a rock-bottom price, most of the cows already carrying calves, and maneuvered him out of Big Red on top of it, she wasn't starting off too badly.

Come to think of it, he could use a slug of brandy himself.

Chapter Five

Shading her eyes from the sunlight, Serena tipped her head back to watch a red-tailed hawk circle lazily against the cloudless cobalt sky. She followed the bird's effortless spirals until her neck ached. How free it must feel, floating above the earth where nothing could touch you. She, too, longed for wings that could carry her away from harm.

The horse beneath her stamped impatiently. "Steady, girl," she murmured. She patted the mare's warm hide. "You want a good run, don't you? But we've work to do yet." With a last look at the tiny black image soaring above her, she nudged her mount forward toward the next fence post.

Thad waited, his thumbs jammed in his back pockets. "Took you long enough," he grumbled. He reached one hand for the metal staples she doled out each time they came across a section of barbed wire that needed tacking down. "What were you starin' at, a pot of gold?"

Serena surveyed her hardworking foreman. "A hawk. You'd have seen it, too, if you'd look up once in a while." She fed three staples into his outstretched palm.

"I'll look up when this fence is fixed. You want your cattle strayin' off into Uncle Carl's rye field?"

"No, Thad, of course not. I was only joking. It's such a lovely morning—my washing is already hung out, I gathered seven eggs and all my other chores are finished." She jingled the staples in her pocket. "I feel lighter than air inside. Besides, I've nothing to do since you insist on hogging the fencing hammer."

Thad pounded in the last staple and snorted. "I'm repairing this rundown tangle your Pa called a fence, Serena. And you're helping me. That oughta be enough."

Serena sighed. "It's not much fun riding fence with you, Thad. You never let me do anything."

Thad's green eyes widened. "Fun! You think banging away on barbed wire is fun? Watchin' hawks is fun. Or…" His eyes took on a faraway look. "Stealing Alice's chocolate nut fudge before it sets up. Or lyin' on my back in a hay field after a spring rain. Or dancing. Now *that's* what I call fun!"

Almost as an afterthought, he shot her a withering look and trudged off toward the next fence post. Serena walked her mare beside him. "Which pasture is Big Red in?"

"This one. That's why I'm fixin' this fence."

"*We're* fixing the fence," she corrected. "I came to learn how it's done."

"Then hush up and learn." His voice softened. "Gosh, Serena, you've been downright dreamy-eyed ever since breakfast."

"Sorry. I was just thinking about…things. My trunk arrived yesterday, and it kind of set me off. I miss my sisters."

"We get your steers to market this fall, you're gonna make a pile of money. Try to think about that, not your sisters. Or hawks." He thrust his hand toward her. "Staples."

Serena scooped up the metal pieces and dropped them

into Thad's palm. "You don't think Big Red's anywhere nearby, do you?" She glanced about nervously.

"Nah. You'd know it by now if he was. With that red shirt you've got on, you're like a lightning rod in a summer storm." He eyed her across the fence post. "You coming into town tonight?"

She blinked at his sudden shift in topic. "Town? What for?"

"Big dance." Thad raised his voice over his pounding. "A social, they call it out here."

"It's called that in Ohio, too. I'm not partial to them." She flinched at the understatement. She hated social gatherings. People whispered and pointed. Now that she'd left Stark County and the wrenching memories of her years growing up, she had resolved never again to go where she wasn't accepted.

"Take your mind off things," Thad offered. "Hawks 'n sisters, like."

Mute, she shook her head.

"Come on, Serena," he urged. "After all, you're half the reason they're holdin' a dance in the first place."

"Me!" Her heart skittered to a halt. "But why?"

Thad rested the combination crowbar-fencing hammer on the top wire and pinned her with a disgusted look. "Because you're new to the valley, you goose. Wildwood Valley folks are being neighborly."

Serena's resolve shrank against her foreman's logic. It was kind of them, of course. A welcoming gesture to a newcomer in their midst. But still...

"I can't, Thad. I just can't."

Thad snatched up the hammer. "You're a coward," he said quietly, not looking at her.

"I'm not!"

"Oh, not about real things, like branding cows or coming out here in the first place. About *imaginary* things. About things you think *might* happen.''

She said nothing, and Thad hammered away on the fence. He was right. But he didn't—couldn't—guess the real reason for her fear.

"Maybe you don't have a dress to wear, is that it? Alice will loan you one. I know she will."

"I have a dress, Thad. It's not that."

He gave her a thoughtful look. "Hellfire, Serena, I'll dance with you if nobody else does, I promise!"

She burst out laughing. Sincere, misguided, gallant lad that he was, Thad thought she worried about being a wall-flower! She almost cried with relief. Being a wallflower was the furthest thing from her mind!

She felt years older than Thad. For all his knowledge about cattle and fences, her foreman could not see into her soul. Thad could not fathom her real reason for being afraid, and for that she was grateful.

And, she admitted, she was grateful to her valley neighbors for trying to make her feel welcome. "You don't have to dance with me, Thad," she said softly. "You dance with whomever you please. Dance with Alice. I can get along for one evening—even at a social—without my foreman."

"You'll come, then?" His eyes sparkled. "Uncle Carl and Alice and the baby are takin' the wagon. There's plenty of room for you, too."

Serena hesitated. She didn't want to be near Carleton. Or his stepdaughter. Alice was brusque and unfriendly, and Carleton... Well, Carleton was unnerving. She felt odd when she was around him, as if bees hummed inside her brain, upsetting her equilibrium.

"I'll ride Sandy."

"Huh! In a dress? Not likely. Serena, are you gonna wear that double-barreled skirt thing for the rest of your life?"

"Is that any business of yours?" she shot back.

"Well no, I guess it isn't. You're my boss, not my sister," he said slowly. "Guess I forgot."

Serena groaned. "You forget all the time, Thad," she said in her gentlest voice. She winced at the exasperation in his eyes.

"Dammit to blue blazes, Serena, your brain's getting plumb roasted out here."

No, she thought to herself, it wasn't. Her brain was clear and sharp, as it had always been. It was her emotions that were getting out of hand. She missed Jessie and Mary Irene, hungered to hear their voices. More than that, she ached to see her mother's calm, serene face, catch one of her father's soft-eyed looks when he thought no one was watching.

Her throat closed as hot tears welled behind her eyelids. She would not cry, she resolved. Not here, in front of Thad Kearney, whom no one had ever hated. And she would not let the bitter anger rise in her mouth, souring the taste of this lovely, sunlit day. She would do as her mother had taught her—let her soul savor the beautiful things of the earth and move onward.

But, oh God, sometimes it hurt more than she thought she could bear.

"Come on, Thad." She struggled to keep her voice steady. "It's noon. Time for lunch. I'll race you to the oak tree."

She turned away before he could see her face. "The first one there gets the fencing hammer this afternoon!"

At dusk they rode back to the hay barn, half of which was now Serena's tiny living quarters. The Double K hands had dubbed it the Hay House. Her hands ached so from gripping the heavy iron and pounding staples all afternoon she could barely hold the reins. But it was a satisfying tiredness. She and her foreman had inspected and repaired nearly two miles of fence.

Dancing would not be a problem tonight. She could barely stay on her feet, and exhaustion made her sway in the saddle. She would relish being a wallflower!

Thad tipped his hat and rode on ahead to the Lost Acres gate while Serena stepped her mare slowly into the yard. When she saw what awaited her, she gasped out loud.

"My clothesline!" The rope Thad had strung from her roof to the post he'd set, together with all the clean garments she'd laundered and hung up that very morning, lay sprawled in the dirt.

She was positive the line had been snugged tight. Thad had yanked on it to test it, had driven the post an extra foot into the hard earth. Despite his efforts, had the rope slipped off the post?

She stepped the mare forward. The entire post had toppled. Or had been pushed over. The rope knot was still intact.

Her breathing stopped. It could have been an accident. Perhaps a horse bumped into the post. Or maybe the big black-and-white dog that lived in the men's bunkhouse at the Double K had tugged on her sheets.

She expelled a long breath and turned away. She didn't want to think about it. She would put it out of her mind, for tonight at least. Tomorrow she'd ask Thad to double-check the clothesline rigging and she'd launder her clothes again. Tonight, she'd heat water for a bath, shake out her sky-blue-sprigged lawn dress, and pack it and her petticoat carefully in her saddlebag. She'd wear her split riding skirt into town and change at Amanda's house.

And then she would force herself to get acquainted with the townspeople she feared, share some supper with them, sit on the sidelines and make conversation with some of the older women and watch the dancing.

It couldn't be too terrible. After all, only the elder Kearneys—Carleton and his brother, Ben, and his wife—knew about her Indian mother. They were the only people in the valley who knew she was half Modoc.

Would it start all over again out here in Wildwood Valley? The harassment, the taunts? The fear? Dear God, she prayed not. There had to be some other explanation for her downed clothesline. There just had to be.

Aching with weariness in both body and spirit, Serena dismounted and dragged herself to the front door of her little one-room house. In all her life, she had never felt so alone.

From the outside, the Dixon House hotel looked as if it had seen better days. But the inside—especially the large wood-paneled dining room, cleared now for dancing with a potluck supper offered on the sidelines—glowed with soft lamplight from the multiglobed chandelier.

The room buzzed with laughter and voices. A bent, be-whiskered man sawed away on a fiddle, accompanied by two guitar players—young, dark-skinned men with fancy tooled-leather boots and high-crowned felt hats. One of them Serena recognized as Ruiz, or Rosy, from the Double K. A well-known Scottish tune soared over the noise of pounding feet.

"Oh!" Amanda Frieder clapped her hands in delight. "They're playing a reel! Come on, Serena."

Serena quelled the flutter of panic in her belly as Amanda tugged her into the room jam-packed with ranchers, townspeople, wives, grandmothers, children and cowhands.

Amanda's honey-colored curls bobbed against her yellow gingham-covered shoulders. "I'll just set my cake on the dessert table." She disappeared behind the crowd of dancers.

Old men, young men, every male in the room, it seemed, had a woman in his arms. Serena searched the sidelines for an empty chair. She spotted one between a horse-faced lady who reminded her of Aunt Letty and a wrinkle-cheeked matron tapping her feet in time to the music, and she edged toward it. Halfway to her destination, Amanda reappeared. The dimpled blonde waved from the arms of Double K foreman Lyle Bartel.

Serena smiled and continued toward the beckoning empty chair. She would enjoy watching the festivity from the sidelines, resting her aching body in a soft chair. *If* she could reach it. Progress through the press of moving bodies was slow.

Deep inside, she longed to escape into the soft summer night and ride through the sweet-scented hay fields toward home. But she couldn't. She'd promised both Thad and Amanda she would stay at least long enough for supper. She would steel herself to make polite conversation with the two elderly females flanking the empty chair and do the best she could about the rest.

Drawing in a careful breath, she paused to avoid a whirling couple and then started forward again.

Carleton Kearney tipped his chair back onto the two rear legs and settled his baby daughter in the crook of his arm. "Like I said, Silas, this year we'll head for the railhead at Winnemucca. Best beef prices around, right before winter sets in."

Silas Appleby grunted over his plate of baked beans, coleslaw, potato salad and three kinds of pie. "Long haul. 'Specially if the weather turns. October can be iffy."

Carleton smoothed his forefinger gently over Sarah's silky dark hair. The color was like Ella's; the texture, his, he guessed. Ella never liked him touching her hair. It was coarse and straight, like Alice's was now. At least it wasn't red, like Si's.

"October's always a gamble," he said as he corraled his thoughts back to his fall cattle drive. "That's why we get such a good price. I've got a good outfit, Si. We'll have extra hands with my nephew, Jem—Ben's boy—and the younger Bartel twins. You're welcome to join us. Another couple hundred head won't make that much difference."

Silas chewed up a mouthful of coleslaw and swallowed. "I'll think on it, Carl. Tell you the truth, it'd feel kinda good bein' on a drive again. That year when I broke my leg kinda lowered my interest level some, but hell, Doc Bartel says the bone's mended and—"

He broke off, pointing with his fork across the room. "Hellfire," he breathed. "Who's that?"

Carleton followed the direction of Silas's gaze.

"Over there," the rancher directed. "Behind Jem at the punch bowl."

Sarah whimpered, and Carleton began to rock the chair back and forth to quiet her. After a moment, he lifted his eyes from his infant daughter's face and scanned the room.

"See her?" Silas persisted. "God almighty."

It was Serena. Carleton's breath hissed in and stayed there when he caught sight of her. It was the first time he'd ever seen her without that two-legged skirt and riding boots and a worn felt hat. Maybe he was dreaming.

She wore a gauzy, soft-looking blue dress that swirled about her ankles when she moved. The long, full sleeves ended at the wrist in a wide cuff with tiny buttons marching halfway up to her elbow. The high, tight neckline had more buttons. There must be a hundred all told. How the devil had she gotten into it? How was she going to get *out* of it? The thought made his belly tighten.

Unable to take his eyes off her, he concentrated on his

slow, gentle rocking and pulling his breath in and pushing it out. "That's Serena Hull," he replied at last. "Jeremiah Hull's oldest girl."

Silas spilled coleslaw down the front of his shirt. "Damned pretty woman."

"She's twenty-five," Carleton said dryly. "You're fifty-six."

"And regrettin' every year of it, believe me. When the gentlemen get a look at her, it's gonna be some show, Carl. Glad I've got a ringside seat."

Carleton saw no point in responding. Silas was beyond reach. Instead, he rocked forward and back, staring across the room at the young woman he'd thought he was beginning to know.

Her hair was unbound. Pulled behind her ears in some kind of graceful twist, it swept down her back like a waterfall of black silk. When she reached her destination opposite him, between Fannie Lindstrom, the preacher's wife, and the widow Boult, Serena bent to speak to the ladies, then turned gracefully and seated herself between them. Her hair swirled with the motion, and Carleton's throat tightened.

The fiddler struck up a waltz, and two young men collided in a race to Serena's chair.

Silas chuckled. "What'd I tell you? Like bees to honey."

A third man, one of the younger Bartel twins—Carleton couldn't tell which one—stepped around the other two and spoke to Serena. She smiled and shook her head. Next to her, Cora Boult's mouth dropped open. The widow shut it with a snap as the young man again bent toward Serena.

Carleton had to laugh. If Serena wouldn't dance with him, Cora Boult would! The older woman's high-button shoes kept perfect time under her chair.

Cora said something and jabbed her elbow into Serena's

ribs. Serena jumped, then rose and moved onto the dance floor. Carleton stroked Sarah's warm, smooth forehead and watched the Bartel boy enfold Serena in his arms.

She danced stiffly, almost as if she were unwilling to be held. Whenever her partner slid his hand about her waist and pulled her closer, she backed away, holding him at arm's length with her fingertips resting lightly on the top of his shoulder.

"Balls of fire," Silas breathed beside him. "What a woman."

Carleton ground his boot heels into the waxed plank floor. "She's a girl, not a woman."

Silas chuckled. "Old age is gettin' to ya, Carl. You mean to tell me you don't see that pretty piece over there, fighting them off like yellow jackets, as a full-growed female just ripe for—"

"Shut up, Silas. I've got eyes."

He wished he didn't. He watched Thorny Duret, Silas's foreman, cut in on young Bartel. Then his own foreman, Lyle, left Amanda Frieder with Jem at the punch bowl and cut in on Thorny. With each partner, Serena stiffened, holding herself so rigid it looked as if her back were pounded straight as a branding iron. Carleton narrowed his eyes.

Something was wrong. She wasn't enjoying the dancing. Being held in a young man's arms seemed to make her uncomfortable. She looked skittish as a mare that'd been whipped once too often. His gut clenched. Good God, it was plain as horse teeth. She was frightened.

He watched Lyle try to settle her close, to no avail. Then Thorny again, then that newspaper fellow from Scottsburg. Slowly, his conviction grew. Serena was terrified of being held by a man.

Carleton rocked his daughter and thought hard. At his side, Silas alternately commented on the goings-on and shoveled forkfuls of cherry pie into his mouth. Carleton ignored him.

And then Thorny Duret made his move. He pulled Serena into a close embrace and with one hand, tucked her head under his chin. She pulled away, but he circled his arms about her and started in again. Evidently, he wouldn't take no for an answer.

He watched her purposely tread on Thorny's toe, but it didn't deter the dapper cowhand one bit. Catching her about the waist, Thorny lifted her off her feet and pinned her hard against his body.

Carleton was on his feet in an instant. "Hold the baby, Si," he barked. Plopping Sarah into the startled rancher's lap, he started across the floor toward Serena.

Chapter Six

Carleton reached Serena in four long strides. In one glance he could see she was shaking; the full gathered sleeves of her dress trembled like aspen leaves. Her chocolate-dark eyes, huge with fear, locked with his.

"Let her go, Duret."

"Now, jes' wait a minute," the muscular ranch hand began. "This has nuthin' to do with—"

"I said let her go. You're hurting her." Carleton closed his fingers on Thorny Duret's shoulder muscle and squeezed. The thick arms opened, and Serena stepped free.

"No offense, Thorny." Carleton held the man's eyes just long enough to reinforce his point. "Just a matter of good manners."

"Damned Rebs," Thorny muttered. "Think they know everything." He turned to Serena. "Beggin' your pardon, Miss Serena. Didn't realize I was out o' line."

Serena sent him a shaky smile.

Carleton touched her elbow, and she flinched. "Outside," he intoned.

She hesitated, then without a word she nodded and moved ahead of him toward the hotel entrance.

He caught her arm. "Not that way. Out the back. You might want to be alone for a few minutes."

She shot him a grateful look. "Yes. Thank you."

Under his fingers he felt her body tremble. A fierce sense of protectiveness welled up inside him, the same surge of feeling he'd had when Sarah was born and he'd first held her in his arms. Only this was stronger, and it was mixed with something else. He didn't have time to question it, just knew it was there, like a deep, quiet river flowing at the back of his mind.

He tightened his hand on her arm and walked her to the rear door and out into the darkened roadway that ran behind the hotel.

Outside, he turned her to face him. "Tell me."

"Tell you what?" Her voice sounded breathy, but the tone was steady. The fear was still there—he could see it in her eyes, feel it in the tension that stretched between them. But her control was back. She hid behind it like a soldier under fire.

"I watched you tonight. Every time a man came within a foot of you, you bolted like a scared filly. Why?"

Mute, she shook her head, her mouth twisting.

"Talk to me, Serena."

"I...I can't. Please, Mr. Kearney, I can't talk about it."

"Something about being close to a man frightens you," he persisted. "Almost as if—" He broke off when she dragged in a shuddery breath. Clasping her arms over her stomach, she bent her head.

"As if you'd been hurt." He watched her face. "Maybe assaulted."

She turned away from him and a long silence fell. He listened to her ragged breathing, heard his own as well, matching hers. Inside the hotel, the fiddle moaned a slow two-step, the music punctuated by the rhythmic chirping of crickets. The hot, still air smelled of dust and honey-suckle and wood smoke.

He didn't know what to make of her, really. Or what to do, outside of extricating her from the clumsy arms of a young, impetuous ranch hand with no sense of timing. Then her low, clear voice sliced through his body like a saber cut.

"It was at home, in Stark County. I was fifteen."

He waited while she collected herself enough to go on.

"I'd been invited to a dance in town. I remember Pa bought me a dress, white with tiny pink roses. On the way home, some men—four of them—caught my horse and dragged me down to the river. Two of them held me down, and…"

Carleton's fists closed into aching rocks of flesh as she struggled to steady her voice.

"They touched me," she said so quietly he could barely hear. "All over. I screamed and screamed, but nobody heard me."

His blood ran cold. "Were you raped?" he said in a low voice.

"N-no. It was just their hands. They tore my dress off and…and underneath, but…in the end, they just touched me."

Thank God, he thought. Enough damage had been done to make her skittish, but maybe she wouldn't be scarred for life. With time and understanding, she'd make some young man a good wife. An extraordinary wife.

"Miss Hull…"

"They didn't even kiss me," she said. Her voice rose to a thready cry. "It's funny in a way, isn't it? I've been *touched* but I've never been kissed."

She opened her mouth, worked to control her gasping breath. Carleton watched her chest rise and fall under the filmy blue material. He pictured a rough, dirty hand on her breast and his jaw clenched. "Damned Yankee bastards," he muttered.

"Yes," she breathed. "That's why I don't like dances, Mr. Kearney. I came tonight just so I wouldn't appear rude to the townsfolk, but—"

"You didn't care to dance."

"I didn't care to dance," she echoed. "Thank you for coming to my aid. And," she continued, dropping her eyes to the ground beneath her shoes, "for letting me speak about it. I never told anyone back in Stark County, not even Mama."

"Or Jeremiah? What about your father?"

"I couldn't tell Pa. He would have killed them."

Carleton bit back a growl. "Back in Carolina, where I come from, horsewhipping would have been a good idea, too."

She stared off into the darkness. "I am getting over it a bit at a time," she ventured. "I waltzed twice with Lyle Bartel, and each time it seemed easier. That's some progress, don't you think?" She lifted her head and looked into his eyes.

Carleton stared down at the white face. The fact that she could stand to be anywhere near a human male after being handled so brutally surprised him. "Yeah, that's progress, all right. 'Course, the way LB was looking at you should have made your hair curl, but I guess you didn't notice."

"I didn't look at him," Serena confessed with a small, tight laugh. "I looked at the wall clock over his shoulder. When he circled us around, I watched Mrs. Boult and Mrs. Lindstrom serving pie. Then I watched Jem at the punch bowl—things like that."

Carleton shook his head and chuckled. She'd been thrown and trampled, but despite her hurt, she hadn't given up. She was a survivor. Not only that, she was uncommonly good-looking. Stunning even, with that long black hair and creamy skin. Within a week, she'd have every male within a hundred miles standing on his head. Even that independent old bachelor Silas Appleby.

"Miss Hull," he said carefully, "I think you are making more progress than you know."

"Good," she announced, speaking slowly and evenly. "I like learning things. Today I stapled barbed wire and waltzed with a man for the first time in ten years. And tomorrow, I'm going to plant seeds in my flower garden."

Impressed by her backbone, Carleton released a long breath. "Life can be awful, can't it?"

"Oh, no, Mr. Kearney. Life isn't awful at all. It's challenging, and it's full of beautiful things, mostly." She faltered. "It's only people, here and there, who are bad."

Challenging, he echoed silently. Beautiful and challenging. Balls of fire, Serena Hull had a lot to learn. She was too young, too vulnerable, not to get hurt out here in the West. Out here, the strong survived, with luck. The weak didn't.

She turned with him back to the hotel, and they moved slowly away from the soft, shadowed evening into the bright lights and throbbing music of the social. He was very careful not to touch her.

"H'lo, S'rena." Jem stood swaying beside her.

"Jem!" She started visibly. "Where did you come from?"

"Over there, near the punch bowl."

Serena smiled at him. "Have you had some lemonade?"

Jem nodded vigorously. "Uh, yeah. 'Lotta lemonade, outside, with th' boys. They called it Tr'ntula Tea."

Carleton shot his nephew a quick look. "Well, now, Jem, looks to me like you've been sampling spirits."

"Sure have, Unc'l Carl. Tasted real good, too, after the firs' one. Only thing is, I feel kinda dizzylike. And my tongue fuzzes when I try t' talk."

"No wonder," Carleton observed with a wry smile. "You're drunk as a lovesick skunk."

Serena bit back a bubble of laughter.

"Come on, kid. Let's get you sober enough to walk home." He laid his arm around Jem's bony shoulders.

"Serena, get him some coffee, will you? Black. And lots of it." He ushered the boy ahead of him through the crowd and out the front door onto the board sidewalk.

By the time Serena arrived with two steaming mugs of coffee, Jem's head hung over the hitching rail. "You won' tell Dad, will ya, Unc'l Carl?"

With one hand, Carlcton massaged his nephew's neck and shoulder muscles. With the other, he lifted the mug out of Serena's hand.

Over Jem's tousled dark hair, Serena met Carleton's steady gaze.

"Seems we're the keeper of secrets tonight, doesn't it?" he said in a quiet voice.

"It does, yes. I assure you, Mr. Kearney, I am a good secret-keeper."

A glimmer of a smile touched his lips. He held her eyes a moment longer than necessary. "I, too, know when to keep my mouth shut. All right, Jem-boy. Drink up."

Jem groaned. "Don' say that, Unc'l Carl. Jus' those words make me feel awful funny. Doggone it, Ma's gonna stripe me good."

"No, she won't," Serena interjected. "She's inside talking to your cousin Alice."

She patted Jem's limp hand and directed Carleton's gaze to the second mug of coffee she'd set on the railing.

"That's how boys grow into men, I suppose."

"Not always. His father, Ben, did his growing when he got bit by a woman. If I'm not mistaken, Thad's going to do his growing up running your ranch."

"And you?" Serena said before she could stop the words.

Carleton was silent for a long minute. "I grew up fighting at Manassas. I was sixteen. Later, I grew up the rest of the way and got old at the same time—when Ella died. Up until then I was just a young fool with a hankering to stay alive and start a family. When she died, I didn't care anymore."

She studied the bronzed face. The weary expression in his shadowed blue eyes made her throat ache.

"But you do care, Mr. Kearney. You care about Jem, and about Alice and Sarah, your daughters. When I was dancing with Lyle, I watched you across the room, rocking your baby girl in your arms. You care a great deal, Mr. Kearney. I admire you for it."

The last words just tumbled out, but it was true. She did admire Carleton Kearney. Any man who could cuddle his infant daughter in one arm and eat pie with his free hand was a unique human being. She watched him steer Jem down the steps and across the rutted street toward the boy's home. It was true that Carleton seemed tired at times, as if he'd given up. Silver frosted his dark sideburns, and his gait, though graceful, was slow and world-weary. Thad and the other men—Lyle Bartel and his younger brother, the twins Jason and Eldon, and Snap and Rosy and the others—all of them were full of vinegar. Full of themselves. Carleton saw things differently.

When he returned, they stared at each other while the fiddler retuned and conversation hummed around them. Then the musicians struck up a lively melody.

Suddenly he held out his hand. "Dance with me, Serena."

Dance with him? Surely he was joking, after what she'd confided to him earlier? She darted a glance at him. No, she could see he was not joking. His eyes looked straight into hers with a question—not would she dance with him, but something else, something deeper.

"It's a Virginia reel," he explained over the scraping of the fiddle. "The man doesn't hold his partner, they just clasp hands. And," he added with the hint of a smile, "nobody can cut in."

She looked at him a long time. Then without a word she set her lemonade cup down and made her way to the line of dancers forming down the center of the room. Carleton followed her. When she turned to face him, the tanned skin around his eyes crinkled.

"Kinda wish you could add some courage to your lemonade, like Jem did?"

"Absolutely not. I will need all my wits about me when I dance—" She bit off the final words just in time. *With you,* she was about to say.

Why did Carleton Kearney muddle up her tongue so? She opened her lips and words she'd never thought of popped out like so many exotic butterflies.

She took a step forward, reached out her arms to start the reel. His warm, strong fingers closed over hers and her breath stopped.

Merciful heavens, she didn't need Jem's Tarantula Tea to make her dizzy! All it took was one dash of Carleton Kearney and the touch of his hands.

Through every step of the reel, Carleton watched the girl across from him. As long as she wasn't pulled close to a man during the whirling pattern of steps, she reveled in the movements of the dance. Her raven black hair swirled about her shoulders in a silky curtain when she spun about, and her dark eyes glowed with inner fire. Graceful and long-limbed, she moved with the same lithe control she showed as a rider. Unusual in a woman, Carleton thought. Ella had never ridden well, and even now,

Alice disliked the activity, preferring to be driven to and from town in the wagon.

Serena, on the other hand, was stronger than her slim, feminine body would suggest and more resilient emotionally than many men he'd known. The joy she expressed in the physical movements demanded by the reel—sashaying up and down the long line of couples clapping in time with the fiddle, leaning slightly backward and pulling hard on his hands when they circled together—these things told him she enjoyed life. He liked the way she met things head-on, the way she relished activity. She was vibrant and alive, exquisitely tuned for pleasure.

His groin tightened. He could understand a man wanting to lay hands on her. Even though he could not abide the brutality of forcing a woman, he felt the same stirrings those men must have felt. He, too, wanted to touch her.

But he would not. Serena deserved more than being the object of a man's desire. When a man lay with her, it must be someone she loved, someone who loved her in return.

He felt the same protective response toward his stepdaughter. Alice was in love with Thad; anyone with half an eye could see it. Anyone except Thad, that is. His nephew half courted, half teased his way into Alice's affections but artfully hid any indication of his own true feelings.

Carleton lost count of the step and suddenly felt Serena's slim fingers intertwine with his own as she pulled him into position for the human bridge under which the other couples ducked. She flashed him a gently accusing smile over the heads of the last couple passing under their outstretched arms, and he raised his eyebrows in mock apology. She laughed out loud.

Abruptly, the reel ended. Out of breath, Serena turned to him, still laughing. Something inside split his heart in two. He wanted to keep her to himself, dance with her again, but something stopped him. He had duties else-where—a baby daughter, a stepdaughter saddled with ranch responsibilities that ate up her youth...

And, he noted with a pang of regret, a cadre of young, eager bucks headed for the slim girl at his side.

He wasn't the one she needed. One of the younger men would be what she'd want, when the time came.

He bowed over her hand. "Miss Hull. It's been a plea-sure."

"Yes, it has, Mr. Kearney. I enjoyed it." Then she added something in a soft, shy voice. "Thank you."

Thad reached her first, and Carleton exhaled in relief. He knew his nephew would not press her, would mostly talk some pretty words and not hold her too tight. She would be safe with Thad.

But instead of satisfaction at the prospect, he felt a jolt of possessive anger. No matter who was dancing with Se-rena, he'd keep an eye on her.

Two hours later, the weary rancher tilted his chair back and narrowed his eyes. In the space of one evening Serena Hull had changed the style of Wildwood Valley dancing from close, arm-encircling embraces to dignified, almost formal placing of fingertips on shoulders. The message was plain: if a man wanted Serena as a partner, he held her as she insisted—with more than a body's width of space be-tween them.

Even Thorny Duret complied with the new practice. Thad was dancing that way with Alice, now, Carleton noted as he scanned the room. Alice didn't look the least bit happy about the change; her narrow face looked even more pinched than usual. Carleton knew it wasn't because of the baby—for most of the evening, Ben's wife, Jessa-myn, or Carleton himself had watched over Sarah while Alice danced.

Lyle Bartel circled the floor with petite, blond Amanda

Frieder held discreetly at arm's length. Lyle didn't look
happy, either, but Amanda bubbled away as usual, and
Carleton had to smile. His foreman never had much to say;
he suspected LB was a better lover than a conversation-
alist. Maybe that was what Amanda was so animated
about.

The younger Bartel twins, Jason and Eldon, fought like
puppies over the same partner—winsome, shy Nettie
Marsh, the undertaker's daughter. The boys were fiercely
competitive; Carleton wondered if she could keep track of
which twin got the most dances with her.

He searched the crowd for Serena. When he couldn't
find her, his chest tightened. Had some randy, lovestruck
cowhand waltzed her outside to snatch a kiss? He relaxed
when he found her at last, over in the far corner trying out
the steps of a schottische with Otto Frieder.

By Jupiter, Otto was half again as old as she was, and
married to boot!

Listen up, he chided himself, *you don't own her. It's
only one dance, not a tryst. Get a grip on yourself.*

Besides, Serena Hull was wise far beyond her years,
maybe because of her Indian mother's upbringing. Her heritage didn't show much on the outside, but Carleton was
beginning to recognize an inner resilience and maturity
few young women had. She had enough good sense not to
angle after some other woman's husband.

His sense of relief was laughable. *You old fool. Serena
has enough good sense not to look twice at a weary,
rancher older than his years, either.*

He needed to go home to bed and sleep off this entire
heart-splitting, upside down night. Pour some of Thorny's
Tarantula Tea in that bitter coffee he was sipping and forget half the things he'd thought about this evening. Better
yet, forget *all* the things he'd thought about.

No way on God's green earth was she going to want a

broken-down widower with an old-maid daughter and a brand-new baby. And no way did he ever want to feel anything for a woman again, especially a girl like Serena— young, full of life, achingly beautiful.

No, by God, never again. One woman was enough. Losing a wife was more than most men could bear. He'd lived through it, but damned if he'd ever risk it again. The pain wasn't worth it.

Chapter Seven

Serena paused after the first paragraph of her letter to Jessie and Mary Irene, so exhausted she could barely lift her pen. Since sunup, she'd been out on horseback with Thad, learning how to cut a cow away from the rest of the herd. Now it was long past supper time, and her backside ached. How she wished she could remember the herbs Mama used to mash up for poultices when Pa hurt his knee that time.

Thad hadn't fared too well, either. He'd ridden to the Double K bunkhouse where he was staying until after the fall roundup with ribs sore from laughing at her. Cutting out a cow was hard to master. Thad said she'd be ready by October, when they left on the drive, but after today, she had her doubts.

With a sigh, she picked up her pen.

"I am not sure Mr. Kearney will let me come along," she wrote. "He'll be the trail boss. Thad says it is most unusual to have a woman in a cow outfit. However, Cora Boult will be the chuck wagon cook. I spoke to her yesterday, and she said I'm a ranch owner just like Mr. Kearney and the other two men, and that I should insist on my rights."

Insist on her rights? With Carleton Kearney? She must be mad. Still, she had to try. Tomorrow she would ride over to the Double K and meet with the other ranchers and try to persuade them.

She hated visiting there. Alice Kearney was always so mean-spirited. Serena suspected Alice was unaware of her Indian heritage, but the younger woman seemed to dislike her enough as it was.

Serena bent over her letter. "The hens, especially Red Wing and Attila, are laying so many eggs all the town ladies are baking angel cakes, which use a full dozen each—just the whites, though. I don't know what they do with all those yolks—maybe give them to the liveryman, Dan Gustafsen, for his pet pig."

She had almost enough egg money saved up to start buying winter feed, providing Mr. Kearney would agree to sell it to her. He was an odd man. He'd been very kind in his actions of late, but he still resented her presence on Lost Acres Ranch. Or maybe it was mostly Alice who resented her.

She tried hard to watch and listen, as Mama had taught her. But while Thad and Alice were easy to understand, Carleton Kearney was a mystery. Certainly he was unhappy after the death of his wife, but he didn't talk about it—or anything else—very often.

"Cora Boult is a dear old soul," her pen scratched across the page. "She says she's never read a book except for the Bible, but she has a keen memory for stories. Jessie, you could fill your writing notebook just listening to her. I told her about my garden, and she said I should go ahead and plant now, even though it is late in the season. 'God knows a seed when He sees one,' were her words."

For weeks she'd soaked the little patch of ground beside the front door with used wash water, and yesterday she spaded it all up while Thad laughed and teased. *He won't laugh when my sunflowers sprout, though—and I know they will.* She'd planted at night when the moon was yellow and almost full, as Mama had taught her.

"Jessie," she continued, "I hope you did not return to school too soon after your last bout with fever. Get out my soft fox fur wrap—the one Mama made for me. It's stored in the old wardrobe. Wear it under your heavy coat to keep your throat and chest warm."

Serena laid her head down on the kitchen table and let her eyelids drift shut. She was so tired she ached all over. *Try not to be discouraged,* she admonished herself. *In the spring, we will all be together again.*

But tonight spring seemed so far away she wondered if it would ever come. And she was lonely. She didn't know where she fit in out here in the West. She knew next to nothing about ranching, and even though Thad assured her she was learning fast, the hands at the Double K avoided her. Alice didn't like her. Amanda wanted her to join the ladies quilting circle in town, but she had neither the time nor the energy after a day of mending fences and hauling water from the spring.

It was already September, a glorious fall, with maple trees turning the hillsides to scarlet and orange. The days were lazy-warm, the nights crisp. It made her think of apples, the way they snapped when you bit into them. Indian summer, the valley people called it. Good planting weather.

She hoped it was good weather for persuading Carlton Kearney to take her along on the drive.

Serena raised her head, shakily dipped her pen in the bottle of walnut ink at her elbow.

"I must close, my darlings—my head is drooping onto the table. All my love to you both. Your Sissy."

Carleton watched Eli Harker pound his bulbous pipe bowl against the kitchen table. "Hell, Thad," the stocky man sputtered. "Whaddya want to take the only girl in this valley God ever made right and waste her on a trail drive for, anyway?" He refilled his pipe with jerky motions.

Thad waited until a match flickered to life and Eli's mouth pursed around his pipe stem. "She wants to come. She's a ranch owner, like the rest of you. Seems to me she's got a right."

Silas Appleby snorted. "You got the papers for that?"

"She owns it, all right," Carleton said in a quiet voice. "I checked with the lawyer in Canton City." He surveyed the three men gathered in his kitchen. "But that's not the issue here."

He himself didn't fancy the idea of a woman on a cattle drive—especially one like Serena. She had courage—he could see that any day of the week. But she looked too...well, *female* to have much strength. A drive all the way to Winnemucca in late fall was serious business; there was no room for error, no time for a tenderfoot with no experience.

Silas slurped the last of his lukewarm coffee. "You're right about the God-made-her-right part, Eli. I ain't seen anybody yet can hold a candle to Miss Serena."

Carleton tightened his jaw muscles. "That's not the issue, either," he growled.

"Mebbe not," the sandy-haired rancher replied with a grin. "But it's mighty interesting verbal lather squeezin' out of Eli's talk-box. Seems I got a rival."

Thad groaned. "No offense, Si, Eli, but you're both old enough to be Serena's grandpa, and besides—"

"That, too, is not the issue," Carleton offered a third time. "But it does suggest one of the problems I foresee in having Miss Hull along on the drive."

"Yeah," Silas breathed on a sigh. "What cowhand's gonna keep his mind on his remuda with *her* around?"

"Old ones," Carleton said dryly. "With good sense and experience. If it comes down to it, *we're* the ones to keep our range rowdies in line."

"If!" Eli shot, his bushy eyebrows dancing. "Great balls of fire, Carl, you can't be serious?"

Carleton regarded the graying ranch owner steadily. He wished to hell he *wasn't* serious. "Might have to be. She's got a point. She's riding over to talk it over—should be here any minute."

Eli straightened. "You got any whiskey?"

"Thad?" Carleton gestured toward Eli's empty cup. "Coffee's on the stove. Whiskey's under the sink."

Thad rose to fetch the enamelware coffee pot and the brown flask behind the sink curtain. "Silas?"

"No whiskey, son." Silas covered his cup with one bony hand. "Wouldn't wanna smell of spirits around Miss Serena."

Thad chuckled as he filled his uncle's cup. "She's a ranch owner first, a woman second."

Silas removed his hand from his cup and Thad poured in the coffee. "Son, you've gotta do something 'bout your eyesight. No matter what she is, Miss Serena is a female first. Yessir, a real honest-to-God ornament in calico."

"Huh!" Eli barked. "More ornamental than useful, I'd guess. Still, I don't want to offend her." He waved away Thad's offer of the whiskey. "Jes' don't want her taggin' along, tangling up my trail boys' spurs. Oh, evenin', Miss Alice."

"Horse coming up the road," Alice snapped. She propped the fretting baby on one hip. "I'm going to give Sarah a bath. She's been crying for the past hour—maybe it'll settle her down." She lifted the simmering teakettle off the stove.

Carleton swallowed a mouthful of coffee. "Give her to me, honey. Maybe I can rock her to sleep."

At the knock on the front door, Alice clutched the child tighter and headed through the hall and yanked the door open.

"Good evening, Alice," Serena said quietly.

"Evening yourself," Alice said over the squalling of the baby in her arms. She made no move to invite Serena inside.

"May I come in? I understood there was to be a meeting—"

Alice swung the door wide and pivoted toward the kitchen. "In the kitchen."

Serena followed the thin figure in a much laundered work dress down the short hallway. "Gentlemen." She nodded at the men seated on either side of the Double K owner.

Alice moved to the stove as first Carleton, and then Silas and Eli Harker rose from their chairs.

"Miss Hull," Carleton responded. "Thad, bring another chair. We were just discussing…"

His words were obliterated by the baby's screaming.

Serena stood before the chair Thad had pulled up for her. "Alice, may I help with Sarah? Let me hold her for you."

"What would you know about young'uns?" Alice huffed over her shoulder.

"Quite a lot, actually. I was almost twelve when my youngest sister, Mary Irene, was born. I cared for her when my mother fell ill."

"Did she die?"

Serena gasped at the brutal question.

"Alice." Carleton's tone conveyed a subtle warning.

"No, she didn't. Not then, anyway. She died…later."

Carleton gestured at the chair. "Sit down, Miss Hull."

Serena sank onto the hard wooden chair and watched Thad splash a dollop of whiskey from the bottle on the sideboard into his cup.

"Alice, my Alice," her foreman crooned. "You got any more of that chocolate cake left?"

"One piece." Alice's voice softened when she spoke to Thad. "It's in the cooler. I'll get it for you."

Before Serena knew what was happening, Alice plunked the squalling infant onto her lap. The child quieted instantly, and Serena raised her eyes to meet the younger woman's startled gaze.

"Well, I never," Alice murmured. She sent Serena a scowl.

Thad coughed into the uneasy silence. "The cake?" he said at last. Alice spun away toward the pantry.

Carleton chuckled. "It's a wonder you're still able to walk after the supper you put away."

"The boy's not overweight, Carl," Silas offered. "He's just a foot too short!"

Thad smiled. "Serena drives me hard, so I got a big appetite. Just yesterday, we were out all day workin' a couple of Snap's cow ponies."

Eli blew a puff of blue smoke into the air. "Yeah? Who was workin, you or the pony?"

Serena settled the baby gently against her chest and listened to the masculine banter. Wherever he was, Thad seemed to get the worst of the ribbing. Probably not so much because he was younger than everyone else, but because he had such a thick skin. None of the men's remarks ever seemed to upset him. Also, he had an irrepressible wit of his own. Only with Alice was Thad ever serious, and that, Serena ventured to guess, was because Alice was an excellent cook.

Carleton cleared his throat. "Miss Hull, I'd like to dissuade you from joining the trail drive. It's a long haul to

Nevada. We could run into some weather this late in the season, and you might not hold up as well as a seasoned hand. You'll be more comfortable staying here at the ranch.''

Silas and Eli nodded in unison. Alice slipped a large wedge of dark chocolate cake before Thad and laid a fork beside the plate. Serena watched him shovel a huge bite into his mouth and pondered how to respond.

"Mr. Kearney," she said at last. "Mr. Appleby. Mr. Harker. I rode all the way from Stark County, Ohio, on a horse so bad-tempered I shook every time I fed it. I wasn't comfortable any part of the trip. It was cold in Missouri and hot in Dakota. I was hungry and thirsty and saddle weary every single day. But I'm here. I own a ranch and thirty head of cattle and I need to sell off my steers to pay for something that's very important to me.''

Thad stopped chewing and stared at her. Even Alice, her back to the proceedings, halted her activity at the stove as Serena went on in a low, clear voice.

"I'm a rancher, just as you gentlemen are. Feeding steers until next spring isn't going to put money in my pocket. I'm going to get them to the railhead if I have to walk every step of the way.''

"Can't do it, Missy." Eli leaned back and blew another aromatic cloud of smoke into the air above him. "Ridin' a fancy hack used to high-steppin' it real slowlike ain't half the job cuttin' steers on a cow pony is. You'll last a day, mebbe two, and we'll have to carry you the rest of the way.''

Silas sighed. "Eli's right, Miss Serena. You'll slow us up. We'll have over a thousand head, countin' Eli's and my stock. We can't take the risk.''

Serena swallowed. They didn't understand and they wouldn't listen. Only Alice, motionless by the iron cook-stove, and Thad, chocolate frosting coating his upper lip, even looked at her. Well, at least that was something. She'd try again.

"Let me ask you gentlemen a question. Is it fair to exclude me just because I'm a woman?"

No answer.

"Well, is it?"

"It's not a matter of being fair," Carleton said after a long pause. "It's a matter of being sensible."

"Practical," Eli interjected.

Silas leaned forward. "You see, Miss Serena, you bein' a female, well, it's not that we don't respect you or anything like that—it's just that, well, you'd be a distraction."

"Mr. Appleby, I assure you I will be so tired and dusty and disheveled I would be the furthest thing you could imagine from a 'distraction.'"

"Yeah, mebbe, but—"

"I can ride, and by the time we leave, I will be able to rope as well. I promise you I will pull my own weight."

Carleton's deep blue eyes met hers across the table. She tried to read the expression in them. Weariness, mostly. And something else she could not name.

"And," she continued, shifting the baby to her other shoulder, "since I intend to work just as hard as any other ranch hand, just as hard as any of you gentlemen, I see no reason why I should be excluded simply because I happen to be *Miss* instead of *Mr.* Hull.

"It won't work," Carleton said, his tone soft. "I'm sorry."

"But why?"

"Because, Miss Hull, I don't need you. I need experienced workers, men like Thad—able to ride all day in the rain and sleep in the saddle if necessary."

Serena looked straight into the hard, tanned face. "Try me."

"Sorry. I don't have time. A cattle drive is all business. None of us will have time to nursemaid a greenhorn."

"Jem Kearney tells me he's going. Is that true? He's only fourteen!"

"Maybe. His daddy's coming with us—he'll take care of Jem."

Serena bit her lip. That was it. She had no family, no one to look out for her. Alone, she was powerless. Or was she?

"Is there no appeal, then?"

"None, I'm afraid. As the trail boss, I have the last word."

Serena digested this in silence. The way was blocked. She could—would have to, in fact—entrust her life's hopes and dreams to someone else.

But it didn't sit right. *She* should be the one with the responsibility. She wanted to be part of it, wanted to be involved, not sit home by the fire and pray that all went well. She wanted to help. She *needed* to help!

She wasn't beaten yet, she resolved. What was it Mama used to say? *The sun appears each morning to light the way of the hunter; the stars guide the warrior home at night.*

She had the help of no man, but she still had herself. She wouldn't give up, no matter what. She worked to corral her thoughts and decide on her next move.

"In that case, Mr. Kearney, I will have to do the next best thing, won't I? Drive my own cows to market. Thad and myself, that is." She waited for the information to sink in.

"Thad!" Carleton set his cup down with such force the coffee sloshed over. "Hell, Sis, I need Thad."

"Yeah," Silas echoed. "He may look dumb, but he'll sure do to ride the river with. Fact is—"

"Shut up, Silas," Carleton interjected. "Fact is, I'd counted on Thad. He's my top hand."

"Exactly so," Serena replied. "That's why I hired him. If you remember, your 'top hand' works for me, now."

Her eyes met his across the table. The dark brows lowered over two cobalt stones that glinted in the lamplight.

"Miss Hull, that's blackmail."

Serena looked back as steadily as she could manage. "Both or none." She held her breath as the owner of the Double K stared at her.

Silas clattered his cup onto the table. "She's got a point, Carl. We need Thad. Hell, better take 'em both."

"Blackmail," Carleton muttered again.

"Shore is," Eli assented. He blew out a puff of smoke and chuckled. "Damn smart move, little lady." He raised his pipe stem in a salute.

"How well does she ride?" Carleton directed the question to Thad.

Serena opened her mouth to reply, but the rancher cut her off. "I'm asking Thad. It's not distance I'm interested in, Sis. A drive takes strength over the long haul and skill on a cow pony." He pinned his nephew with a look. "How well?"

Thad grinned at his uncle. "Well enough." He sent Serena a surreptitious wink.

Carleton studied her in silence. Serena felt her belly turn a slow somersault.

"Get yourself some britches," he barked. "I don't want any of my hands flapping around the herd in a skirt. Makes the cows nervous."

"Whooee!" Thad slapped his palm against his thigh. "We'll be ready, won't we, Serena?"

Serena nodded in the direction of her foreman, but it was Carleton's gaze that held her. In the hard, shuttered face the man's eyes darkened with an emotion she could not read. Uneasy, she shifted her glance to the other two ranchers. Both men looked at her with grudging respect.

Carleton cleared his throat. "Britches," he reminded.

"Certainly, Mr. Kearney." She breathed a sigh of relief. "First thing in the morning, I'll ride into town and visit the mercantile." She'd won! Merciful heavens, he'd taken her on as one of his hands for the cattle drive. Now all she had to do was get ready—practice on the cutting pony and learn to throw a rope. She'd die before she'd let Carleton Kearney find fault with her.

Silvery moonlight illuminated the road leading from the Double K to her own ranch. Serena walked her horse to the Lost Acres entrance, dismounted and opened the gate. Thad had repaired the rusted hinges, so the heavy pole barrier swung noiselessly inward.

The mare moved through the opening, and Serena released the top rail, letting the gate slide home with a click. She stuck her left toe into the stirrup, grabbed the saddle horn and started to pull herself up.

Just as she lifted her leg, a sound directly under her made her check the motion. She peered down, straining to see in the pale light. The horse sidestepped, and she clung to the saddle with both hands.

A dark, rounded shape scuttled out from behind the horse, and Serena's breath whooshed in.

A chicken! Her hens were outside!

Lord, somehow they had gotten out of the henhouse!

Chapter Eight

In the shadowy light, Serena made her way on foot to the henhouse. Not once but twice she had checked the latch before shutting Speckle and Attila and the other chickens inside at dusk. Now the wooden door hung open.

She lit a kerosene lamp and set out to find her missing flock. Unless a fox or a coyote—or the Double K bunkhouse dog—got them, once they wandered out of their shelter they would most likely hunker down in the open. The question was where? She moved toward the Lost Acres entry gate, holding the lantern high over her head.

Unseen chickens clucked in the darkness. She stumbled over one directly in her path, set her lamp on the ground, and bent to pick up the bird. Cradling it under one arm, she tramped back to the chicken house and shut it inside. In the next hour, she searched for and found the other four hens. Her back ached from her workout on the cutting pony that afternoon, and her head throbbed from her encounter with Carleton Kearney after supper.

She trudged into the henhouse with the last chicken under her arm. What was it about that man that made him seem so forbidding? He never raised his voice, never used the fractured grammar that marked the speech of the other ranch owners and their hands. And Mr. Kearney rarely smiled. He was a hard man. Not mean, just determined. Set in his ways.

But, she thought with an inward smile, she'd won the last skirmish. She'd forced him to take her on the drive. Not willingly, but he'd consented all the same. After all, she owned a herd, too, small though it was. It was only right and fair that she go with the men.

An odd feeling swept over her—half elation, half apprehension. Could she really carry her share of trail responsibilities among a bunch of trail-wise cowhands? *Male* cowhands? She already rode passably, Thad assured her, and tomorrow he would begin teaching her how to throw a lariat.

But Thad had no idea how uneasy she felt in the close company of men. Except for Widow Boult, the chuck wagon cook, Serena would be the only female around for weeks on end.

The old panic squeezed the air out of her chest, closing her throat over a cry. At the dance last month, she'd made some progress in her struggle to conquer her uneasiness around men. Thanks to Mr. Kearney, she had survived an entire evening of close contact with strangers—men—and emerged shaken but intact. Stronger, even. She'd grappled with her fear of being near men and had managed the social amenities in spite of it.

Papa would be proud of her, pleased at the way she fit into his world. Mama would, too, even though she knew her mother had felt torn between two worlds—that of her Indian ancestors and the white man she loved. Mama had suffered for loving a man, but she had tried hard to fit in. Serena could do no less.

She would stay close to the chuck wagon and Cora Boult, she resolved. And she would tolerate the close proximity of Mr. Kearney and the other men as best she could.

Those were the terms in her own private war; if she wanted to go on the drive, she had to cope with men.

She shut the henhouse door, then jiggled the catch to be sure it was tight. The chickens couldn't have gotten out by themselves; someone had unlatched the door on purpose. A shiver crawled up her backbone. Maybe the harassment she'd endured in Stark County was starting again.

Apprehension swept over her as she unsaddled the mare and draped a thick blanket over her back. It was three o'clock in the morning. She was too tired to think about it now.

The lariat left her hand, circled erratically over her head, and dropped over her own shoulders.

"Jehosaphat, Serena," Thad Kearney yelled. "Watch what you're doin'!"

"I am watching," she retorted through gritted teeth. "And flapping my arm and flicking my wrist and everything else you ordered! I just can't do it!"

"Don't be a goose, of course you can. Now watch me once again." He retrieved the rope from where it had hung about her body, shook out the kinks and coiled it in his left hand.

"Keep your eyes on your target and lift your arm as you toss the loop." He sailed the rope out and yanked it taut around the fence post. "See? Now, try again."

Serena accepted the rope, checked the loop at the end, and began coiling the braided rawhide into a loose circle. Her neck and shoulders ached. She longed to just shut her eyes and forget about learning to rope. Instead, she squinted into the sun and assessed the distance to the cedar post.

She could tell by the sun it wasn't noon yet, and she was dead tired. Of course she'd been out raking and watering her newly seeded sunflower bed at four o'clock this morning. Maybe she shouldn't have bothered, but the night was balmy and moonlit—just right for planting seeds. After last night's confrontation with Carleton Kearney, then chasing her hens and shutting them in the chicken house in the middle of the night, she needed to do something positive, something that would eventually produce something of beauty, just for its own sake. Growing a flower garden would balance the bitterness of finding herself the butt of another small but unfriendly act.

First the clothesline had been knocked down, then her chickens let out. She'd credited both events to her own carelessness, but underneath she knew better. She wasn't careless—especially not with her own property, and particularly not with her hens. The money she earned selling eggs to Mr. Frieder brought her closer every day to her goal of building a house and purchasing train tickets for Jessie and Mary Irene. Sunflower blooms would be something to look forward to, to sustain her.

She eyed the post, mentally transforming it into a steer, drew back her arm, and shut her eyes as the rope hummed in the air above her. With a snap of her wrist she loosed the lariat. Almost of its own volition, it zinged over the post. Automatically she jerked it snug.

"I did it! Look, Thad—I lassooed a cow!"

"Horsefeathers," her foreman told her with a snort. "You roped a fence post that wouldn't move if a fire burned under it."

"But—"

"It's okay, Serena. You're improving, all right. Come afternoon, we'll go over to the Double K corral and practice on a real calf. I'll try to find one that looks like a fence post!"

"Thanks," she said dryly. Some days she could do without Thad's quirky sense of humor. But she did value what he had taught her. She'd always wanted a brother;

now in a way she had one. When her own Lazy A cattle sold, she'd owe him three months back wages. The amount wouldn't be half enough for Thad's hard work and earnest efforts on her behalf.

She liked Thad. He reminded her there were some good men on this earth. She liked his younger brother, Jem, too. But Jem was only fourteen. Both Thad and Jem were her friends—the only ones she had outside of Amanda and her parents, Otto and Anna-Marie Frieder.

"Let's break for noon eats, boss. My belly's about caved in."

"You eat, Thad. I'm not hungry."

"You'd better have at least a sandwich or somethin'. Otherwise, you won't last 'til supper. Ma sent out some fried chicken, but I gambled most of it away playin' gin in the bunkhouse after breakfast. There's two pieces left— you can have 'em if you want."

Serena watched him coil up the rope and hang it on his saddle horn. She didn't think she could stomach fried chicken now that she'd given names to all her hens. She expelled her breath in a long sigh. Maybe Mr. Kearney was right—she wasn't cut out for ranching.

Oh, yes, she was! she reminded herself immediately. She had to be. Her life, and the lives of her sisters, depended on it.

"You're right, Thad. I should eat something." She followed Thad to the spreading oak midway between the pasture and her house. "I'll try a piece of chicken, please. A small one."

The calf her foreman roped for her to practice on after lunch looked nothing at all like a fence post. Serena's heart sank as she watched the frightened animal dodge and tug on the end of Thad's lariat. When he dragged it into the corral yard, the mother cow—a sloe-eyed Hereford with a bulging udder, nosed the corral fence and bawled her distress.

Serena's heart caught at the mournful cry. When the separated calf answered, the sound cut into her belly.

Thad tossed her the rope. "Come on, Serena. Try it. Drop it right over his head, like I showed you."

She circled the wary calf, trying not to listen to the anguished mother outside the fence. If she managed it quickly, cow and calf would be reunited all the sooner.

Resolutely she dangled the lariat in her right hand and edged near the quivering animal. Soft brown eyes gazed at her with distrust.

The mother cow bawled again, and the calf answered. A shard of pain knifed into her chest. She had to rope it and get it back to its mother. She swung the lariat into the air, began to spin a lazy circle above her head.

Out of the corner of her eye she saw a lean figure climb onto the fence rail. Then another, a cigarette dangling from his lips. Snap. She recognized his cocky strut—like the banty rooster Mama had raised back in Canton City.

She concentrated on her lariat, studying the calf as it circled and dodged. *Come on, rope her!* she ordered herself. *Put an end to her suffering.*

She made one final circle with her roping arm and felt the tears sting into her eyes. Her vision blurred. The calf bawled again, and Serena dropped the rope and started forward. Wrapping both arms around the trembling animal's neck, she held on while choking sobs rose from her belly and racked her body.

"Haw, haw, haw!" a masculine voice penetrated her weeping. "Lookit that, will ya! Missy Tender Heart is fallin' in love."

"Shut up, Snap," a low voice ordered.

"Aw, come on, boss. A bit o' funnin' don't hurt none. 'Specially not for—"

"Shut up or clear out," the voice growled.

"Now jes' hold on a minute—"

Serena released the calf and sank to her knees on the hard-packed earth. "Oh, God," she wept. "I can't do it."

She heard a muffled sound behind her. Carleton Kearney strode toward her, slapping his black Stetson hard against one jean-clad thigh.

"Get up," he barked.

Trembling, Serena forced herself to her feet and faced the grim-faced rancher.

"Miss Hull," he began, his voice menacing, "unless you want not-too-gentle ribbing from here to Nevada, you'd best toughen your hide. No cowhand worth spit's going to wait around while you nursemaid each calf you rope."

He thrust her rope into her hand. "Now, try it again. When you tag it, lean backward or she'll pull you over."

He moved away from her with long, easy strides and climbed up on the fence rail, watching her. From all the way across the yard she felt his dark, intense eyes bore into hers. *Do it, and do it now,* his look said.

Setting her jaw, she determinedly coiled the lariat, set the spin, and moved once more toward the nervous calf, purposefully screening out the jeering voices of the men ranged around the corral perimeter.

Serena let the lariat fly. The loop settled over its body and she let it drift down to its forelegs. Then she snapped it tight and leaned back against the animal's weight.

Thad's voice rose above the general tumult. "Once more, Serena! Do it again!"

Again! Merciful heaven, wasn't once enough? Evidently not, from the expression on Carleton Kearney's face. Impassive, he stared at her across the yard, waiting.

Damn the man. Meeting his expectations tested every

ounce of strength and courage she had. She'd caught one calf, met his challenge. What more did he want?

She coiled her rope slowly. On second thought, maybe she'd just go him one better.

Afraid she'd lose her nerve, she allowed herself no time to think. She eyed the calf Thad had just freed, grasped her rope, and tossed a wide, circling loop into the air. The calf dodged and ran, brushing Carleton's pant leg in its mad dash for freedom. Serena steadied her nerve, flicked her wrist and let the rope fly toward her target.

It dropped neatly over the ranch owner's shoulders, and, with an inward smile, she yanked backward with all her strength.

Carleton Kearney toppled off the fence rail and sprawled into the dirt.

Snap's raucous "haw, haw, haw" rose over the guffaws of the Double K hands. This time it echoed her own feelings exactly. She could almost hug the stocky wrangler for expressing what she held rigidly inside—jubilation at bringing the high-and-mighty rancher to his knees.

Without a word, Carleton picked himself up and brushed off the dirt. As she began to coil the rope, he strode across the corral toward her.

An ominous silence fell. Except for Snap's wheezy breathing, there wasn't a sound save the occasional bawl from the cow. Suddenly terrified, Serena found herself unable to take a single step. So forbidding was the expression on the ranch owner's tanned, angular face her feet simply refused to move.

"Miss Hull," he said when he was within hearing distance. "Next time you prove your point…" He kept moving toward her, his eyes glinting like two polished stones.

She quailed inside. He was almost on top of her when he stopped, so close she could smell dust and the faint scent of bay rum rising from his skin.

"Next time," he repeated, his voice a low rasp near her temple, "I'd hog-tie a man good and certain. That way you might live through the experience. Otherwise..."

He drew in a long, slow breath. Serena watched, fascinated, as his chest expanded to strain the buttons in the navy canvas shirt.

"Otherwise, Miss Hull, you can count on possibly a happy but predictably short life." He gave her a long, steady look and turned away.

She swore she saw the glimmer of a smile touch his lips, and her heart cartwheeled into an erratic rhythm. She'd played a trick on the king of the mountain and she'd survived! He must like her a little bit—otherwise, he would surely have laid into her with more vituperative words, or even—she shuddered—a horsewhip!

Well, *that* was something to think about. There was a good deal more to Carleton Kearney than met the eye. She wasn't sure what, but she wanted to discover it. Mr. Kearney was definitely out of the ordinary. For no reason other than that, he deserved watching.

She grinned at the gawking ranch hands. Happier than she'd felt for days, she watched the calf trot out the open corral gate and bolt toward its mother. A surge of well-being filled her with a buoyant, sunny feeling. She hadn't felt this good since the day she'd arrived in Wildwood Valley!

In the next instant, her euphoria vanished. An even bigger challenged faced her now—the cattle drive to Winnemucca. It would be long and difficult. And dangerous. How, she wondered with sudden misgivings, would she measure up? How would she get through it?

Not only that, would Carleton Kearney be watching her, assessing her every step of the way?

He would. She knew he would.

Just as she was beginning to watch him.

Chapter Nine

Serena narrowed her eyes to peer through the cloud of dust-laden air. Ahead of her, the hooves of a thousand head of cattle plodded down the main street through town. Somebody on the board sidewalk waved as she rode by. Jessamyn Kearney, she guessed. Ben's wife. They were just passing the newspaper office. The haze was so thick, she couldn't really be sure.

Her eyes smarted. The acrid smell of cow dung choked her throat. Under the bandanna she had tied around her face, she ran her tongue around the inside of her dry mouth and over her chapped lips.

A few yards to her left, ranch owner Eli Harker expertly guided his mount through the swirling brown air. A small, tough man with sunburned ears that stuck straight out from his head like seashells, Eli seemed unperturbed at the prospect of having to eat dust all morning.

"Doin' okay, gal?" he called out.

"Sure," she yelled back. When she closed her mouth, dust gritted between her teeth. It felt like chewing bits of gravel.

"Keep your head down," Eli advised. "And tip your hat over your face."

Serena tugged her black Stetson down over the thick braid she'd coiled about her head at five o'clock this morning. At least her hair would be reasonably clean tonight. The rest of her—her shirt and jeans, and every inch of her skin—would be filthy. And sweaty. Already, rivulets of perspiration trickled down her neck and between her shoulder blades. She felt sticky all over, as if she'd been dipped in molasses. She longed to roll up her blue denim shirtsleeves, but when she unbuttoned one cuff, Eli had stopped her with a gesture.

"Worse," he warned in a single word. He pantomimed heat coming off the skin of her forearm, and she nodded in comprehension. Sunburn. Windburn, too, probably. Nothing lay between the scorching rays of the sun and her delicate skin but protective layers of clothing.

Never had she felt so at the mercy of the elements. Even when she'd come out west from Stark County last spring, she'd been able to stop and rest under an occasional shady tree or cool off in a meandering stream. But on a cattle drive, she was part of a team. She couldn't leave her designated post unless the trail boss ordered it.

But the trail boss, Carleton Kearney, was at least a mile ahead, separated from her by a milling mass of cattle on the move and a thick cloud of dust-laden air. He neither knew nor cared how she fared.

Serena consciously straightened her spine. He'd assigned her to ride drag, and ride drag she would. She was low man on the totem pole, and she knew she had lots to learn. She only hoped she could live through the experience.

So far it hadn't been too difficult. All she had to do was corral the laggards and keep the occasional stray cow from turning back or wandering off. It was the constant thirst and breathing dust through her bandanna that took its toll as the hours passed. Hell, she thought, with its searing flames and anguished souls persecuted by pitchfork-wielding demons, must have been conceived on an ancient cattle drive.

A yearling dropped behind the herd. Serena spurred the cow pony forward and chased it back and forth until it finally settled back in line. Dust sifted into her eyes. Panting from the exertion, she sucked more of the gritty stuff into her mouth and nose.

She repositioned the pony on Eli's right, noting the effortless, graceful way he moved atop his horse. The diminutive, gray-haired man was an expert rider. She'd have to live to be a hundred before she could control a horse with that much skill.

The rancher caught her gaze and sent her a swift thumbs-up gesture. Stunned, Serena felt her spirits soar. Carleton Kearney might not applaud—or even notice—her struggle, but at least *someone* did. *Bless that man, Lord. And, please, keep him at my side the rest of this day.*

Thad had warned her about the rough hazing greenhorn trail riders often endured. Eli's quiet approval encouraged her. Maybe she *could* make a go of this venture.

Buoyed up by her small success, she sent the man a smile, then realized he couldn't see it because of the bandanna covering the lower portion of her face. Without thinking, she snapped a smart salute instead.

She was rewarded by Eli's low, gentle laughter as he cantered off after a stray cow and her calf.

Invigorated, Serena picked up her pace and went to help him.

Eli Harker nudged his mount close to Carleton's as the tail end of the long line of cows reached Vinegar Flat and spread into the lush pasture to rest. "Pushin' kinda hard, aren'tcha?"

"Got to," Carleton replied through dry, cracked lips.

"Need to move the herd far enough from home that they won't keep turning back."

Eli nodded. "She's ridin' drag, you know."

"I know." He'd purposely assigned Serena the worst trail position. If she tossed in the towel this first day out, she could always turn back. "How's she managing?"

Eli blew out a long breath. "She's not complaining. Fact is, she's not sayin' much of anything. I figure her throat's so clogged with Oregon trail dust she won't talk for a week."

"Can't be helped," Carleton muttered. "I won't have a hand that can't pull his—or her—weight. It puts lives in jeopardy."

"Yeah. Well, she's pullin' what little weight the good Lord loaded onto them tiny bones of hers. See for yourself." With a jerk of his head, the older man drew Carleton's attention to the solitary rider just now arriving at the noon camp.

"How'd she get so far behind?"

Eli spat onto the ground at Carleton's feet. "Chasin' cows, how d'ya think."

"She'll get the thin part of dinner. Both Thad and Hog ate already. I sent them on ahead to scout for a campsite."

"How far ahead?"

"Six, maybe eight miles. Around Sandy Bottom Creek. We need good water."

"Sandy Bottom, huh?" Eli's matter-of-fact tone failed to disguise his concern. "She'll never make it that far ridin' drag, Carl."

Carleton studied the wizened man on the tired pony. "She'll make it. A thick steak, a fresh horse...she'll make it." He hoped his tone of voice masked his worry about Serena. He wanted to show her the hardships of a drive, trail-break her, not kill her.

Eli turned his mount toward the remuda encircled by

Snap's hastily fashioned temporary rope corral. Carleton fell in behind him. Both their cow ponies, ridden hard for the past four hours, were played out. All the hands, including Serena, would get fresh mounts when they saddled up after the noon meal. Carleton hoped Snap would select a strong, steady horse for the young woman to finish out the day.

With a glance at the last of the cows now moving into the broad meadow where camp had been set up, he dismounted, lifted off his saddle, and turned his horse into the remuda corral. Then he strode toward the chuck wagon, where Cora had the noon meal waiting for the hands. He'd be about the last one to feed, he figured; the men ate in shifts so the herd was always watched.

The buxom cook plopped a sizzling hunk of beef onto his blue enamelware plate, and he moved on to the huge skillet of fried potatoes, dished some out and drowned the entire plate in gravy.

Cora bustled between the makeshift grill where the steaks cooked and the kettle of gravy hung from a hook over the fire. "I don't believe in luggin' a stove around in a wagon," she muttered. "I'd rather cook in the open."

"That's why the Double K is still known as a pot rack outfit," Carleton remarked, raising one dark eyebrow at the cook.

"Maybe so," Cora huffed. "But hands compete all year long for the privilege of working a Double K drive—now I wonder why that is?"

"Smells good, Cora," he remarked, changing the subject.

"Oughtta," the woman snapped. Her china blue eyes sparkled. "Been fryin' the last hour, waitin' for you. What took you so long?"

Carleton spooned a last dollop of gravy over his meat and grabbed a tinware coffee cup. "Checking ahead for tonight's camp. Make sure Jem pulls the wagon close to the creek, will you? And fill the water barrels before the herd gets there."

"Anything special you want for supper tonight?"

Carleton sent the elderly woman a conspiratorial look. "Yeah. Add some whiskey to Serena's coffee."

Cora pursed her lips and nodded. "Rough on her, ain't it?"

Carleton gulped a mouthful of scalding coffee. "Yeah. And going to get rougher." He squatted on a ragged patch of dry grass some yards away from the cookfire, settled the coffee cup on the ground beside him, and dug into his food.

He watched Cora busy herself dishing up a plate just as Serena walked up. Holding her body pretty stiff, he noted. She untied the bandanna about her face, shook the dust out and stuffed it into her back pocket. A mask of dark trail dust outlined her eyes.

"My stars, child," Cora sputtered. "You look like a raccoon! Dip some water into your hat and sponge off afore you eat."

So tired she could barely move, Serena moved to the water barrel and scooped two full dippers of water into the crown of her Stetson. Using her bandanna, she scrubbed at her nose and cheeks until the pale skin showed, then rinsed her hands and tossed the grimy water at the base of a parched-looking bush.

"Here." Cora shoved her loaded dinner plate into Serena's hands and stuck a fork in her shirt pocket. "Sit a spell while you eat."

"Can't," Serena said, her voice low. "I'll never get up again. I'll eat standing up."

Spearing a gravy-slathered potato slice, she poked it into her mouth, chewed once, then leaned over to spit it out. Without a word, Carleton handed her his cup of coffee.

She took a big swig, swished it around the inside of her mouth, and spit again. "I do beg your pardon, but my mouth was full of grit." She swallowed another mouthful and returned his cup.

"Kinda dusty back there," the trail boss observed. He concentrated on slicing up his steak with his pocketknife.

"A bit." She stabbed another potato, forked it past her chapped lips. She wouldn't complain if it was the last thing she ever did.

Out of the corner of her eye, she saw the redheaded Bartel twins race up, tumbling over each other trying to reach the chuck wagon first.

"Hold it," Cora ordered. "Don't allow no horseplay around the chuck box. Kicks dust into my dinner pots."

"Sorry, ma'am," the young men chorused in unison. "Can we eat now?"

"What've you boys been up to that you're so late?" Carleton inquired without lifting his eyes from his plate.

Eldon jerked to attention. "Well, Mr. Kearney, me an' Jason, here, an' the rest of the boys, well, we had a kind of a bet goin,' and—"

"I'd eat instead of gamble, if I were you," Carleton interrupted. He could imagine what the bet was—probably something about Serena. Would she last the morning, or beg for relief from riding drag the rest of the day? He flashed a quick look at the young woman standing an arm's length from his shoulder.

If he knew anything about boys on a trail drive, he knew they'd be laying for Serena—not only because she was a tenderfoot, but because she was female.

"When you finish eating, boys, stash your plates in the wash bucket and get back to the herd. We head out in fifteen minutes."

On the other hand, if he knew anything about Serena,

he guessed she would cost whoever was betting against her a tidy pile of money.

He drew in a long breath, studying the dark head bent over her plate. Lord, she looked like she couldn't hold up one more minute, let alone through the long afternoon shift.

Chapter Ten

"Hear them cattle bawlin'?" Eli Harker shouted to Serena over the rumble of hooves. "That's Sandy Bottom Creek up ahead. They smell the water."

Serena signaled her understanding. At last! Reaching the creek meant their first night's camp was just over the rise, and the day was mercifully over. The first thing she'd do when she got off this sorry excuse for a cow pony would be to throw herself, clothes and all, into the creek and wash off the dirt that caked her skin and her outer garments. The thought of submerging her hot, dust-caked body in cool, soothing water brought tears to her eyes.

The horse jerked under her, dancing sideways in the erratic pattern he had displayed all afternoon. An animal this fractious shouldn't be part of a trail remuda, she reasoned. She wondered at Snap's selecting such a jittery mount for a drag position rider. Dodger, what a name for a horse! He'd been difficult to control ever since she'd settled her backside onto the saddle. Thank goodness he'd have two or three days of rest before being ridden again; today he was definitely out of sorts.

At the crest of the small hill, she peered through the brown haze at the herd circling ahead. Yipping cowhands drew the animals tighter and tighter until they barely had room to lie down. Smoke rose from the fire pit dug near the chuck wagon, parked upstream from the herd. Two black iron Dutch ovens swung on a crude rack directly over the fire. The scent of supper bubbling in Cora's collection of pots made her stomach gurgle. She couldn't tear her gaze away from the lidded utensils.

Torn between her imagined bath in the creek and filling her belly, Serena grappled with the effect of exhaustion—the inability to make a simple decision. By this time, chasing a laggard cow required no thought whatsoever; it was simply a reflex action. The pony did most of the work—all she had to do was stay seated.

But whether to eat or wash? Her beleaguered mind couldn't decide.

Another hundred yards and she could rest. She heaved a shaky sigh and wondered if her legs would support her when she dismounted.

Thad met her at the improvised corral gate. "You look plumb saddle-silly, Serena. Let me help you down."

Too tired to respond, she tipped toward him. He hauled her out of the saddle and steadied her with one hand while he loosened the cinch. "I'll bring your gear. Why don't you go have a dip in the creek. Everybody else has already washed up—you and Eli are the last ones into camp."

Numb with fatigue, Serena nodded at her foreman and stumbled toward the beckoning ribbon of silvery water. Before she went three steps, Jem popped up at her elbow.

"Uncle Carl said to 'ccompany you down to the creek in case you want a bath. 'N Cora sent some soap and a towel." He proffered a square of clean huck toweling. "And she said to tell you 'bout the chamber pot she keeps in the wagon in case you..."

Serena choked back a laugh. God knew she had no need of a chamber pot! She'd relieved herself behind a clump of vine maples early this morning, and the rest of the day she'd been so parched she hadn't felt the need. She accepted the towel and the cake of soap.

"Thank you, Jem. A bath sounds wonderful." She sent the boy as much of a smile as she could muster. "You can stand guard for me."

"There's a pool half a mile upstream. Gosh, Serena, you look kinda peaked—think you can make it that far?"

"For a bath? I could walk a *whole* mile for a bath!"

Maybe she could, maybe she couldn't. But she wouldn't admit that to Jem.

The boy positioned himself in front of three spreading cottonwoods which screened her from view. Serena stepped to the creek bank, stripped off her shirt and jeans and then her underclothes and plunged into the clear pool.

Ten minutes later, she emerged, teeth chattering from the cold water, rebraided her hair and donned the fresh clothes she'd grabbed out of the leather wallet containing her personal belongings. With Jem beside her, Serena headed back to camp. As they neared the fire pit, Cora's voice carried to them.

"Come and get it or I'll spit in the skillet!" She clanged two pot lids together like cymbals.

Jem grabbed her hand. "Come on, Serena. I don't want any of Cora's spit on *my* biscuits!"

All the men except Silas Appleby and one of the Bartel twins, out circling the herd on horseback, sprawled in a semicircle around the cook fire, tin dinner plates balanced on their knees.

"Beans and bacon, biscuits and gravy," Thorny Duret announced, his voice hinting hungry admiration. "That woman's a genius at marrying breakfast and dinner."

"Now ain't that romantical," Snap chimed. The wrangler waggled his fork at Thorny. "Hearin' wedding bells, huh?"

"Nope," Eli Harker offered in his usual mild tone. "Not wedding bells. Just bells."

The men guffawed. Cora handed Serena a plate piled with two tall sourdough biscuits and a spreading circle of beans. "I made spotted pup for dessert, so save some room," the cook cautioned.

Serena settled herself between Thad and a thickset man she hadn't seen before today. He sat somewhat separate from the close circle of men. She arranged her plate on her lap and heard him murmur, "Winston Hartley, ma'am. Pleased to meet you."

"Mr. Hartley." Serena inclined her head in his direction.

"Ever'body calls him Hog," Thorny volunteered, his mustache twitching. "Don't pay to ask why."

It was already apparent why. Winston Hartley—Hog—shoveled his plate clean in a scant minute while making an odd humming sound, punctuated by heavy, irregular breathing and much lip smacking. Serena shifted her position so she wouldn't have to look at him.

"Didn't you learn no manners down in Texas?" Snap growled out of the side of his mouth. "Feedin' you is jes' like sloppin' a pig."

Hog's soft brown eyes rested briefly on the chunky wrangler. "Never been in Texas, Snap."

"Well, where the hell was you brought up?"

Hog spit on his thumb and smoothed his black mustache. "Arizona, mostly." He burped so loudly Serena jumped.

"Here's your coffee, honey." Cora set the tin cup at Serena's feet and patted her shoulder. "Drink it all up, now," the older woman intoned before she bustled back to her array of pots.

Hog rose and followed the cook. "Did you say spotted pup, ma'am? With raisins?"

"Hey!" One of the Bartel twins leaped to his feet. "Don't let Hog at that pudding—there won't be a speck left for the rest of us."

"Mind your own business, son." Carleton Kearney's voice carried around the circle with quiet authority.

"Or eat faster," Carleton's brother, Ben, added.

Serena smiled down into her coffee cup. As apprehensive as she was about being surrounded by men, she enjoyed the rough humor of the tired hands. For one thing, it gave her time to figure out who was who. Keeping the names and faces straight taxed her brain.

She took a big swallow of coffee just as Thad returned to her side, his plate covered with the raisin-filled pudding.

She gasped as the whiskey-laced brew went down. Across the campfire she caught Carleton's fleeting smile. Were they *all* drinking spirits in their coffee? She reached for Thad's cup and took a small sip. Just coffee.

Had Cora surreptitiously dipped into the locked drawer containing the medicinal liquor? She glanced at the bulky cook's face. The expression under the worn brown felt hat was studiedly impassive.

No, she reasoned. Cora would never do such a thing except in an emergency. The trail boss would have had to order the cook to add whiskey to Serena's coffee, and at this moment, Carleton Kearney looked... She glanced at the sun-lined face under the gray Stetson.

Guilty!

Suddenly she felt warm all over. He had done exactly that. He'd done it because... what? As a reward for sticking out a full ten hours of riding drag? Because he knew how her thigh muscles quivered and her back and legs ached and he wanted to ease her discomfort?

She pulled her attention back to her plate. No matter. She intended to drink every drop.

"Serena," Thad said softly when he'd swallowed his

first mouthful of pudding. "Thought you'd like to see something I picked up today." He dropped a smashed thistle head into her lap. "Found it under your saddle."

She picked up the prickly burr and closed her hand around it. "That's why Dodger was so skittish," she breathed.

Thad nodded. "Keep eating while I tell you something else."

Her appetite dwindling, Serena picked at her beans.

"Half the boys are bettin' you don't make it through tomorrow. The rest of us—" he paused to gobble another spoonful of spotted pup "—are bettin' you will."

"Is Carleton Kearney in on this?" Serena whispered.

"Dunno. I do know he rode a lot of circles today, keepin' his eye on the rear of the herd. Must have ridden twenty extra miles, just checking. Should be plumb tuckered."

"I wonder what he's got in *his* coffee," she said without thinking.

Thad surprised her with a grin. "He asked Cora to put whiskey in yours, didn't he? That old fox. He did the same for me on my first drive, too. 'Bout came to blows with Dad over it. I was only fifteen."

In the flickering firelight, Serena stared at the Double K trail boss. His tall body bent forward, Carleton conversed with his brother, Ben, and Eli Harker, scratching a crude map on the ground with the handle of his fork. Absorbed as he was, Serena felt free to study him.

His tanned face in profile was lean and chiseled, softened by the silky black mustache and the sensual mouth beneath it. The muscles in his forearm, bare where he'd rolled up his shirtsleeve, flexed as he sketched lines on the ground with the fork handle. He drew a semicircle, talking all the while to Ben and Eli. She couldn't hear the words, only the rich timbre of his voice.

"You like him, don't you?" Thad observed quietly.

Serena jerked. "Certainly not! I do respect him, though. He is quite an admirable man."

"Respect him," Thad echoed, watching her face.

"Yes, respect. And that is all."

Thad's grin widened. "Just wondering. Let me know if you still think so come morning."

Serena frowned. "What's happening in the morning?"

Before her foreman could reply, Carleton's quiet voice brought the hands to attention.

"Listen up, boys. Tomorrow we'll cross the South Umpqua where it bends at Beal Flat. I sent Lyle on ahead to scout a fording place. Should be back before sunup."

Serena bent forward to hear the soft voice over the crackle of the campfire.

"We'll head south through Cow Canyon Pass and camp the other side of Fern Flat. I'll want Thad and Eli on point, Hog—you and Silas take swing and keep Eldon Bartel with you. Ben will cover the flank position, along with Rosy and Serena. Thorny, that other young Bartel pup should settle down a bit ridin' drag with you."

Serena could barely believe her ears. She would not have to ride drag behind the herd tomorrow? A returning sense of well-being flooded her. *Thank you, Lord.*

"No need to push too hard from now on," Carleton continued. "We're far enough from home the cattle won't turn back, so you can keep the herd moving nice and slow. I don't want to run the fat off them."

Thorny recrossed his legs. "What about the night guard, boss?"

"I'm just coming to that. We'll run three-hour shifts. Silas and Eldon are out patrolling now. Around nine, Thad and the other Bartel boy, Jason, will take over. From midnight until three, Serena and Hog will do, and from then 'til breakfast, Ben and myself. We've got twelve working hands—not counting Snap. That's enough for each of us to take every third night off. Anybody want to talk on it?''

Silence.

"That's it, then."

The men shuffled off for second helpings of pudding, dropping their plates in the wash bucket when they finished, and began to bed down for the night.

The warmth that had flooded Serena earlier dissipated in a heartbeat. He'd assigned her to night duty, after riding drag all day? How *could* he? He must know how tired and achy she was. Every square inch of her hurt!

He could, she reminded herself, because he was the trail boss. A cold lump settled into the pit of her stomach. Carleton worried about the cattle. He neither knew nor cared how she—a mere human being, and a woman at that—was managing.

With resignation she ate the remainder of her biscuit and a half slice of bacon and a few beans, and then she gave up. She knew she had to keep her strength up, but it was work even moving her fork from her plate to her mouth.

But she did drink her coffee, down to the very last sip.

It didn't help. Nothing would help the sting of cruel truth. To Carleton Kearney, cows were more important than people on a trail drive. Maybe for him, cows would *always* be more important. She guessed that was how big, successful ranches were built out here.

Sick at heart and sore in body, she dropped her plate in the wash bucket and rolled out her pallet.

"Serena." A low voice spoke in the darkness.

"Thad?" She rolled over and sat up.

"Time for your guard shift. Take your jacket—it's breezy."

Gritting her teeth, Serena threw off the single blanket covering her and pulled on her riding boots.

"Your horse is waiting for you—a nice little roan. I...uh...already checked under the saddle blanket."

She clapped on her hat and hoisted her saddle. "Thanks, Thad. Sleep well."

"Sure, Serena. Ride soft, now." He wrapped himself in his blanket and rolled away from her.

When she reached the remuda, she halted. Snap insisted that no one cross the rope corral perimeter without his permission. The wrangler lifted her saddle from under her arm and settled it in place, pulled the cinch tight and adjusted the stirrups. Only then did he walk the animal out of the enclosure and hand her the lead.

"Ain't exactly got any lady-broke horses," the wrangler grumbled. "So, this one'll hafta do."

Serena did not reply. Before she mounted, she considered checking under the saddle for burrs, but with Snap following her every move with cold, hard eyes, she thought better of it. Murmuring a quick prayer, she settled her rump into the saddle and reined away from him.

A hulking shadow moved his mount past her at a walk. Hog, she guessed. Her night herding partner.

"You go 'round t'other way, ma'am. Hope you don't mind my singin' none."

"Hush up!" Snap ordered. "Only s'posed to whisper around cows at night. Now, git."

Serena stepped the roan in the opposite direction, listening to a mellow tenor voice begin to hum. Halfway around the herd the words of Hog's song floated to her ears over the still night air.

"I got me a horse, I got me a pal. Ain't nuthin' much better, unless it's a gal. Come a ti-yi-yippee..."

Serena began to hum the simple melody under her breath as she circled the sleeping cattle. Hog met her halfway around the far side of the circle, still singing softly.

Without interrupting his song, he thrust a fistful of wild-flowers at her—blue chicory and bachelor's buttons.

"I got me a pie, I got me a pan…"

"Why, thank you, Mr. Hartley."

"You kin call me Hog, ma'am. I don't take no offense."

Even in the dark she could see the gleam of his white teeth as he grinned. "Gotta keep movin, ma'am." He clicked his tongue and the horse ambled off.

"…Gonna bake me a six-foot tall gingerbread man. Come a ti-yi…"

On their next meeting, he again presented her with something—this time, a small cocklebur. The next time around he spoke.

"I reckon you know a good use for a cocklebur, ma'am?"

The soft tenor voice carried a hint of amusement.

"You *know*," she whispered. "*How* do you know?"

The big shoulders shrugged. "Jes' inelegant, I guess."

Serena choked back a bubble of laughter. Surely he must have meant *intelligent*. "Thank you again, Hog. Yes, I'm sure I can find some good use for such a fine specimen."

Chuckling, Hog moved past her into the dark.

They conversed that way most of the night—a few words here, a few more words on their next meeting half-way around the circle. Serena learned some things she hadn't known before.

About Lyle Bartel, for instance. Foreman at the Double K, LB, as he was called, resented Thad's assured status at his uncle's ranch as well as his place in his cousin Alice's affections. That came as a surprise to Serena. Surely Lyle could see that Alice was in love with Thad? How could Lyle possibly come away with anything but a broken heart?

She resisted asking Hog. She knew he'd already told her more than made him comfortable. Cowhands, she was learning, rarely talked about personal things—theirs or anyone else's. But she could tell Hog was lonely. Poor man. He needed a friend.

Still, she wouldn't bargain friendship for information he would later regret having shared. She would simply offer him what she could and let it go at that.

On their next pass, their last of the night, Serena formally shook his hand and again thanked him for the flowers.

And the cocklebur. She could hardly wait until the hands saddled up in the morning.

Chapter Eleven

Balancing her saddle on her hip, Serena approached the firelit camp. Letting the heavy leather seat slip to the ground, she searched the blanketed mounds of sleeping men for Ben and Carleton, who were to ride the next shift. Finally she spotted two long, slim forms, toes pointing to the fire.

Ben's gray Stetson covered his face. Next to him, Carleton's silver-touched hair emerged from beneath a carelessly thrown blanket, as if someone else had covered him up after he fell asleep. Ben, probably. Tired as she was, Serena smiled to herself and bent to touch Carleton's shoulder.

In the next instant, five fingers closed like bands of iron about her wrist. A cold steel muzzle jabbed her rib cage and a gun hammer clicked.

Serena sucked air into a mouth suddenly gone dry.

"Don't ever touch a sleeping man, Sis. It'll get you killed." With care, Carleton lowered the hammer and slid the weapon under his saddle.

"It's t-time for your shift," Serena stammered.

Carleton ran one hand through his tousled hair. The gesture made Serena's breath catch. His hands were extraordinary—tanned and lean, like the rest of him, the fingers long and slim. Purposeful.

"Ben." He spoke the single word so quietly Serena was sure it couldn't be heard over the crackling of the campfire.

"I'm awake," a low voice drawled from under his hat. "Thought I'd wait and see whether you shot her or not."

"Go to hell."

"Gosh, thanks, boss. Better than night riding any day of the week." He sat up and surveyed Serena. "And lots better than ridin' drag." He gave her a lazy wink.

Both men threw off their blankets and began pulling on their boots. Serena moved away toward the chuck wagon, located her bedroll in the dark, and plopped her saddle next to it. Too exhausted to remove her boots, she stretched out full-length on top of the blanket, laid her head in the curve of her saddle, still warm from cushioning her backside for the last three hours, and folded her hands across her middle.

Next to losing Mama and Pa on the same afternoon back in Stark County, this has been the longest day of my life. From now on, she resolved, she would take more heed of her mother's teachings. *Look for the small joys hidden even in the darkest moments,* Mama had said. Chickadees and meadowlarks in a green pasture. Sunlight dappling the rope swing hung in the oak tree. The scent of violets and sweet woodruff under her feet. Mary Irene's cool, smooth cheek pressed against hers. Jessie's laughter.

All these things were blessings that no one, not even a brusque, uncaring trail boss or a grouchy wrangler or a hundred trail hands betting she would fail, could take away from her. No matter what the coming weeks brought, she would take each day, each hour, as it came. She would search out and savor the good part of each and every minute.

And the rest...the heat and dust and endless hours in the saddle...the rest she would let blow away on the wind.

Even blunt-spoken, trigger-prone and definitely disturbing Carleton Kearney.

Especially Carleton Kearney.

They stopped for dinner near the entrance to Cow Canyon. After a morning spent chasing cows, Serena thought she'd never tasted anything better than sourdough biscuits and venison gravy. Cora topped off the meal with sweet applesauce and coffee so strong it made Serena's eyes water. Pleasantly full, she leaned her shoulders back against the wagon wheel and closed her eyes for a moment.

In the next instant, everything changed.

"Now you listen to me, Missy," someone shouted from the other side of the cook fire. The voice grew louder.

"Nobody, *nobody,* messes with the wrangler. My horses are off-limits, you hear?"

Snap bent down and shook a meaty fist under Serena's nose. *"Off-limits!"*

His face was purple, contorted with rage. Opening his hand, he dumped three stiff, spiky burrs into her lap. "Found these under my saddle," he growled.

Three? But she'd slipped only...

Serena stifled an urge to laugh. Someone—two other someones—had done exactly the same thing she had.

"What'cha flappin' your jaw about, Snap?" Thorny planted his thick legs in front of Serena and faced the shouting wrangler.

"Lookit this!" Snap stabbed a finger at the three prickly burrs Serena now cradled in her palm. "Under my saddle. I like to kill myself afore I got suspicious and checked underneath. Damn little—"

"Just a minute," Serena said. "Why do you accuse me of this?"

Snap's mouth twisted. "You done it for revenge, plain and simple."

"Not so plain or simple," Serena replied, working to keep her voice calm. The menacing circle of men gathering about her made her heart pound. It was hard to hold her own against the hulk of one man leaning over her; more than one man she perceived as a threat to her safety. Unreasoning panic obliterated everything from her conscious mind but the hammering of her heart. If one of them laid a hand on her, she would scream.

"For revenge against what?" she asked over a lump in her tightening throat.

"For—" Snap stopped suddenly and narrowed his eyes. "Now ain't that jes' like a woman," he gritted. "Tryin' to trap me, huh?"

Thad stepped to Serena's side. "If I were you, Snap, I'd take your lumps and call it a draw."

"You would, wouldja? Well you ain't me, sonny. You got no right tellin' me what to do."

"I think he's got a point," Thorny interjected. "Seems to me you're even with the lady now."

"Even! Why, I only put—" Snap bit off the rest of his sentence.

Despite her fear, Serena almost laughed out loud. "There are three cockleburs here," she managed to say in an even tone. "I should think one would be sufficient."

Jem's jaw dropped. "You mean somebody else 'sides Miss Serena…"

Snap jerked as if somebody'd lassoed him. "Now just a damn minute. I say it's her. Just her."

Carleton materialized from nowhere. "Shut up, Snap."

"But, boss—"

"Drop it, I said. Miss Hull has one-upped you, and from what I hear, you deserved it. She spent all yesterday afternoon trying to control a horse so cut up under the saddle it's still bleeding.''

"Well, I didn't have nuthin' to do with—"

"No one crosses the remuda rope but you, Snap."

"Yeah," a few voices echoed. The forest of legs encircling Serena retreated, and her breathing began to return to normal.

Carleton positioned himself between Snap and Serena. "You're a good wrangler, mister. But maybe just a bit short on judgment when it comes to a woman."

"Woman, hell, she's a damn—"

The trail boss cut him off with a gesture. "Drop it, Snap. It's over."

"Not for me, it ain't!"

"Drop it," Carleton repeated, "or draw your pay."

The air crackled with tension. Serena looked up and was surprised to find Carleton's steady blue eyes on her. No doubt he'd reprimand her later, in private. In his expression she read disapproval.

"Aw, come on, Snap." Thad laid his arm across the older man's shoulders. "You had your fun with our tenderfoot, and she funned you right back. She and two others, looks like to me."

Murmurs of assent came from the other men.

"So whaddya say we mount up and get back to work?"

A glowering Snap jerked his shoulder from under Thad's arm and stomped off toward the corral.

Serena knew the matter wasn't finished, no matter how skillfully Thad smoothed things over. She could still feel the fury radiating from the wrangler, and she knew from her mother's teachings that a white man nursed his grudges.

In the next instant something occurred to her that made her want to dance. She *had* been the butt of Snap's mean trick, but his animosity wasn't because of her Indian heritage. He resented her because she was a woman on a traditionally male cattle drive! A tenderfoot.

Dear God in heaven, it didn't matter that she was half Modoc. It mattered only that she was female and green at cattle ranching.

Her heart sang. About her heritage she could do nothing. About her gender she could likewise do nothing. But about being a tenderfoot, that she *could* do something about, and do it she would. Just as fast as she was able.

Starting right now. She got to her feet and brushed off her jeans. "Guess I'll go saddle up. They tell me it's a long ride through Cow Canyon."

Turning her back on the assembled hands, she marched off toward the remuda and her afternoon's work.

Chapter Twelve

Carleton gazed past the bend in the river and out across the sea of marsh grass known as Fern Flat. Beside him Lyle Bartel sat his dappled roan with barely concealed impatience. He removed the wide-brimmed brown hat and ran his fingers through his chin-length blond hair.

"She's splitting the hands, boss."

"That so?" Carleton narrowed his eyes, searching for the campsite he'd used on last fall's drive.

"They're layin' bets, Mr. Kearney. Some of us think she'll turn back by sunup tomorrow. The rest of the boys are so smitten they're dropping silver dollars sayin' she can't do no wrong."

Carleton refocused his attention on Lyle. "*That's* what's dividing my trail crew? Hell, LB, we've had greenhorns on drives before. You yourself were inexperienced once, if you recall. We all were, once. And we've had bets riding on the outcome before, too."

"This is different, boss. There's more riding on the lady than some loose silver."

Carleton studied his foreman. He trusted Lyle, but for some reason he'd never liked him. He'd cast his covetous eye at the Double K spread too many times to be misinterpreted. Lyle was land hungry. He'd decided against being a doctor, like his father; said he wanted to raise cattle instead. But he didn't have a ranch. Carleton suspected Lyle's attention to his stepdaughter, Alice, was spurred by his interest in the Double K, half of which would someday be Alice's inheritance.

He exhaled on a long sigh. "If it's more than silver, then name it."

Lyle idly flicked the ends of his reins against the saddle horn. "She's small. Not toughened. When the chips are down, she won't be reliable."

"You might have a point there," Carleton conceded. "And? What else is at stake here?"

Lyle hesitated. "Drives have always been run without women."

"LB, it strikes me you're too young to know how things have 'always' been done."

Lyle readjusted his hat. "You ever been on a drive with a woman before? Not an old lady like Cora, but a real woman?"

"No," Carleton replied, his voice matter-of-fact. "I haven't. Have you?"

Lyle blinked. "Well, no, Mr. Kearney. That is, I haven't experienced it directly, but—"

"Well, then, we both might learn something on this trip." He lifted his reins. "Chuck wagon's about reached the riverbank. Let's go help the old lady swim across."

Lyle's mouth thinned. "Yes, sir, Mr. Kearney."

"And Lyle…"

"Yeah?"

"Thanks for passing on the information. A riled up trail crew is next to useless." He wheeled his bay in the opposite direction and started for the river.

And, he thought with an inward grin, a land-hungry foreman would work hard to keep peace among the men.

A quarreling crew meant a careless drive and lower profits for the Double K.

"*¡Bien, señorita!* Very good. I, Antonio Ruiz, tell you this and it is so. You ride like a *vaquero.*"

"Thanks, Rosy." To hide her pleasure, Serena gazed at the canyon walls rising on both sides of the herd. Lichen-etched gray stone formed a pass through the mountain range. She corraled a pesky cow—the same one Rosy had roped and returned to the herd before entering the canyon over an hour ago, then trotted back to her position on the Spaniard's left.

Rosy pointed out the river where the cattle would cross.

"Rosy, will it be dangerous, crossing the river?"

"*Sí,* if the current is fast. This river will not be so fast. Quicksand, perhaps, but not fast."

"Quicksand!" The hair on the back of her neck bristled.

The Spaniard laughed. "Trust your horse, *señorita.* And if you fall off…" He shot her a twinkly-eyed look. "*Agárrese su cola.* Grab onto his tail. But I think you will not fall off."

"Why not?"

Rosy's grin widened. "Because already you hold on too tight."

Serena looked down at her hands, knotting the reins in her two balled fists.

"Grip here." Rosy slapped his knee. "And when the horse he start to swim, do not leave your boot so, in the stirrup."

Instantly she grasped his meaning. If the horse slipped or was swept away, a foot caught in a stirrup could mean death. With a shudder, she pulled her attention back to the lowing cattle plodding on through the canyon. She wouldn't worry about the river until it was time to face it.

An hour later, Serena watched the cows boil out of the

narrow canyon and gather on the banks of the tumbling south fork of the Umpqua. Ahead of her, at the bend in the river, Snap's remuda splashed into the swirling current. She squinted her eyes and unconsciously held her breath until the last horses emerged on the opposite bank.

The chuck wagon would be next, then the herd. She watched Jem wrestle the reluctant mules into the river. The water rose over the huge wooden wheels and finally lifted the wagon off the river bottom, where it bobbed jerkily behind the two struggling animals. Cora clung to the bench with both hands. Even at this distance, Serena could hear the fear in the elderly woman's voice as she shouted at the mules, at Jem, at the river and at Snap, who stood on the opposite bank, guffawing at the cook's discomfort.

A knot formed in Serena's belly. Rosy coiled his lariat, and she did the same, checking the knot at one end of her rope three or four times just to settle her nerves. If she had to rope a steer and pull it to shore, she wanted to be ready.

The milling cattle moved forward, prodded by the shouts of trail hands anxious to get to Fern Flat and supper. The lead steer hesitated at the sandy bank, and the other bawling cows piled up behind him until the animals finally edged into the river.

The cowhands yelled from the sidelines and snapped their ropes over their heads. Four men—Ben Kearney, Lyle, Hog and Jason Bartel swam their mounts alongside the first of the herd. Thorny waited to cross with Serena and Rosy when the last batch of cows would cross.

Before she knew it, in they went. Icy water lapped at her ankles, crept up her thighs. Remembering the Spaniard's warning, she slipped her boots free of the stirrups and gripped the swimming pony with her knees. Ahead of her, Thorny suddenly turned upstream. Off balance, he grabbed for a handful of his horse's mane, tipped precariously and splashed into the river. He yelped as he went under.

Serena froze with horror. Thorny's head bobbed to the surface, and he shouted a single word before he disappeared again. "Current!"

When the trail hand resurfaced, he was twenty yards away and being swept farther downstream every second.

Rosy yelled something to her, but Serena was already swinging her lariat. She sailed her rope out, but it fell short. Desperately, she recoiled the braided rawhide and pressed her mount toward the bank.

Once on solid ground, she headed downstream. Ben and Lyle thundered past her, but she noted the current was as swift as their horses. Serena choked back a sob. They weren't going to make it.

Ben held one end of his rope and threw the other toward Thorny. Lyle rode on downstream. Without thinking, Serena dug her heels in the pony's side and raced along the bank past both men. When she neared Thorny, still struggling in the churning water, she loosed her rope.

It sailed out and settled on the water and then caught on something. She leaned back and pulled with all her strength.

Thorny yelled and disappeared. But the rope remained taut.

Then his wrist appeared above the surface, encircled by her lasso. By some miracle, she'd snagged one of his hands! She fought to hold on against the tug of the current.

Lyle crashed into the water ahead of her. "Wrap it!" he shouted.

With hurried motions, Serena wound the rope end three turns around the saddle horn. Then she stepped her pony backward.

"Pull," the foreman ordered.

She nudged her horse back another step. *Dear Lord, let*

there not be quicksand on this bank! At the thought, sweat gathered on her forehead, dripped into her eyes. She brushed one arm across her face.

"Pull!" Lyle shouted again. "You've got him! Drag him closer!"

The foreman let his own lariat fly. Just as Thorny's head reappeared, the rope circle settled on the water and the gasping cowboy managed to shrug it around his shoulders. Lyle snubbed the rope and began backing his own mount away.

Serena pulled her rope tight as Lyle's horse slowly dragged the sputtering Thorny to shore. On hands and knees, the sodden trail hand crawled up the bank, slipped the ropes from his wrist and shoulders and vomited up some water.

"Good job, Serena," said a voice behind her. It was Ben Kearney. She hadn't realized he was there until he spoke.

"Yeah," Lyle added in his controlled tenor. "Not bad for a girl who's still pretty green."

Both men dismounted and hauled Thorny to a standing position, holding him upright between them.

"Not bad for one of *any* color," Ben countered with a grin. "Come on, Serena. We all need some of that whiskey Cora's got locked in her medicine box."

Rosy caught Thorny's horse. The saddle cinch was still tight, and he helped the wet cowhand mount.

Thorny sent Serena a brief look of gratitude. "Did you say whiskey, Ben?"

"You know, Duret," Ben began, shoving his hat back with his thumb. "As I get older I get more and more forgetful. Did I say lemonade?"

"Whiskey," Thorny insisted.

"Whiskey," Lyle agreed.

"Whis-key," Rosy pronounced with care.

"Goshamighty." Ben raised his palms in a shrug. "I coulda sworn I said 'whiskey,' but if you say it's lemonade, it's lemonade!"

Supper that night in Fern Flat promised to be a celebratory affair. Jem and Snap had built a blazing cook fire, and two Dutch ovens of stew bubbled over the coals. Cora also fried up a skillet of corn fritters and baked two apple pies flavored with molasses—Thorny's favorite.

The quart bottle of Child's whiskey made the rounds twice before Cora recorked it and hid it away under lock and key. When the cook heard all the variations and embroideries of Thorny's near drowning, she cut an extra slab of pie and plopped it onto his enamelware plate. Then she cut another one for Serena.

"You deserve it, child. Rosy told me all you done today. Lyle's plumb struck by your rope-throwin' arm."

"Oh, Cora." Serena knew she was blushing. Her face felt hot, her neck and chest prickly. She stared down at her boots. Grateful when the high-spirited joshing started up again, she bent her knees and sank to a sitting position, her back resting against the wagon wheel.

"Anybody else have a mis'ry needs doctorin'?" Cora called out.

"Snap does," someone said. "Got a sore butt. Kinda got cocklebur-bit."

"Nah, he ain't been bit," Thorny drawled. "Just busted up some."

"What's broke, then?" Cora lumbered to her feet, ready to retrieve her collection of ointments and elixirs.

"His pride, mostly," someone volunteered.

His face purpling, Snap puffed himself up like a bullfrog. "Ain't my pride. It's my sense of pro...pro...propri'ty."

"I've got just the thing for that," Cora said in a soothing voice. "Some of my hot sassafras tea."

"I got a swole-up lip," Silas Appleby confessed.

Cora turned an attentive face toward the middle-aged rancher. "What from?"

"Not enough kissin', I guess. Seems like years since we left town."

"Too *much* kissin's more likely," someone joked. "You'd think by your age, Si, you'd grow outta that habit."

Cora harrumphed and gave Silas a hard look.

"Sassafras tea!" chorused a number of male voices.

"I got a rope burn," Eldon Bartel offered.

"Comin' or goin'," a voice quipped.

Eldon hesitated, unsure of the joke.

"Maybe Hog didn't work you hard enough ridin' drag today, son."

Eldon glared at the speaker through the firelight. "Oh, he worked me plenty hard."

"Musta been goin', then," the voice said.

"Hog'll hafta tie your leash tighter tomorrow, so it don't slip."

Another "sassafras tea" chorus rose.

Serena laughed with the others in spite of herself. She liked the easy banter among the hands, the sense of companionship and camaraderie among men who daily entrusted their lives to each other's care. Here was another beautiful thing to balance the harshness of life on the western frontier—the unique, sometimes even grudging trust between men. Out west, betrayal of a friend was a bigger sin than stealing cattle or even killing someone.

What a wild, fiercely independent breed of men these were! She both feared and admired them.

Some of them, anyway. Instantly, Carleton Kearney's visage rose in her mind.

And in another way, she reflected as Cora clanged her pot lids a second time to signal the end of supper, men were the biggest obstacles to civilizing this rough, raw country. They could be rude. Crude. Even mean.

A cold breath of fear washed over her. Men could also be violent. They could harm her. And they could do it on purpose.

She shuddered.

Thad squatted beside her and spread his jacket over her shoulders. "Cold?"

"No. You missed supper. Where have you been?"

"Ridin' with Eli and Lyle and Uncle Carl. Scouting tomorrow's route."

"You'd better hurry and eat. Cora's washing up already."

Thad rose in an unhurried motion and approached the buxom cook. Slipping his arm around her ample waist, he crooned in her ear. "Cora, my Cora, what's left for supper?"

"Sassafras tea!" Thorny shouted in high spirits.

"Mon— Monog— Monogamy!" Hog yelled.

"Monogamy?"

"Yeah." The brawny trail hand cocked a bushy eyebrow. "Ain't that what people allus drink at Christmas? Cora said she's gonna make some tomorrow, providin' we're all still alive and able to swallow."

"That's *eggnog*, you dumb Texan," Thorny corrected. "Monogamy means marriage."

"More like monotony," came a dry voice.

"Nah, marriage is like mahogany," someone else chimed in. "Shiny and hard. Shiny at the beginning, hard after the honeymoon."

Serena laughed softly. Poor Hog's malaprop would be an endless source of humorous ribbing. Tired as she was, she looked forward to it. Laughter eased her anxiety about being the lone female in the campfire circle.

"I had a mahogany gun once," Thorny began. "Polshed it up so's it shone like glass. Couldn't shoot it, of course, seein' as how lead bullets spoiled the balance. But t shore killed a lot of folks. Why, I'd just shine it in their eyes and blind 'em—then hit 'em over the head with the gun barrel.''

The men chortled. Rolling cigarettes, they stretched their legs toward the fire and settled down to joke back and forth. Serena watched and listened, keeping her back pressed against the wagon wheel.

"Cora," Hog shouted. "Whaddya got for a dying sense of humus?"

"Humor," someone corrected. "Humus is some kinda bone in the arm."

Cora splashed two more plates into the bucket of soap-suds at her elbow. "What I got for both of you is brain food," she snapped. "Venison heart, calf liver and—" she paused dramatically, lifted her soap-covered hands to her waist "—beef testicles. Prairie oysters." She plunked another dish into the bucket.

"Testicles! Hellfire and brimstone."

"Guess you won't want any breakfast, then, Hog," Cora observed.

"Hell, no, I don't— You wouldn't serve 'em for breakfast, now wouldja, Cora?" Hog's voice shook.

"Oh, I'll disguise 'em. I can make 'em look like fried eggs real easy. Or flapjacks with lumps. Pigs in blankets. Or even..."

Serena heard the cook chuckle under her breath. "Creamed oysters. Then there's prairie oyster cobbler and, let's see... Oh, land o'Goshen, I almost forgot. Prairie oyster shortcake."

Shouts of laughter regaled the now-silent Hog. Serena felt a stab of pity for the huge man, but then he began to laugh along with the others, and the joshing started up again.

Serena stopped listening. At the outer edge of camp three shadowy figures approached the circle of firelight. One of them, she could tell by his easy, controlled walk, was Carleton Kearney. She barely glanced at the other two men.

The trail boss was the one that held her attention. He was headed straight toward her, his eyes hard.

Chapter Thirteen

"Miss Hull." Carleton Kearney planted his long legs in front of her and looked down at her. "If you're not too busy, I'd like to have a word with you."

Serena's heart settled in the pit of her stomach. "What about?" she said, trying to keep her voice steady. The cold, determined glint in his blue eyes gave her the shivers. "Have…have you had supper yet?"

"Not hungry," he growled. "Come on, stand up. We'll talk over by the corral."

Serena rose to her feet. Clutching Thad's jacket about her shoulders, she took a step forward.

Without a word, Cora thrust a loaded supper plate into the trail boss's hand and jammed a fork in his shirt pocket. "There's apple pie," she announced to no one in particular. "And fresh coffee."

"Later, Cora." Carleton set the plate down on a barrel and headed away from camp, his strides so long Serena struggled to keep up. She followed him to the roped-off area that held the horses, wondering at each step what was bothering him. He already knew about the cockleburs Snap had found under his saddle; she thought that issue over and dealt with. Was there more?

Obviously there was. The set of the trail boss's shoulders told her something had made him angry—something about her. But what?

He turned toward her. Night shadows obscured his face, but his low, gruff voice hinted at exasperation. "I heard about your antics in the river today."

"Antics?" Baffled, Serena stared at the tall man.

"You made it across the river, then you rode along the bank, where it was soft. Damn fool thing to do."

"A man was drowning! I couldn't just stand by and watch—"

"You could," he said, his voice ominously quiet. "And should have. More experienced hands than you have died riding their horses on banks that haven't been scouted."

"I had no choice," Serena protested. What ailed the man? Wasn't he glad Thorny was alive and uninjured?

"I just—"

"You didn't think," Carleton interrupted. "Any trail hand worth spit calculates the odds in an emergency. If it's riskier to offer aid, then sit back and let others handle it."

"Sit back!" The words came out sharper than she intended. "I'm sorry, Mr. Kearney. By the time I *thought* about whether to sit back or try to help, it would have been too late. The man would have been dead."

"Maybe. Maybe not."

"But don't you see? I had to try! I couldn't live with myself if I didn't at least try!"

Carleton fell silent for so long she wondered if he'd heard her.

"I see, all right," he said after an excruciating minute. "And maybe on a human level you're right."

"What other level *is* there?" she snapped.

"This is a cattle drive, Serena, not a study in morality.

And for the next six weeks you do as I say, understand? *Exactly* as I say."

"I'm not sure I can do that, Mr. Kearney."

"You can. If you're half the *vaquero* Rosy says you are, you can learn to take orders. It's part of belonging to a trail crew."

Fierce pride at the trail boss's backhanded compliment and Rosy's apparent praise of her sucked the angry wind out of her sails.

"Mr. Kearney, I apologize for acting in haste. You know why I did so, and I know why you are reprimanding me. It won't happen again."

"Sure it will," he said with a hint of amusement in his voice. "There's no road that doesn't have a bend or two in it. Greenhorns don't get trail-wise overnight."

"Just don't send me back," Serena said in a small voice. "Please don't send me back."

"I hadn't even considered it."

She blinked. "You hadn't?" She took a moment to digest this. "You know about Snap and the cocklebur and the bet and...everything, don't you? And you're not going to send me back?"

"No."

"You're concerned about my actions. They were ill-advised in your view, essential in mine."

"I am."

"And you're still not going to fire me?"

"No."

She noticed Carleton's answers got shorter as her questions probed deeper. He was hiding something. Every fiber of her being told her so. There was something he didn't want to admit.

"Why?" she demanded. He was an honest man. He would answer truthfully or give her no answer at all.

"Why? What difference does it make if Thorny drowns or I do?"

The question hung in the chilly night air for some moments. Crickets screeched in the flat. Off in the distance somewhere a coyote howled. At last, Carleton cleared his throat.

"Thorny can take care of himself. I don't want you to get hurt."

Serena's heart stopped. Stunned, she stared at him, noting how his hand shook. "You mean sometimes cows are *not* more important than people?" She held her breath waiting for his answer.

"Sometimes,"   he   said   quietly.   "Not   often, but…sometimes."

Lord in heaven, could a human heart beat under that denim shirt and dusty leather vest?

She doubted it. Carleton Kearney was single-minded, pragmatic—a successful rancher, as desperate to get his herd to market before winter as she was. He had as much at stake as she did, maybe more—his ranch, feed for his stock, the future welfare of his baby daughter and his stepdaughter. She knew he would stop at nothing to accomplish what he'd set out to do. Neither would she, and for the very same reason—survival.

She was learning that survival out here in the West took hard work and sacrifice. But at least she understood him a little better. He was a good man. A caring man. Maybe even a lonely man, considering the load he carried on his shoulders.

She pivoted away from him and moved back toward the campfire. "Good night, Mr. Kearney."

He made no response.

"Don't forget about Cora's apple pie."

In the darkness she heard his low, rich laughter.

Serena moved behind the circle of firelit faces and sat

down unobtrusively between Thad and Rosy. The minute she was settled, Jem bobbed at her elbow. "Want some coffee, Serena?" He handed her a brimming tin cup.

"So, like I wuz sayin'," Thorny continued from the other side of the campfire. "Snap, I figure you owe me twenty dollars. Lyle, you owe me...lessee here...thirteen. 'S plain as freckles on a redhead—no offense, Jason—Serena's gonna stick it out."

She stiffened at the mention of her name.

"I ain't payin'," Snap grumbled.

"Hell, I won it, fair and square!" Thorny's voice rose in accusation. "You jes' don't want to admit you misjudged the lady!"

"Didn't neither."

"Did so. Snap, that current was so fast the water got hot!" He winked broadly at his now attentive audience. "Damn near melted my belt buckle."

"It's yer brain that got melted," Snap shot back.

Lyle Bartel stood up suddenly. "You two are actin' like a couple of mail-order cowboys. Only a fool argues with a mule."

"Or a skunk!" Snap hissed.

"Or a cook," someone added in an undertone.

"The way I see it," Lyle continued, "you two mules can go on buttin' heads or you can draw your pay. Mr. Kearney's not gonna smile on two stubborn old buckaroos that can't think straight."

"I think straight enough," Snap growled.

"Me, too." Thorny stuck out his hand. "You kin owe me 'til we get paid, an' I won't charge any interest."

"Interest! Why you old— Okay, it's a deal." Snap pumped Thorny's hand up and down once. "Think Cora'd break out some whiskey to celebrate, LB?"

Lyle held up a cautionary hand. "Don't get too happy, boys. The old man hasn't forgotten the river incident yet.

He was pretty steamed up when he heard about it. I figure he'll have some words for some of you boys.''

"Here he comes now," someone admonished.

Snap and Thorny retreated to opposite sides of the campfire. Lyle moved to the chuck wagon for more coffee. As he passed near Serena, he slowed his step.

"None of this would have happened if you'd stayed home where you belong," he said in an undertone.

She wasn't about to let that slip by. In an instant she was on her feet, dogging Lyle's footsteps. "I've got fifteen steers in this herd, Mr. Bartel. I mean to see they get to market."

Lyle made a half turn toward her, leaned against the chuck box with lazy nonchalance. "That's what men are for," he drawled. "That, and a few other things."

He inspected her frame from boots to Stetson with an appraising look. "Women should stay home in the kitchen or the parlor or..." he licked his lips deliberately and grinned "...in bed. *¿Sabe?*"

She *sabe*'d all right. Her blood boiled at the look in the insolent cowboy's eyes.

"*¡Váyase al diablo!*" Serena spit the words out without looking at him and stalked back to the fire. *Oh, my!* she thought. *Where had those words come from?* She'd learned more from Rosy today than she'd realized.

Lyle stared after her until Cora appeared from somewhere, snatched the cup out of his hand and threw it into the wash bucket.

"Hold on a minute, old lady. What're *you* mad about?"

"You talk too much," the cook snapped.

"I don't think so," Lyle said slowly as Cora retreated around the corner of the chuck wagon. "Here's a lady with a thousand-acre spread that needs a man. In fact, I think I haven't said near enough. But there's time."

He drifted toward the back of the wagon. "Yessir, there's six whole weeks. Plenty of time."

Squatted on his haunches, Carleton continued speaking just as Serena rejoined the lopsided circle of hands grouped around the campfire. She sat with her back against the chuck wagon wheel, behind the cluster of men and out of their view as much as possible. She didn't mind men by themselves or in twos so much any more, as long as they didn't touch her. But four or five men in a group sent a warning shiver up her spine. Even though it was ten years ago, that night back in Stark County when she'd been assaulted was never far from her thoughts.

The trail boss quickly dictated tomorrow's herd assignments and outlined the plans for the day. His voice drifted to Serena over the splash of Cora's dishwashing and the exploding sparks from the fire.

"…up Fire Mountain. It'll be a long, steady climb, and it'll be dry."

"Jehosaphat, boss," Thorny sang out. "That's a dang mountain of glass, the rock is so slippery. There ain't no better route?"

Carleton pressed his fork handle in the dirt. "It'll pay in the long run, when we get through the pass. We'll dinner at Garnett Cutoff and camp tomorrow night in Tin Pot Valley."

"What about Indians?" Hog queried.

Serena's body seemed to turn to stone. *Indians?* Surely not Modocs—her mother's people—or other Klamath River tribes? All at once she didn't know who she was beneath the sweaty plaid shirt and dusty jeans—a Scot with Indian blood or a Modoc with a Scottish father?

"Maybe some Yoncalla, a few Molalla here and there," the trail boss answered patiently. "They're generally peaceable."

"'Cept when they're hungry," Snap interjected. "I'd better hobble the horses."

"We'll post a night guard around the remuda," Carleton said. "If they look hungry, cut out a couple of steers for them. They've got wives and families, too."

Her mind numb, Serena half listened to the remainder of the trail boss's words. She knew he'd finished when he rose and headed for the coffeepot at the back of the chuck box. His long legs brushed so close by her side she could smell his leathery, wood-smoky scent.

Eli Harker began tuning the guitar he'd stashed in the wagon. After a few chords, Thorny produced a small nickel-plated harmonica and they lauched into "My Old Kentucky Home." Tears stung into Serena's eyes. She missed Jessie and Mary Irene so much it was like a pain that never eased.

The guitar switched to "Beautiful Dreamer." Thorny waited one verse before joining on his harmonica. The talk quieted as the men listened, and then all of a sudden Hog began to sing. His mellow tenor brought an ache to Serena's throat. She swallowed a convulsive sob, drew in a deep breath and raised her head.

In the firelight's flicker, she met Carleton Kearney's steady gaze. His eyes held hers for what seemed an endless minute, until she closed her lids to shut out his face.

Something soft and insistent stirred deep within her. Her mother's voice floated on the back of her mind. *Look at him, Daughter. So it was that I fell in love with your father.*

Her throat tightened with longing. She opened her eyes to find Carleton still looking at her through the evening shadows.

An invisible hand reached across the few feet of ground separating them, and a veil dropped over the two of them. Serena felt her entire body go still. The plaintive, sweet sound of the guitar and the murmur of the song held her spirit suspended in time, and still she stared at the man facing her. Her blood thrummed in her head. She would remember this moment for the rest of her life.

Chapter Fourteen

Carleton reined in his mount, twisted in the saddle and surveyed the straggling line of cows and men on horseback plodding up the trail behind him. The chuck wagon, along with Snap and the remuda, had already begun its descent down the other side of Fire Mountain pass. He was more concerned about the bulk of the herd, laboring up the long grade following Old Moses, the lead steer.

Already, Carleton had traded off one horse for another in his string. This one, a tough little gray mare, had been fresh and ready to go an hour ago; now she seemed to have lost her zest for riding up and down the mountain.

He wondered how Serena was managing. He'd teamed her with Ben and put Rosy and young Eldon Bartel on the other side of the herd. Gazing down on the scene before him he couldn't tell which of the two smaller riders Serena was, they'd changed sides so often. Rosy was easy to pick out. The silver conchas banding the Spaniard's high-crowned felt hat flashed in the sunlight. His belt was also studded with conchas, making him easy to spot from a distance. The smaller figure on the droop-headed roan must be Eldon. That meant the tall figure and the shorter one, on almost matched black geldings, had to be his brother, Ben, and Serena.

He watched them for a few moments, then headed back down the mountain to consult with Lyle and Thad, riding point a half mile behind him. Something struck him odd about Lyle's constant, low-voiced questions regarding Serena and the little heart-shaped spread she'd inherited from her father, Ben's deputy, long ago. Lyle had the same hungry look about him he wore when he was around Alice. Carleton wouldn't put it past his foreman to covet Serena's thousand acres.

Or... The thought gave him pause. Or did Lyle covet the woman who owned it?

Approaching his point men, Carleton reined his horse to fall in alongside Thad.

"Mornin', Uncle Carl. Haven't seen you since noon dinner. Anything up ahead but sagebrush and gnats?"

"More sagebrush. No gnats, just mosquitos."

"Figures," Thad said with a laugh. "Hog says there ain't no God north of Arizona. I'm beginning to believe him."

"Sometimes Hog doesn't have both feet in the stirrups, if you take my meaning."

"Sings real pretty, though," Thad countered, slanting his uncle a sly look. "Last night you looked plumb spellbound. It *was* the song, wasn't it?"

"Sure," Carleton said, his voice noncommittal. "And Cora's apple pie. And that big handful of stars overhead. Real nice night."

"That's all, just pie and stars? Hell's bells, Uncle Carl, it's gotta be more 'n that. I ain't seen you so dreamy-eyed since Aunt Ella told you she was... Oh, 'scuse me, Carl. Didn't mean to bring her up."

"I *haven't* seen," Carleton corrected, keeping his voice even.

"Well, I ain't. Oh, all right, *haven't.* Gee willikers, Carl, you change topics quicker'n a skunk can stink up a hen-house."

Carleton raised his eyes heavenward. "Think you could learn how to talk if you went back to school, Thad?"

"See, there you go again! Dammit, Carl, I want to know about Serena."

"Well, what a coincidence," Carleton drawled. "So do I."

"Huh? Well, why in the hell didn't you say so?"

"Can't see much from the hilltop—too far away. How's she doing?"

"Okay, I guess. She's with Ben. I haven't ridden back down there in a while. Too hard comin' back up. Boy, this sure is one steep mountain."

"When you do ride down, check her canteen, will you? Make sure she's drinking plenty of water."

Thad chuckled. "Anything else? You want to know what she's thinkin' about?"

"She's thinking about her fifteen steers and the money to build that house she wants," Carleton said dryly.

Thad chortled. "Think so?"

"Know so."

"Want to lay a little bet?"

Carleton studied his nephew's suntanned face. He had to admit Thad knew more about women in general than he did. But not about Serena, he'd wager. Serena wasn't like the other women in the valley. She was more determined, more headstrong. And a lot more quiet and self-contained.

What a combination—a real handful for a man, if one could even get close enough to court her. She shied away from close contact with most males except for Thad and young Jem, preferring to stay on the fringe. Night after night he'd watched her lean against the chuck wagon wheel, hidden in shadow, rather than rub shoulders with the other hands around the campfire.

Carleton brought his thoughts back to Thad's challenge. "Ten bucks says she's thinking about her parlor layout."

"Ten bucks says she's thinking about you."

"Me! I'm nothing but a worn-out old rancher with more cares than cattle. It'll be Lyle she'll cotton to."

Thad snorted. "Carl, you ain't got the brains God gave a bird's nest."

"*Haven't,* Thad. *Haven't* got the brains." He hid a smile. "Guess you're right about that in a way. Shouldn't send a young pup back there to check on her if he can't talk straight."

He threw a friendly punch to his nephew's arm and wheeled the mare away. Tipping his hat to Lyle, a quarter mile off on a big roan gelding, he started up the hill again.

At the summit, he turned to look out over the herd strung out below him. Thad's horse kicked up a cloud of dust as he dropped back to the flank position. Carleton watched him approach the small figure on the dark horse dancing alongside a bawling stream of cattle.

He would have gone himself, but he didn't want to see her up close for a while. Last night in the middle of Hog's heartbreakingly lovely song, something that felt like the biggest horse's hoof on God's green earth had kicked him square in the solar plexus. All he could see as he rolled and tossed on his pallet during the long, hot night was Serena's oval, suntanned face, her nose and cheekbones windburned, her dark eyes shimmering with unshed tears. Finally at three o'clock in the morning, he'd gotten up and taken Silas's night herding shift, much to the surprise of the sleepy ranch owner.

"Whazza matter, Carl?" the man had inquired. "Somethin' on your mind?"

"Something like that," Carleton mumbled. "Need to ride a bit."

He'd night herded until sunup, grabbed a cup of Cora's morning coffee—coffin varnish, the men dubbed it—and rode ahead to scout the route up Fire Mountain. When Old Moses headed up the trail behind Thad and Lyle, riding point, Carleton had breathed a sigh of relief. A moving herd would keep his mind occupied.

But even that hadn't kept his thoughts off Serena. Maybe nothing would this morning. Tonight, though, he'd be damned if he'd stick around listening to Hog sing again. The words of last night's song had punched a hole right in the center of his heart.

God in heaven, he was a lonely man.

He was also tired and dispirited and too damned scarred to start over. He turned the mare toward the marshy creek visible just beyond Garnett Cutoff. He'd best check it out. With the early rain this season, it could be boggy.

The horse veered to avoid a slippery patch of pebbled riprap. He'd have to keep his mind on his business, or he'd slide right off the mountainside and injure a good horse!

Tightening his grip on the reins, Carleton slowed the mare and bent his head to peer at the rock-studded ground ahead.

Serena gulped a swallow of tepid, slightly salty water from her battered metal canteen. Army issue, Ben said. The canvas cover was so frayed in spots the tin showed through. She wondered which army. She knew both Ben and Carleton had fought for the Confederacy. Ben had evidently mellowed over the years, gotten the hurt out of his system. But she wondered about the brusque, taciturn loner Carleton Kearney seemed to be. Maybe he was embittered by the war, or by the loss of his wife a year ago. Or both. She didn't know. She didn't want to know, really, because then the hidden man would become real to her, and an even greater threat.

Trusting a man, any man, even if he professed to be a friend, was dangerous. Once she'd trusted that young Matthews boy, her schoolmate. He'd walked her home one afternoon, and then the very next night he'd let his older brother and two friends attack her. An icy chill washed over her at the memory.

"Hey, Serena?" Thad reined his horse close to hers. "Uncle Carl wants to know if you're managing all right?"

Serena nodded and recapped the canteen. "Ben says I'm ready to ride the river. I guess that means I'm doing all right." She lifted her hat, brushed the stray tendrils off her sweaty forehead.

"More than all right."

"Sure is hot, though. And poor Blackie here..." She leaned forward to pat the gelding's warm hide. "He's about played out. Does this mountain ever end?"

Thad pushed back his Stetson. "Yeah, it does. Eventually. There's a pass a couple of miles ahead, then it's all downhill 'til you come to Dead Horse Creek."

Serena shuddered. "What an awful name."

"Lyle will want to get the cattle across before we let 'em drink, kinda get 'em running so they won't stop and mill in the creekbed. Just thought I'd warn you—don't get between a thirsty cow and water. Stick close to Ben."

Serena nodded again. "Anything else?"

Thad shot her a quick grin. "Yeah. You look real serious today, Serena. A penny for your thoughts."

Serena inspected the young man gazing at her with a twinkle in his soft green eyes. Just what did he want to know?

She shouldn't take offense. Her young foreman was just being friendly.

"I was thinking about...the War Between the States."

Thad's eyebrows rose. "You funnin' me?"

"I was thinking about Ben, your father. And about Carl—Mr. Kearney. Your uncle. How different they are."

Thad's grin widened until the laugh lines around his eyes crinkled. "They're not so different, really," he said slowly. "It's just that Uncle Carl... Well, Carl married real early, right after the war. A widow with a young daughter. Aunt Ella was real nice, but she never liked it out here much. She never complained or nuthin', just kinda froze up inside."

He shot a look at her. "Carl was...well, maybe I shouldn't be sayin' this, but he blamed himself when Ella died. Thought if he'd taken her back home to Carolina like she wanted, maybe she'd have been stronger when the baby came."

Serena stared past Thad's shoulder at the vista spread below the straggling band of cows moving up the mountain. A line of dusky green pine trees in the distance marked their starting point this morning. Since sunup they had climbed upward. It had taken them hours to come this far, and still the summit and Fire Mountain pass were ahead of them. It seemed a never-ending struggle.

Like life. You worked hard, sweated, bit down on your pain for a few fleeting, fragile moments of triumph. If such an existence was blessed with the joy of love, of family, then it was all worthwhile. If not, life would be bitter as gall and all tasks and suffering endured for nothing.

"Men meet life in different ways," she said quietly. "Ben has found peace. He is at the summit. Carl is still struggling. Hurting. And you..."

She looked into Thad's suddenly thoughtful face. "You are young, full of hope and confidence. You—and I—are just starting out. We're both as green as those trees down there."

And as vulnerable, she acknowledged. Any living thing was vulnerable in this rough land.

Her foreman turned serious eyes on her. "You like him, don't you, Serena? And you're afraid of him, too."

"Who? Ben? Certainly I'm not afraid of him. No one could be kinder to a tenderfoot on a cattle trail. He—"

"Not Ben. Carl."

Serena hesitated. "I don't know what you mean."

Thad chuckled. "God love you, Serena, you're no good at lyin'. Your face is as readable as the front page of Ma's newspaper."

Serena yanked her hat brim down to partially hide her burning cheeks. "You are a nosy, mouthy, irritating boy, Thad Kearney. I don't know why I put up with you!"

"Oh, yes, you do," Thad countered with a snort of laughter. "You like *me,* too."

Serena drew back her fist and knocked his Stetson into the dirt at his feet. "Well, I'm not afraid of you, you big know-it-all!"

She spurred her horse away from him in time to evade his long arm reaching for her own hat.

"Thanks, Serena," he shouted after her. "I found out what I wanted to know. And now I'm ten bucks richer!"

Serena pulled the gelding to a halt. Hands fisted on her hips, she stared at him. "What did you say?"

Thad retrieved his hat with slow, nonchalant motions, slapped the dust off against his denim-clad thigh, and jammed the Stetson on his head.

"I said—" Thad struggled to speak over his laughter "—he likes you, too!"

He was off like a shot, pushing his bay back up the steep trail toward the summit. Hellfire, she could boggle a man quicker'n blackberry brambles. He released a satisfied sigh. "Just what old Carl needs, ain't it?" he murmured to the laboring animal beneath him. "I mean, *isn't* it?"

Still laughing, he looked back at Serena, sitting her gelding like an angry queen, her back stiff as a ramrod, her features hidden beneath the wide-brimmed black felt hat.

"Well, I'll be switched," he chortled.

Even at this distance, he could tell she was laughing, too.

"Yessir, just the thing for old sobersides Carl. Come on, Panther, let's make some tracks."

Serena shook her head at Thad's retreating back. He was right, of course. He was always right—about attending the Wildwood Valley social last summer, teaching her to rope and work a cutting horse, even backing her up when she threatened to withdraw him from the drive.

The slim figure on the dark horse disappeared over the top of the hill, and suddenly Serena realized they were only a half mile or so from the pass.

"Come on, you sons of steers," she heard herself yell. "Get along there, you good-for-nothing bunch of cows!"

Merciful heavens! Had those words really tumbled out of her mouth?

They must have. No one but her would utter such a thing—all the other trail hands knew that steers had no sons!

At the top of Fire Mountain pass, the tired cattle picked up speed, tumbling down the other side of the mountain toward the meandering creek. Serena could now see where the trail leveled off into a long, flat valley covered with brown-tipped cattails. In the late afternoon sunlight, the wide, lazy stream shone like liquid metal.

As the lowing animals smelled water, the front-runners began to trot. She understood now why Thad and Lyle, riding point, wanted the cattle across the creek before they let them double back to drink. Too many thirsty cows on the approach side would slow the crossing to a crawl, increasing the risk. It wasn't deep, she deduced from the ease with which the chuck wagon splashed across. But it did look marshy.

"Keep moving!" Ben shouted from his side of the herd. "Move along, now, you Oregon dogies. Mind your manners!"

Serena took his lead. "Get along!" she yelled. "Move, now. Move!" She added a few 'yips' for emphasis.

Ben looked up, grinned and tipped his hat. She pulled her bandanna over her mouth to filter the dust and kicked Blackie into a canter to keep up with the herd. Down the mountain they thundered, straight for the creek.

On the bank, Rosy, Hog, ranch owner Silas Appleby and the Bartel twins worked frantically to keep the cows moving. The first of the herd was already across, milling about in a wide arc as Thad and Lyle drove them downstream to drink. Beside her, Eli Harker and Ben snapped their lariats over the backs of the bunched-up cows. Blocked from the glut of animals being manhandled across the expanse of shallow water, the bulk of the cattle slowed.

She tagged the rear end of a stubborn steer with her rope, then flicked it against the hide of a cow turning broadside, blocking the way. "Yi-yi-yip! Get along, there!"

The cattle bawled, surged ahead, bumping into each other until they picked up the pace again.

"Yip! Yip!" She snapped the rope again and pressed on toward the creek.

The ground felt soft and spongy. Instinctively, the gelding slowed and stepped cautiously into the now-trampled area of cattails and tough, big-leafed ferns. The cattle at her side moved more slowly, too. Finally they came to a complete stop.

Rosy and Silas swooped down, shouting and ki-yi-ing. "Got one stuck," Silas shouted. "Move 'em downstream."

The men turned the cattle slightly off course, veered for the bank a dozen yards off. Serena rode like the wind to turn them, with Ben and Eli's help, and then plunged into the slow-moving water.

Halfway across, she saw what was causing the problem. A steer stood mired in midstream, its legs slowly disappearing into the sandy muck. Underneath the trail brand on his hide she deciphered a curved letter A.

Lazy A. Her own brand. Lord God in heaven, the steer was one of her precious band of fifteen!

Serena headed for the men clustered around the terrified animal. Ben tried to intercept her.

"Don't watch, Serena!" he shouted.

She plunged past him. "I have to—he's mine!"

The steer struggled, sank another inch.

"You think it's a suckhole?" Lyle called to Thad.

"Quicksand, more'n likely."

Quicksand! Dear God, no! Serena panicked.

"Let it go, then," Lyle shouted. "Leave this one. Get the rest of the herd across."

"No!" Serena screamed the word. "I want to save my steer!"

Lyle turned to her. "It's only one animal, lady. We've got near a thousand others to think about."

"You can't just abandon it, let it die like that!" She struggled to keep her voice from breaking. "Please, Lyle."

Thad nudged her gelding's nose with his knee. "You want me to shoot it?" he said, his voice low. "It'll be quick, and he won't suffer."

"No! It's my steer! It belongs to me, to my ranch. Help me get it out!"

Thad pushed back his hat and gave her a long, penetrating look. "I'll go get Carl. Let him decide."

"Oh, hurry, Thad. Please hurry!"

Thad spurred his bay up the marshy bank and streaked

away to the south. Serena thought she would die of an-guish as she watched her steer sink up to its knees in the rippling sand. It had stopped thrashing and now stood, head drooping, waiting for inevitable death.

Serena clenched her jaw tight. She wouldn't let the an-imal die. She couldn't. She needed to sell it at the railhead to build the house for Jessie and Mary Irene. *Oh, please, God. I have to build that house for my sisters. Please, please, let me have my steer back.*

She did not hear Carleton and Thad ride up behind her. Only when their mounts splashed into the water did she jerk back to reality.

Carleton closed his hand on her upper arm. "He's mired too deep, Serena. His legs are thin. They stick in the sand like anchors. No way in hell to break him free."

"There must be *something* we can do?"

"Not much, Sis. I wouldn't want to risk men and horses for just one—"

"Mr. Kearney, please." Serena heard her voice begin to choke. She swallowed hard and continued. "That's *my* steer there—one you sold me last summer."

"I see that." Carleton's tone was low, his voice oddly gentle. His eyes looked straight into hers. "I know it's hard to see this. Go on up to the chuck—"

"No, thank you," she said as calmly as she could. "You're a fair man, Mr. Kearney. Hear me out."

Behind her, the steer bellowed, a desperate cry for aid. The fine hair on her forearms rose.

Clenching her hands into fists to keep them from shak-ing, she held the trail boss's steady gaze. "That's one-fifteenth of my life savings stuck in the sand. As a rancher, you know what getting your stock to market means—it can make the difference between survival or failure. Life and death. I need the money that steer will bring, Mr. Kearney. Every penny of it. Twenty-five dollars is enough

for a roof on the house I plan to build, or maybe a pump
in the kitchen, or a wash porch. I'm not going to give up,
you hear!''

Clamping her trembling lips together, she gazed into the
face of the man who held her future in his hand.

Chapter Fifteen

Carleton's eyes held hers so long she wondered if he could read her thoughts. After a long moment, he laid his gloved hand over hers. "All right, Serena, we'll try."

Tears stung under her eyelids.

"Wait just a damn minute." Lyle's pale eyes blazed. "It's just one lousy animal. It's crazy to risk lives for one lousy steer. Let the lady rancher take her lumps."

Carleton studied his foreman for a long moment. "Yeah, LB, I know that's how you see it." He turned his gaze on the steer. "Come on, boys. We'll have to dig him out by hand."

Shaking, Serena listened to his calm, clear orders.

"Rosy, Thad. Crawl out there on your knees, and keep your body weight centered over your calves. When you get to the front legs, burrow down around each one and double it back at the knee. Then tie it good. Ben, you and Silas slip your lariats around those two, just in case."

Ben already had his rope looped around Thad's shoulders. Silas quickly had Rosy similarly secured.

Carleton continued talking in a low voice while coiling his own rope. "Hog, you and Thorny get the back legs."

"I'll do it," Serena blurted. "I'm small and—"

"No way, Sis." Carleton's quick, dry response surprised her. "That's an order. Now, get your horse out of here. Thorny?"

Stung, Serena retreated to the far side of the creek.

Thorny swung his leg over the saddle horn. "Right, boss. Come on, you tub o' Texas lard," he sang at Hog. "Let's get started."

Hog snorted. "What a mammary you got! It's Arizona, not Texas."

Serena couldn't even smile at Hog's mangled English. She watched Carleton's lariat catch Thorny's broad shoulders just as he shuffled into the creek on his knees. Lyle tossed the loop at the end of his rope to Hog, who settled it over his own brawny frame.

With caution, the four men approached the steer. Hunching over their calves, as Carleton had dictated, they dug desperately through the silty muck with their bare hands. Gradually the steer's callused knees were exposed, then the forelegs, finally the hooves. Quickly they bent the legs back and bound them in place with lengths of rawhide.

Carleton's quiet voice carried over the steer's frenzied bellowing and the grunts of the men. "Okay, boys. Back out of there real easy."

When the mud-caked quartet reached solid ground, Carleton flipped his lasso free of Thad's shoulders, recoiled the rope and sailed it over one of the steer's horns. "He's trussed. We'll try pulling him out with the horses."

Four other ropes settled over the animal's curving horns—one of them Serena's, thrown from her position at the edge of the creek.

"Pull," Carleton ordered. "Slow and easy."

The steer began to emerge from the sand so slowly Serena thought she would scream with impatience. Her horse danced under her as, inch by inch, the creek relinquished the exhausted animal. With a final sucking sound, the legs pulled free and the steer rolled onto its side.

In the next minute, five horses dragged the struggling steer to the bank, and Thad leaped to cut the rawhide ties. Freed, the animal stood stock-still for a moment, then lumbered off to rejoin the herd.

Serena felt the knots in her stomach begin to unravel. She never dreamed the life of one single steer could be so important to her! She recoiled her lariat with hands that fluttered like windblown leaves, her entire body trembling so violently she wondered whether she could control her horse for the next hour. Maybe Cora would lace her coffee with whiskey tonight.

She edged her gelding forward until she could speak to the trail boss. "Mr. Kearney?"

The tall man waited, his coiled rope in one hand, his blue eyes unfathomable.

"Thank you," she whispered. "I am in your debt."

"Don't count on it, Sis. It's a long way to Winnemucca."

Serena stared at him. Whatever did he mean by that?

But just before he reined his mare away, she saw his lips twitch into a smile.

That evening before supper, Serena found a small bouquet of blue flowers tucked under the tie of her bedroll. On impulse, she stuck them in her hatband, then went to wash up for Cora's supper of biscuits, chili beans and baked cobbler made with tinned peaches.

She dished up her plate and seated herself next to Hog, who stayed apart from the other hands, evidently because of the ragging his table manners provoked.

"Howdy, Miss Serena." The stocky giant attempted a gallant bow over his supper plate. When he straightened, a tomato-tinted spot appeared on the lower third of his dusty work shirt.

Serena studied the toes of her boots until she could speak without laughing. "I wanted to thank you for what you did today, pulling my steer out of the creek."

"T'weren't nuthin, ma'am."

Serena ignored the slurping sounds he made as he attacked his food. "It meant a great deal to me," she observed softly.

A grin split Hog's dripping chin. "Them bluebuckets look real purty on your hat, ma'am."

Serena choked. He must mean the bluebonnets.

"Thank you for picking them, Hog. I didn't see any close by—where did you find them?"

"Oh, *I* didn't pick 'em, Miss Serena. Kinda wish I had, though, they look real nice. But t'warn't me."

Not Hog? Then who? Serena wondered. Cora? Jem, maybe? Thad, because he'd annoyed her asking questions about Carleton?

The puzzle was still unsolved an hour later, when she drew the first night-herding shift. As soon as the trail boss stopped talking, she rose, dropped her empty plate in Cora's hot wash water, and went to saddle her horse. Her entire string, except for her own mare, Sandy, were Double K horses, tough and so well trained she had only to point out a cow needing corralling and the horse did the rest.

That was Carleton's doing, she acknowledged. He trained all the Kearney ranch horses. Thad had helped him until the young man had taken the job as her foreman; now Carleton used Rosy. Snap, she noticed, never worked with the animals, just took care of shoeing and maintaining the tack.

By the time she stepped Sandy out to the quiet herd bedded down for the night in a field of horse fern, it was getting dark. She rode slowly around the circle, keeping some yards clear of the cattle. The afterglow of sunset lit the mountains far to the south with warm, gold light. Trees dotted the nearer hills like dark silhouettes reaching toward a cloudless, purple-black sky.

The country out here was beautiful. And changeable. Tonight the air was soft and balmy. By morning, there might be frost on the ground, with a sharp wind cutting at her back. And by ten o'clock, with the sun a blazing orange ball against the sky, sweat would be soaking her shirt.

The approaching rider, her night guard partner, emerged from the shadows and came toward her. Someone tall, but it was too dark to tell who it was. Ben Kearney, maybe. Or Lyle.

She hoped it wasn't Lyle. She felt uncomfortable near him, especially in the dark. Serena's instincts told her Lyle was like two people—a trustworthy, trail-wise foreman on one hand, a determined predator on the other. She never liked being around him, especially at night. Something about the way he looked at her made her uneasy, as if he could see right through her clothes.

She sucked in her breath as the rider drew near and tipped his dark Stetson. ''Good evening, Miss Hull.''

''Mr. Kearney!'' Her heart began to pound. ''I didn't expect to find you herding tonight.''

''I didn't expect to be here. Silas is nursing a toothache. I told him I'd cover his shift.''

Serena suppressed a smile and nudged the mare forward. ''Silas sleeps well on a cattle drive, with ten trail hands to cover for him. His teeth must be in terrible condition. For a man who doesn't miss much, you didn't notice this?''

''I didn't sleep much last night and I've been riding hard since sunup. A man misses a good deal if he's tired enough.''

His eyes flicked to her hat. ''Most unusual headgear I've ever seen on night duty.''

Serena's hand flew to her Stetson. Oh, the flowers! She'd completely forgotten about them. "Bluebuckets, Hog said. I think he meant bluebonnets."

Carleton's mouth relaxed. "That's Texan for silver mountain lupine. Blooms in the fall up here in the high country. Blooms all the time in Texas."

"Arizona," she corrected. "Hog's from Arizona."

"Bluebonnets in Arizona, too. Mighty pretty." He lifted his reins.

"Evening, Miss Hull." He tipped his hat and moved past her, headed in the opposite direction.

Carleton listened to her mare's slow hoofbeats fade into silence, and gradually became aware of the chorus of crickets rising from the darkened valley floor. He'd come to dread nights like these, the still air full of nature's sounds—night birds, a bullfrog or two, maybe a coyote off in the hills. It was as if the earth had stopped turning and waited for something. All his senses were pricked into awareness as he listened and waited, too.

An ache gnawed inside him. Deep down, where he had to face himself, he needed to confront and accept the knowledge that he'd failed as a man. He felt as if he were wrestling the devil for his soul. A night like this was seductive, driving into the quick of the old feelings—desolation and body hunger.

And the new feelings of surprise and desire whenever he looked into Serena's dark, quiet eyes.

He'd best keep moving. Otherwise, the night, and his thoughts, would last forever.

On his next pass by her, he waited to see if she reined her horse in. She did not. Relief and disappointment warred in his brain. He'd like another good look at those flowers. Somebody had ridden a good distance to pick them. He wondered who it was.

"You don't sing, do you?" Her voice startled him. He'd

come halfway around the herd again and met her in the middle of the loop. This time she halted.

"Not often, no. Not since…it's been a while now."

"I do. But Rosy told me not to. He said my voice was so much higher than a man's it'd spook the herd."

"So it seems we're both quiet tonight," Carleton said.

She half smiled. "I'm usually quiet. Except lately, herding cows. The sounds I hear myself make are most unladylike."

Carleton chuckled. "There's no genteel way to get a thousand head of cattle up a mountain and across a boggy stream. You did fine."

"You weren't listening to me today," she said with a laugh.

"Yes," he countered. "I was. 'Sons of steers.' Very inventive."

"You heard me!"

Carleton bit back a laugh. Right before his eyes, Miss Iron Spine had become an appealingly winsome child, anxious to please. The contrast made his gut tighten. She was made of layers, like the Charleston Summer Cake his mother used to make. Sweet brandy-laced whipped cream spread between crisp butter pastry rounds that shattered at the touch of his tongue. The image he conjured made him suck in his breath. There were all kinds of places he'd like to put his tongue right now.

He felt his groin swell, tried to smile at her and forced himself to step the gelding on past her.

He knew she was staring at his back, her dark eyes probably widening in surprise at his abrupt exit. The urge to look almost overpowered him. He listened to the *clop-clop* of her mare, closed his eyes and let his horse follow the circuit it knew by rote.

Dammit, somehow she'd gotten under his skin so deep he felt he was drowning. He wasn't in love with her—not yet, anyway. But he was sure as hell in *something* with her, and he wasn't sure he liked it.

Nope. Not true. He liked it, all right. Just wasn't sure he could handle it.

Her.

Serena needed a younger man, someone with a future. Someone without the encumbrances of a marriageable stepdaughter and the infant child of another woman.

And what did he need?

Someone to believe in him. Trust him, need him. Want him, as a man.

That about tears it, then. Serena felt none of these things for him, especially not the *want* part. Hell, she was so skittish around men she'd barely talk to any of the hands except Thad and young Jem Kearney.

Still, the bluebonnets in her hatband stuck in his mind. Where they came from didn't signify. What did matter was that she'd stuck them up there as a decoration, the kind of small, seemingly unconscious gesture women did when they wanted to attract a man's attention.

All at once, Carleton found himself grinning. He began to hum an old, old tune from his war years. "Lorena."

Yeah, she'd done it—stuck those blue blossoms on her hat. He'd bet next year's feed bill she hadn't a clue what her innocent gesture suggested to any red-blooded man with half a brain.

He kicked the gelding into a faster pace. On his next circle around the herd, he'd have a question for the Summer Cake lady.

Chapter Sixteen

"Serena?"

The voice out of the darkness jarred her, and she pulled the pony up short.

"Lyle! What are you doing out here? It's not time for the next shift yet."

"Yeah, I know. I came early. Want to talk to you."

Serena stiffened. "I can't talk now, Lyle. I'm riding night guard."

"Yeah, I know that, too. Stop for just a minute." He blocked her way with his big roan.

"I can't do that. As a ranch foreman, you should know I can't leave the herd unguarded. Let me pass." She lifted the reins.

"Not so fast, lady." He caught her bridle and brought her mare head-to-head with his. "I said I want to talk."

"Talk, then," she snapped. "Get it over with."

"Serena..." He leaned forward, slipped his free hand around her waist. "I'm sorry about not volunteering to rescue your steer this afternoon."

She tried to pull away. "It's perfectly understandable. Now, let me go." She tried to move the mare past him, but he held her bridle in an iron grip.

A needle of fear pricked her spine. "I said let go!"

"You're needin' a man, Serena," he said, his voice silky. "To run your ranch, and to run you." He pulled her closer, pressed her knee with his.

"Mr. Bartel, take your hands off me!"

"Not yet, pretty lady. Not 'til I'm done." He yanked her forward, nuzzled her temple with hot, dry lips.

"Let her go, LB." Carleton's low voice cut through Serena's tumbling thoughts.

"Boss, I was just—"

"Do it now!"

"Damn," Lyle muttered under his breath. He dropped his hand from her waist.

"Release her horse."

Shaking, Serena stepped her mare away, moving close to Carleton on his bay.

"Listen to me good, LB. You lay one finger on Miss Hull between here and Winnemucca and I'll fire you so fast your head will spin. You got that?"

"Yeah, I got it. Maybe I was a little out of line."

"A little," Carleton said, his voice flat and even. "Now, go take a cold bath in the creek and stay out of my sight 'til morning."

Without a backward glance, the lanky cowhand jerked on his reins and jolted away. The herd rustled uneasily, some raising their heads, others hunching to their feet, then flopping over to lie on the other side.

Serena drew in an unsteady breath. She wanted to weep, scream, break something. The memory of Lyle's hot, groping fingers made her shiver. "I don't want to talk about it, so don't ask me anything," she said through gritted teeth.

"Don't have to." He laid a hand on her shoulder.

Serena leaned into him, buried her face against his chest. He dropped his reins and pulled her closer. "If you're going to cry," he said, keeping his voice low, "try to muffle it against my shirt. The cattle are uneasy."

Carleton wished he could take her somewhere out of earshot and let her cry it out. Unfortunately, until they were relieved by Eli and Thorny at midnight, neither one could leave their post.

Serena grasped his shirtfront with both hands and pressed her mouth hard against one fist. Sobs shook her body, racked her entire frame in silence. Except for little hiccuping sounds, she made no noise.

"Damn him," she choked out. "Damn all men, but especially him."

Carleton said nothing. Holding her shuddering body for even these few moments was a gift from heaven. He didn't want to let her go.

At last, she swiped at her eyes, pulled out her bandanna and blew her nose. "He wanted to—"

"I know. I heard most of it. When you didn't show up at the checkpoint, I figured you were in some kind of trouble."

The feel of her nestled in his arms sent his senses reeling. She smelled like a cowhand—wood smoke and coffee and trail dust. But she felt like a woman. He lifted her hat off. Even after four days on the trail, her hair still smelled faintly of lilacs and sweet clover.

Without thinking, he pressed his mouth to her forehead. She went perfectly still.

"Serena," he whispered. Very, very slowly, she raised her face to his. "It's all right. I won't hurt you."

You're damn right you won't hurt her, you old fool. Now get your hands off of her. This isn't what she needs right now. Maybe not ever. And even if it is, you're not the one to show her.

"You were going to kiss me, weren't you?"

"I— Well I was, until I thought about it."

"You can, if you want," she breathed. "I've always wanted to know what it would be like. I've been wanting you to."

His groin tightened. *Go slow,* he ordered himself. She was offering, but he could see she was skittish. "You're scared," he said, his tone gentle.

"Oh, no. I'm terrified. No one's ever kissed me before."

"I see," he said with a soft laugh. "I hope you like it." Very deliberately, he tipped her chin up, bent his head and covered her mouth with his.

Her lips were cool and soft. Against his chest he could feel her heart flutter like the wings of an imprisoned bird. Something cracked inside him, and a warmth like molten sunlight spilled into his heart. She tasted of coffee and cinnamon.

He should never have done it. He should have ridden on by her, or at least waited. God in heaven, he couldn't get enough of her. He deepened the kiss, then lifted his lips from hers, his blood thrumming in his ears. He wanted to kiss her again, but he didn't want to frighten her. He ached to haul her tight against him, dip his head and lose himself in her softness, her taste.

He brushed her mouth with his. "Serena," he murmured. "Do you want me to stop?"

She opened her eyes like a sleepy child. "No, don't stop. I like it with you."

Carleton's heart catapulted into his throat. "You sure?"

"Y-yes. It makes me feel...floaty. Unreal, as if I'm dreaming. I didn't like being close to Lyle," she confessed in a whisper. "But then I don't—"

He kissed her again, felt her lashes flutter against his cheek when he pulled away. She opened her lids and looked straight into his eyes. "I don't respect Lyle the way I do you. I don't trust him."

Carleton's breath dammed in his chest. "And you trust me?"

Oh, *God,* she had to trust him. She was a lot like a fine, sensitive horse that had been cruelly broken. She had to be gentled very slowly, shown that hope and faith were still possible in a flawed and violent world. Trusting a man would be the first step toward healing the damage.

Serena smiled and nodded her head. "Yes, I do. I do trust you."

An odd, protective feeling surged through him. He wanted to keep on kissing her, wanted to feel her skin under his hands, hear her moan his name. But more than that, he wanted to keep her safe from harm. No matter how he yearned to feel her mouth under his again, he would not press for more just now. She'd given him the most valued gift—her respect and trust. He would do nothing to weaken the fragile bond building between them. Not even if it meant lying sleepless on his pallet all night with a swollen, aching groin.

Deliberately, he lifted his hands from her shoulders and straightened in the saddle. "Come on," he said, his voice hoarse. "Time to wake up our replacements and get some rest."

He laid the mare's reins in her hand, pointed its nose toward camp. "I'll wait here. You go wake up Eli."

He slapped the horse's rump and forced his own mount to move in the opposite direction while her mare clopped off in the darkness.

For the next two days, while the drive met the Klamath River at Hazel Glen and paralleled it south to Snowball Gulch, Serena took special pains to stay out of Lyle Bartel's path. She also avoided Carleton as much as possible, but for different reasons.

Lyle made her nervous. Carleton made her body sing

with excitement at the mere sight of him. His rangy frame, his lazy, graceful way of mounting his horse or joining the circle of men around the evening campfire were pure pleasure to watch. Every evening he rolled up his shirtsleeves, revealing the fine dark hair on his forearms, and her breath would catch. She longed to run her fingers over the tanned skin, feel his body heat under her palm.

The very thought astounded her. No respectable young woman in Stark County would dream of such a forward act. But perhaps things were different out here in Oregon.

Or was it she who was different? Had taking over Lost Acres Ranch made her more clear-eyed and forthright than she'd been as a girl? Or had she been so all along, and starting her new life on her father's ranch had merely rubbed away the protective layers she'd hidden behind for so many years? For hours at a time she thought the matter over while herding cattle along the trail.

At Carson Crossing, they forded the river with only one mishap. Eldon Bartel got dumped in the icy water when his horse swam out from under him. Thad and Eli Harker rescued the thrashing youth, dragged him to the bank where he waited with chattering teeth while Silas Appleby rounded up the boy's horse.

"No harm done," the lanky ranch owner remarked amiably as he led the animal back to its owner. "Fit as a fiddle."

"W-well, I'm n-not," Eldon stammered. He yanked the reins out of Silas's grasp. "I'm p-plumb fr-froze from my w-waist down."

Serena could see the boy trying to control his shivering. He'd head for the chuck wagon and some of Cora's hot sassafras tea as soon as he could mount. The brew was such a cure-all she wondered why Silas didn't use it for the toothache that plagued him at night.

"Now, that's bad, kid," Silas drawled. "Yessir, mighty

hard to thaw things out down there.'' He jerked his thumb at Eldon's crotch. "The cold shrinks it, see, and— Well, I'm real sorry to be the one to tell you this, son—but it don't ever regain its former size.''

Eldon wet his lips. "You—you mean n-never?''

Silas nodded. "Yep. No more calico catchin', if you take my meaning.''

Thorny pricked up his ears and joined in. "Aw, he kin still chase 'em. Just can't do nuthin' once he's got 'em spread flat and wigglin'.''

Serena sucked in her breath, sure that the joke had gone too far. It didn't bother her that the men had completely forgotten her presence, or the fact that she was female. In fact, she rather liked it. She was accepted as "one of the boys," and at this moment was being ignored.

What bothered her was young Bartel's horrified reaction to the scandalous, coarse yarn Silas and Thorny were busy spinning.

Thorny stalked over and clapped his hand on Eldon's shuddering frame. "But the worst part is not havin' the capacity no more. Even a little guy can please a lady, ya know. But if you can't even... Gosh, I'm sure sorry, kid. Might have to come up with a new name for ya, to reflect yer new status.''

"N-new name?''

"Yeah. Whaddya think, Silas?''

Silas erased the grin from his face. "I think he had it and now he's lost it.''

"That's it!'' Thorny chortled. "Hadit! From now on, we're gonna call you Hadit Bartel.''

Eldon blanched. Quickly he mounted his horse, wheeled, and raced for the chuck wagon while Silas and Thorny slapped each other on the back and guffawed.

That was too much for Serena. "You ought to be

ashamed of yourselves, tormenting a gullible boy like that!''

Silas's hand froze in midslap. "Jehosaphat, I forgot all about you, Serena. Well now, ma'am, I really do beg your pardon.''

"Oh, you do nothing of the kind, you big liar! You're not a speck sorry. You neither, Thorny.''

Thorny's mouth dropped open. "Me! What'd I do?''

Serena pinned him with a look. "You know perfectly well. You aided and abetted Silas in hoodwinking that poor young man into thinking he's...he's... Oh, you know what I mean.''

She sniffed and spun away.

"No offense, Serena. Just meant to have a bit of fun. He'll get over it.''

She didn't turn around. She couldn't. The ridiculousness of the joke had her convulsed with laughter. Merciful heavens, what was happening to her! She stifled a giggle.

She was more trail hand now than lady, laughing at a joke in shockingly poor taste, made at the expense of a perfectly innocent young man who happened to fall off his horse midriver.

With a sigh, she headed for the chuck wagon. Maybe she and Eldon—no, Hadit, she remembered with a grin—could think up something in retaliation.

Chapter Seventeen

It took the rest of the day to herd the cattle onto one of the two log ferries and float them across. Using ropes and pulleys, the hands worked to keep the heavy craft from escaping downstream, pushed by the swift current.

Serena rode drag all day, along with Eli Harker, pushing the tail end of the herd to the ferry at the river's edge. When the last of the bawling cows arrived on the opposite bank, Serena and Eli, dusty and exhausted, stepped their mounts onto the raft and were pulled across.

Cora's chuck wagon and the remuda had long since traversed the water and set up camp on the south bank of the Klamath. When the cattle were settled into a grassy meadow downstream, the hands headed for a long-awaited supper. Serena headed upstream for a bath, taking Jem with her to stand guard, at Cora's insistence.

"Don't know who might happen by, and if you're nekkid in three feet of water, not much you can do if they ain't friendly."

Jem packed his father's Winchester, "just to be on the safe side," he assured her. His green eyes looked so earnest, Serena had to smile.

Safe or not, she had to have a bath, even if it was only

a quick dip in the icy Klamath. When Jem stationed himself under a cottonwood tree with his back to her, she stripped off her clothes, took a deep breath and plunged into the river.

She lasted three, maybe four minutes before her legs began to ache from the cold water. She clambered up the bank, teeth chattering, and donned a clean shirt and jeans. Then she scrubbed her dust-caked garments on the rocks lining the bank and wrapped them in her damp towel, finger-combed her wet hair and headed back to camp and supper.

Cora guarded the iron stew pot bubbling over the fire pit like an apron-clad avenging angel, wielding an oversize spoon instead of a sword. "Supper ain't ready 'til I say it's ready," she warned the men as they sidled close enough to sniff the contents of the pot. Overeager cowhands got their knuckles rapped.

Serena knew the feisty cook had delayed until she and Jem returned; otherwise, the hungry hands would gobble every scrap, leaving nothing for latecomers. Jem's appetite increased daily—a missed meal for him would be a calamity.

Loading her plate with sourdough biscuits and venison stew, Serena sat down to eat and watch the fun she and Eldon—Hadit—had cooked up after Silas and Thorny had teased him so unmercifully earlier in the day. Things started with her first bite of supper.

"My stars, Thorny," Cora said as the bulky cowhand held out his plate. Her raspy voice was full of concern. "Lemme take a look at you."

The cook peered up into the suntanned face and her eyes narrowed. "I thought so. You look positively spinotic."

Thorny's empty plate clattered against the rim of the stew kettle. "Spin—what?"

"It's a form of spinosis. That's somethin' even my sassafras tea can't cure."

"Spinosis?" the trail hand ventured, his tone wary. "Whazzat?"

"You outta ask Lyle about it—he's had some medical training." Cora lifted her spoon and turned back to the stew.

Ben Kearney backed away from Thorny. "Spinosis! Hell's bells, why didn't you say so before we left town?"

"Well, I…"

"*Spinosis?*" Hog and Rosy sang in one voice. "Is it dangerous?" Hog asked in a quavery voice.

Rosy struck his head with one hand. "*Ay, Santa Maria,* my uncle in Chihuahua, he had it. Beeg purple spots come, and then…" He crossed himself dramatically.

"Spots?" Thorny said in a choked voice. He cast a furtive glance at his bare forearm. "What kinda spots?"

Serena stared down at her plate to hide the smile she could not control.

"Beeg ones," Rosy reiterated.

"Purple," Ben added. "Sometimes even blue. The blue ones—that's the next stage—they're the worst."

With a shaking hand, Thorny ran his hand over his face. "Don't feel too bad," he murmured.

Cora sniffed. "That's a mercy. That means you ain't tainted yet. You can stop it altogether, if you hurry."

"Stop it? How?"

"Gotta take a real cold bath for five minutes and then fast for two meals."

"What's *fast* mean?"

"Don't eat," Cora snapped. "Nuthin'. Not even coffee."

Thorny groaned.

Ben clapped the trail hand on the back. "Think I see a spot or two on the back of your neck."

Thorny dropped his plate and began unbuttoning his shirt. Tearing it free from his trouser waistband, he headed for the river.

When the splash came, seven heads rose, looked at each other in conspiratorial silence, and went on eating.

"Hey, boys." Silas ambled up from the corral and stopped short at the whooping noises drifting from the river. "What's all that commotion?"

"No commotion, Mr. Appleby," the Bartel twins replied in unison.

"Unless you mean that love noise comin' from the river." Ben chewed for a moment, then added as an afterthought, "Oh, guess I wasn't supposed to say anything about that in front of the young'uns." He glanced at Eldon and Jason.

Silas's eyebrows rose. "Say anything about what?"

More screeching noises rose from the direction of the river.

"Jehosaphat, what gives?"

Hog plunked his oversize frame down across from Serena and settled his loaded plate onto his knees. "Well, Silas, it all started when this little bitty gal, all dressed up in ruffles an' lace, rode into camp a while back. She said she wanted to indulge in absolution."

"Ablution," Serena murmured beside him.

"Yeah, that's right. Pollution."

Ben forked another bite of stew into his mouth. "We couldn't send her off alone, now could we? So Thorny..." he took his time chewing and swallowing "...Thorny took her off to the river for a..."

Silas's hazel eyes gleamed. "Which way'd they go?"

Serena bit back a shout of laughter. Silas's reputation with the ladies was legendary among cowhands and townsfolk alike.

"Can't tell you that," Hog said over a mouthful of biscuit. "'Twouldn't be gentlemanly to spoil a fella's fun, now would it?''

Another splash broke the stillness, followed by a high, anguished cry.

Silas pivoted in the direction of the sound, his hands already at his belt buckle. "Well, now, I been needin' a bath myself after a hot, dusty day like today. Think I'll mosey on down to the river and…'' His voice faded as he disappeared into the shadows.

Hog laid down his fork and threw back his head. "Haw, haw, h—'' His mouth still open, the cowhand looked past Serena, his eyes widening. One by one, the men gathered around the campfire followed his gaze and fell silent.

The hair on Serena's neck bristled. She glanced behind her and stifled a gasp.

Out of the shadows emerged four figures on horseback. Indians. One, his head encircled by red-and-black feathers, carried a long spear. The other three carried rifles.

"Jem,'' Ben said quietly. "Go get Carl.''

Behind her, Serena heard the boy dart away toward the corral where Carleton met Snap each evening to check on the remuda.

Very slowly, Ben got to his feet. He addressed the first man in a strange-sounding language. One of the men answered, a brawny fellow in worn deerskin leggings, a tattered army shirt and a rifle.

"Molalla,'' Ben said. "At least one of them is. Renegades, probably, from around Fort McDermitt. The big fellow in front might be Nez Percé.''

"Ask what they want,'' Lyle said.

Thad spoke from the chuck wagon. "Might be smarter to welcome them,'' he countered. "Give them some food if they're hungry.''

"Not *my* stew,'' Cora announced. "I spent all afternoon cuttin' up potatoes.''

"Didn't mean *our* supper," Thad said, his voice calm. "I meant meat on the hoof."

Ben spoke again in the odd language. The man in the frayed shirt settled his rifle across his knees and pointed a finger at Serena.

Rooted to the spot, she found she was unable to draw breath. What could they possibly want with her?

Ben moved slowly forward, positioning himself between her and the Indians. Over his shoulder he spoke a single word. "Hog."

The burly ranch hand motioned Serena to his side. Very deliberately, she set her plate on the ground and, creeping on all fours, edged her body around to the opposite side of the campfire. Just as she reached Hog's bulky form, Lyle stepped forward. "If it comes to it, she's mine. Not Hog's."

"If it comes to it, LB," Ben replied, "take the one on your right. My rifle scabbard's under my saddle."

Rosy inched his way closer to Serena. Turning his back to the mounted Indians, he hunched over Serena. "My pistol, *señorita*. In my pocket." He patted his short wool jacket. "You take."

Serena reached her hand into the pocket. Closing her fingers over the barrel of the gun, she lifted it out and lowered it to her lap. While Ben spoke at length to the four mounted men, Rosy slipped off his jacket and dropped it over the weapon.

"*Bueno, señorita,*" he whispered. "You can shoot?"

She shook her head. Reaching under his jacket, Rosy cocked the hammer for her. "Do not aim. Just point and pull the trigger."

She tried to breathe slowly and quietly as Rosy pressed her forefinger into the trigger guard. Then he sat back on his haunches and moved a few inches to the left, giving her a clear shot.

Oh God, she couldn't! She was Indian, too. How could she kill one of them and live with herself the rest of her life?

Ben's voice rose and fell as he conversed with the tall man in front. The Indian kept shaking his head and repeating something.

When Carleton strode into the firelit circle, Serena wondered whether the gun strapped to his thigh was loaded. *Don't let him shoot,* she prayed. *Please, God. Don't let him kill one of them.*

"What's up?" The calm, authoritative voice cut through her thoughts.

Ben spoke in a low tone. "Our friends here say they're looking for a runaway squaw called Little Feather. They think Serena might be her."

Carleton nodded. "What do they really want?"

"I think they want a woman," Ben replied. "Any woman."

"Guns?"

"Three rifles. Old ones. Single shot. We got two revolvers—mine and yours. Three, if you count Rosy's."

Carleton advanced to the leader, and Serena held her breath.

"Tell them I'm the boss here."

Ben spoke some words, and the tall Indian made a sign.

"Now tell them this woman is not the one they seek."

Ben spoke again. "He wants to know why you are so sure."

Carleton was silent for a long moment. Serena thought the gun would slip out of her hand her palm was sweating so profusely.

"Tell them I know this to be true because she belongs to one of us."

Ben exchanged more words with the well-built man.

"He wants to know which one owns her?" he translated. "And how many horses it would take to—"

"She's mine," Lyle blurted. "My woman."

Serena stiffened as he moved behind her and knelt at her back.

"Just relax and play along," he intoned. "Boss ordered me not to touch you, so don't worry—I'm not gonna."

She caught Carleton's steady gaze. His head bent in an almost imperceptible nod.

Go along with it, he was telling her. *Play the ruse.*

In a voice meant only for her hearing, Lyle spoke near her ear. "I watched you bathe in the river today, Serena. I was upstream a ways. You couldn't see me, but I saw you."

The foreman's voice dropped even lower. "I saw you real good. You need a man to spend all them female charms on. 'Specially now since I'm your protector, you might say. Without me, you aren't gonna be too safe around here."

Serena's entire body froze. Instinct told her she wasn't safe with Lyle, either. The tall cowboy was young and capable, and not bad looking with his long blond hair and penetrating brown eyes. But no matter what his manly attributes, she knew she didn't want to be anywhere near him.

"Now, pretty lady," he breathed at her back. "You owe me. Yessir, you owe me."

The four Indians conferred in gutteral tones. Finally, the tall one spoke, his words spit from between lips curled in distaste.

Ben listened, then turned to his brother. "They want her anyway."

Serena's scalp prickled. Every fiber of her being warned against relying on Lyle's offer of protection, but she could see no way out. Unless...an alternative came to her. The cost of that, too, would be great. It was a risk, she acknowledged. But one she'd have to take.

She stood up slowly, keeping the revolver covered under Rosy's jacket. "Tell them," she said over the hammering of her heart, "that I am no man's woman. Tell them that I am the granddaughter of Chief Black Eagle of the Klamath River tribes. And tell them that Black Eagle's spirit, and the spirit of my mother, Walks Dancing, will hound any man who touches me against my will."

Every man present stared at her. Carleton held her gaze until her eyes burned.

"Tell them," she demanded in a quiet voice. "They will not dare take me then."

At Carleton's nod, Ben spoke to the Indians at length. Halfway through his speech, the tall man jerked visibly, then raised his spear over his head and let out a raucous cry.

Serena's blood turned to ice water as she waited for Ben's translation.

"They will honor the memory of Black Eagle. They will not defile the granddaughter of his heart."

Relief swept over her like waves of intoxicating wine. Already the four braves were turning their horses away from the fire.

"Wait!" Carleton ordered. "Ben, ask them to accept a gift in Black Eagle's memory. Hog, Rosy, cut two steers from the herd and bring them around."

Ben spoke quickly, receiving a grunt of assent from the leader. Serena watched in stunned silence while the four men saluted her, and then Carleton, and at last slipped into the shadows.

Her limbs trembled so violently they would no longer support her. Sinking to the ground, she gingerly pushed Rosy's pistol away, bent her legs and buried her face against her knees.

What had she done? Short of killing all four men, she'd offered the only thing she could think of that would save her—the truth of her identity. But now the entire trail crew knew she was a half-breed.

"Land sakes!" Cora exclaimed when the hoofbeats died away. She stared around the campfire at the silent trail crew. "Stew's gettin' cold, biscuits gettin' soggy. Finish it up now, boys."

Shaking, Serena accepted Ben's hand and pulled herself upright. She was more unnerved by Lyle's offer of protection, and the implied price, than the Indians' demand to hand her over. At least that was direct. Mama always said the white man was more devious than the red man.

She knew Lyle wouldn't lay a hand on her for the time being for fear of losing his job. But there were other, more insidious ways of coercion. She shuddered at the thought.

Thorny strode back into camp at that moment, accompanied by a shivering Silas. "K-kin we have s-some whiskey, Cora?" he stuttered. "We're m-mighty c-cold."

Silas nodded as vigorously as his quaking frame would allow. "And s-some humbled, t-too. Who p-planned this little sh-shindig, anyway?"

Unaccountably warm, Serena squirmed. Now that she had revealed herself, she expected to be betrayed at any moment. Most of the hands hated the Indians. Now that they knew she was half Modoc, they would hate her, too. She waited, her fists clenched, for someone to speak the words.

Silence.

Then Rosy, his face impassive, said, "*No sabe,* Señor Appleby. *¿Qué es un* 'shindig'?"

Silas gazed about the studiedly innocent faces of his comrades. "Aw, forget it. None of you's gonna weasel on a friend. Anyway, it was a mighty g-good joke on us."

"M-mighty good," Thorny growled. "How 'bout that whiskey, Cora? My t-toes are 'bout froze off."

"To say nuthin' of yer..." someone ventured, purposely leaving the sentence unfinished.

Serena saw Cora glance at Carleton, then saw the trail boss nod.

"Sure, short whiskey all around. Seems to me you've all—" he flicked a look at Serena, his blue eyes twinkling "—been workin' pretty hard lately."

He paused to retie his holster flap. "Silas, Thorny. Don't get too drunk to take the midnight shift. And you'll both get to ride drag tomorrow, along with Eldon. Kinda help you three get reacquainted."

"Hold on a minute, Mr. Kearney," Eldon interjected from the chuck wagon. "Name's Hadit now."

Thorny guffawed and strode over to slap the red-headed boy on the back. "You're a good man, Hadit. Now," he said in a conspiratorial tone, "what're we gonna do about your brother's name? Jason. If that ain't a citified moniker, I never heard one."

Eldon grinned. "I been thinking about that ever since he was born, Thorny. Two bits says Silas an' you 'n me can cook up a doozy of a name tomorrow. A feller's gotta talk about something other than the dust when you're ridin' drag."

Carleton rolled his eyes. "Just one round, Cora. Got to have some sober hands tomorrow. It'll be a dry drive for the next three days."

The men lined up at the chuck box, where Cora unlocked the medicine drawer and lifted out the quart of Child's.

Serena stayed behind. One teaspoon of such a substance would completely destroy her shaky composure.

She could hardly believe not one man had revealed her part in the trumped-up joke on Silas and Thorny. Especially now that they all knew she was part Indian. A half-breed. It was too much to hope that it didn't matter.

Or did it? From across the campfire, Lyle Bartel made a prolonged, embarrassingly complete perusal of her body his insolent gaze moving slowly from her toes to the top of her head. His look made her flesh crawl.

She turned away to find Carleton beside her as she headed for the back of the wagon. He adjusted his long, loose-limbed stride to match hers.

"Seems you made a few conquests tonight," he observed.

"I made an enemy, too." She shifted her eyes sideways to Lyle.

Carleton grinned. "I wouldn't worry, Serena. A man who has no enemies, has no friends, either. Same goes for a woman."

The warmth in his voice slid over her like sweet melted butter. She could not believe she had friends among the rough cowhands who were her trail companions.

Trust no man, especially a white man. Her mother's words.

But she did. She trusted Thad. And young Jem. And, she acknowledged as an odd heat flowed through her veins, she trusted Carleton Kearney. Trusted him, and liked him, as a person. As a man.

The realization made her heart stop. Liking the man was probably the biggest mistake of her life, but she couldn't deny her real feelings. She knew Carleton didn't want to like her—but he did. She could tell by the gentleness of his mouth on hers, the respectful way he had held her, spoken to her in his low, quiet voice.

A silence rose between them, waves of tension emanating from their two bodies moving side by side so close together. To break its power, Serena posed a question.

"What is a 'dry drive'?"

Carleton released a long breath. "No water. Cattle get edgy. The trail hands get strung up pretty tight."

"Oh," Serena breathed.

"We'll skirt the lava beds to the east," Carleton continued, "then head for Captain Jack's Spring at the far end of Firewater Gulch. If we're lucky, we can make it in three days. After that, the cattle will start to die of thirst."

"What if we're not lucky?"

"Well, Sis, then you're not gonna build a house for your sisters come spring."

Chapter Eighteen

The trail boss had been right, Serena thought as she chased after an ornery steer, driving the animal back in line with a shout and a flick of her lariat. Driving cows that hadn't had a drink in two days was exhausting. It required constant vigilance to keep them moving forward instead of turning back toward their last watering place, and the farther they traveled from the Klamath, the more short-tempered both cattle and trail hands became.

Now, pressing on for the third day without water, even Ben Kearney, riding the shoulder position with Eli Harker and herself, lost his usual benign acceptance of the foibles of cows and men. Serena winced as he swore again, using even more colorful language than before.

"Move, you damned spineless sons of—"

"My," observed Eli in a dry tone. "Sure gettin' poetic in your old age."

"Sure gettin' nosy in yours!" Ben retorted.

Serena listened to the banter between the two men and a bubble of well-being rose in her chest. Despite the searing afternoon sun and the thirst-tormented dryness of her throat, she sensed another one of those special moments.

The raw, treeless hillsides were so thickly cloaked with

dry, golden grass they looked like lumps of dappled velvet. The haze of late afternoon washed the slick black rocks with amber light. And Ben Kearney's flair for imaginative language, punctuating the lowing of a thousand head of cattle headed for market, reminded her that the human spirit was never vanquished as long as one could laugh.

When the day drew to a close, the cattle safely bedded down in a dry lake bed and all but the two hands riding guard had gathered at the chuck wagon for supper, the quiet contentment of the day and her satisfaction at a job done to the best of her ability reminded her to count her blessings. She would get her steers to the railhead and ride home with enough money to build a fine house. Her cup was running over.

Hog and Rosy had been assigned to watch the remuda, an extra detail Carleton had ordered after the Indian incident two nights ago. Tomorrow she and Rosy would ride flank again; maybe she'd pick up some more Spanish.

Her muscles aching from hours on Dodger's broad back, she climbed into the curtained chuck wagon at Cora's invitation and indulged in a spit bath. It took only a quart of the cook's precious supply of wash water. When they reached the spring at Firewater Gulch tomorrow, the first task would be to refill the two water barrels in the wagon. She prayed they would meet no delays; the dust coating her skin was so thick the bath felt as if she were merely smearing a layer of dusty paste around the surface of her body. She longed to wash her shirt and jeans, her undergarments. Her hair.

Tomorrow. When they reached Captain Jack's—

A gunshot splintered the still evening air. And then an odd rumbling began, like thunder, only she could feel it through the soles of her feet.

"All hands but the cook!" a male voice yelled. "Stampede!"

For an instant, Serena froze in her bloomers. Then she threw on her shirt and stiff, dirty jeans, grabbed her hat and headed toward the corral.

Carleton grabbed her arm as she raced toward the remuda to saddle her horse. "Whatever you do, don't get caught in the herd," he shouted. "Stay clear, but try to keep up."

"Yes, I understand!" she yelled over the din of shouting men and drumming hooves. She wasn't sure he heard her.

He preceded her into the rope corral. "Give her my gray," he ordered Snap. "She's surefooted and smart."

He turned to Serena. "Let the horse do the work, Sis. Just stay away from the front of the herd."

She threw her saddle over the tough little pony Snap led forth. The deafening noise of pounding hooves rolled over her like a wall of cacaphonous drumbeats. She tightened the cinch, and Carleton adjusted the stirrups. Then he mounted a piebald gelding and caught the gray's bridle, tugging the horse forward so he faced Serena.

"We'll try to herd them southeast, toward Firewater Gulch."

"How far is that?" She had to shout to make him hear.

"Ten miles. When we can get ahead of them, we'll try to turn the herd. They'll run 'til they're exhausted, but we'll try to maneuver them into a circle."

Serena nodded, slipped her leather gloves out of her jacket pocket and hurriedly drew them on. The dust choked her throat. "Is it dangerous in front of the herd?" she shouted.

"Not for experienced men. I don't want you or the Bartel boys anywhere up there, is that clear? If you get lost or hurt trying to keep up, just wait it out. We'll come back for you."

She nodded again. For once she didn't mind being assigned a minor role. Branding and roping were one thing;

she had no desire to try her hand at turning a stampeding herd of cows.

A strong hand gripped her shoulder, squeezed hard and fell away. The piebald gelding dashed ahead, along with seven other mounted men, pounding down the trail after the cattle barely visible in the silvery light of a half-moon.

A metallic taste flooded her mouth. Fear. She was afraid for Carleton and the other men out battling for control over a thousand head of rampaging cows.

She kicked the pony and it leaped forward. She galloped hard to catch up.

The sound of bawling cows and the thundering mass of huge animals so near was terrifying. Riding alongside the herd, she swerved out of the way when the maddened cattle suddenly hurtled in her direction. The heat from their laboring bodies washed over her in sickening waves whenever she got too close.

Snap joined her. She knew the wrangler was riding with her just to keep an eye on her. He'd double back when they had the herd under control, then drive the remuda and the chuck wagon forward to a rendezvous later.

"Come on, boys!" he yelled. "Them cattle are runnin'!"

The redheaded Bartel twins shot by her, whooping with glee at the prospect of an adventure.

"Damn young fools," Snap yelled. "Get themselves killed tearin' off like that."

"They're just trying to grow up," Serena called to the irate man. "If I weren't so scared, I'd join them."

Snap snorted. "You're plucky, Missy. Not dumb."

She wasn't feeling plucky, she admitted. She was scared spitless. Still, there was a job to be done.

To the ranch owners, a stampede brought the possibility of losing part of the herd, maybe all of it if things went wrong. At the very least, a stampede meant body weight lost in the run. Each animal meant money in the bank. Cowhands, on the other hand, were a dime a dozen.

For Serena, the prospect of losing one human life far outweighed the value of meat on the hoof. The Bar H and Double K ranches, along with Silas Appleby's Mariah Two spread, the ranch he'd named after the girl who'd jilted him long years before—all based their livelihood on cattle. So did she, but not at the risk of a life.

Resolutely, she guided the pony nearer the herd, longing to close her ears to the raw, animal sounds made by the frightened cows. Dust choked her nostrils. She slid her bandanna up over her mouth and nose.

They caught up to the main part of the fear-maddened herd after a half hour of hard riding. The crazed animals had bunched together and spread sideways into a solid driving wedge eight or ten cows deep. Ahead of the beeves, Thad and Carleton and the others struggled to turn the roiling mass into a mill, allowing the cattle to run but drawing them into an ever-tightening knot.

Serena fought back panic as the uncontrollable tide swerved toward her. The gray pony danced out of harm's way, and then as the herd veered away, it raced ahead. Thank God the animal knew what to do! Heart pounding against her rib cage, her mouth dry, Serena clung to her mount and tried to anticipate what the wild-eyed mass of trail-toughened Herefords would do next.

Hours passed and still the animals hurtled on. She had no idea how many miles they had run. All she knew was that she'd never ridden so desperately in her life, and she never wanted to again as long as she lived. The ground under her blurred as she raced to keep up.

Dimly she noticed that the landscape she could see in the waning moonlight began to change. The last tree she'd seen was miles behind her; now only an occasional wind-stunted juniper leaped at her out of the darkness.

The horse skillfully avoided every obstacle on the end-less flat plain—straggly patches of wild alfalfa, clumps of dry rabbit brush, prairie dog holes that studded the ground. If one hoof accidentally plunged into such a depression, it would likely kill them both.

She fought for calm, struggled to withstand a choking fear. *She didn't want to die!* Not like this, not before she'd built the house for Jessie and Mary Irene. *Oh, God, please let me live through this! I want to see my sisters again!*

Near the front of the herd, Carleton rotated one arm in the air, signaling that the cattle were turning.

Thank You, Lord! Maybe if Thad and the others near the front could get the animals circling, this terrifying night would be over.

Snap wheeled away and headed back down the trail just as Thorny raced past her, waving his hat and yelling.

"They're turning! All hands to the front!"

Serena started after him. Like a giant wheel, the herd jostled itself into a huge, roiling circle, the cows packed so tight it looked like a solid wall of hides. She saw Thad ahead of her, riding in so close he was almost pushing the cows into the mill. Carleton and Ben and the others were doing exactly the same thing, and her throat tightened. She knew it was dangerous to get that near thousands of pounds of uncontrolled animal flesh.

A big steer pushed sideways into Ben's gelding. The horse reared and retreated, but not before two more huge beeves veered away from the main mass. Suddenly, Thad's horse was trapped between them.

Someone yelled, but it was too late. Thad disappeared into the milling mass of animals.

Too horrified to even scream, Serena watched Carleton plunge after his nephew, turning his horse into the center of the circling cattle while Ben tried to clear a path. She clenched the saddle horn with both hands and tried to pray.

Any second, all three of the men—brother, father and son—would be trampled to death.

Before she realized what she was doing, she kicked her pony forward to help.

Rosy caught her bridle. "Is too dangerous, *señorita! ¡Vamanos!*" He tugged hard on the bit to turn her horse, then grasped her reins and led her away.

The muddling herd slowed. All at once a space opened up and Carleton's horse appeared in the middle of a knot of cows. The saddle was empty.

Ben shouted for help. Her heart in her throat, Serena watched while four mounted men rode pell-mell into the melee to break up the knot. Foot by foot, they fought their way toward Ben. One of the riders—Eli Harker—grabbed for the piebald's bridle. Still slowing, the cattle split around the now screaming gelding, and then Serena realized what was happening. Thad and Carleton must be huddled among the cattle, fighting to avoid the sharp hooves.

Before she could draw another breath, one man stood up. Thad. Dusty and bedraggled, her young foreman grinned shakily, then accepted his father's extended arm and swung up behind him on the big roan. In the next moment, Eli and Hog dismounted, bent down and hoisted Carleton to his feet. Protected by a cadre of mounted riders, the three men lurched forward and stumbled their way to safety.

Thad looked rumpled, and he'd lost his hat. Carleton, his face twisting in pain, moved with difficulty, supported by the two men on either side of him. She could not believe they had survived.

She turned her face away, unable to watch Carleton struggle to hide his agony. Dead cows littered the wide, dusty path, trampled by the stampeding herd.

A sick feeling settled in her belly. Some of those dead animals could be hers. She wondered how many.

The trail hands rode in circles around the remaining cattle, soothing them with low talk and lilting songs. Hog's clear tenor rose above the shuffle of hooves and the raspy breathing of the exhausted herd. Hearing him revived Serena's spirits. Surely if the burly cowhand could still sing, things couldn't be too bad.

Except for Carleton. She turned her attention to where the trail boss sagged between Hog and Eli.

"Get Cora's medicine kit," Carleton said between gritted teeth.

Eli shot a glance at his boss's torn shirt. "The chuck wagon's miles back, Carl. And anyway, you'll need more than sassafras tea this time. Looks bloody and the skin's all busted up."

"Get a count of our losses," the trail boss demanded. "I want to know how bad we've been hit."

"Huh!" Hog let out a grating snort. "Cow musta' stepped on his head, too—rattled his brains. Ain't no way we're gonna be able to count cows at night. Can't see the brands. It'll hafta wait 'til mornin'."

Suddenly realizing he was giving orders to his boss, Hog looked to Eli for affirmation.

"He's right, Carl. Let the herd settle down and give the chuck wagon time to catch up. Snap and fresh horses oughta be here in another hour. Ours are too played out to be much good."

Hog hitched Carleton's body over a hillock, and the trail boss groaned. "Dammit, man, watch where you're dragging me! Hurts like a son of a—" He sucked breath in between clenched teeth as Hog sidestepped to avoid a chuckhole.

"Eli!" Carleton barked when he could talk. "Get this giant off me!"

Ben rode up on his big gelding. "Just what the devil were you thinkin' of back there, Carl?"

"I wasn't thinking," he muttered.

"Well, hell, Carl—that's not like you. Nor Thad, neither. What in God's name possessed you to ride smack into a bunch of fear-crazy cows?"

Eli shot a look at the mounted man. "Hell, Ben, he won't remember. But I saw a good bit of it. Carl went into the herd after Thad. When the kid lost his horse and went under, Carl crawled on top of him. Steer prob'ly would have killed your son, seein' as his head was unprotected. Carl took it on the shoulder instead."

Ben whistled. "Hellfire. Am I the only Kearney with any sense? Coulda killed you both!"

"Didn't," Carleton retorted.

Ben bit his lip, then bent and reached one hand out to grasp his brother's shoulder. Eli warned him off with a look.

"I owe you my thanks, Carl."

Carleton sent his brother a lopsided smile. "How's Thad?"

"Bellyachin'. Wants to find his hat. And his horse, but Silas and Rosy won't let him up. Rosy's sittin' on his chest."

Carleton's grin twisted as Hog negotiated a few yards of rocky terrain. "Gotta lie down pretty quick," he muttered. "Think I'm gonna..."

He crumpled into a heap at Hog's feet.

Serena started forward, but Eli waved her away.

"Don't try to rouse him, Missy. Hurtin' the way he is, might be better to leave him unconscious. Why don't you ride on back and check on Cora and the wagon. Tell her we'll need to rig up a sling. And we'll need some laudanum when he wakes up."

Serena's vision dimmed. Dizzy with relief that both Carleton and her foreman were alive, she turned the gray pony around. Unable to help herself, she glanced back at Eli.

"Now, don't worry none, Miss Serena. Lyle's had some doctor training. He'll take care of the boss."

She bit her lip and started back down the trail.

Two hours later, under a high, silvery moon, Serena followed the chuck wagon into the makeshift camp the trail hands had set up. Off to one side of the now sleeping herd, Snap's remuda shuffled within the confines of the rope corral. Dust-caked and weary, her bones aching for relief, she plodded past the glow of firelight, unsaddled her horse and turned it over to the wrangler.

Within fifteen minutes, Jem had a cook fire going and Cora bustled about the chuck box doing three things at once—frying bacon, mixing up an apple cake and sorting through the medicine drawer for bandages and whiskey.

"Darn fool men," she huffed as she forked the thick bacon slices around the huge skillet. "Jem, come keep your eye on my cake while I go see to your brother and your uncle. Least *you* got sense enough not to go traipsin' off to dance with a bunch of rowdy steers."

Jem's mouth tightened and he narrowed his eyes at the chattering cook. Serena knew exactly what he was thinking. The boy wished he *had* been in the thick of things instead of spending the night shouting threats at the mules. A slower wagon team than Ruby and Pandora she could not imagine.

As soon as she dismounted, she followed Cora to the area near the campfire where Carleton lay stretched out on his pallet, a blanket spread over him. Thad and Ben crouched at his side.

Lyle bent over his trail boss, feeling his bared shoulder with both hands.

"How many?" Carleton's breath rasped in as the probing continued.

"Over a hundred," Ben answered, his tone quiet. "And two horses. Thad's pony was trampled. And the piebald mare you were riding broke its leg. Snap had to shoot it."

Serena's knees turned to jelly. Carleton had given her the surefooted gray pony. Would he have escaped injury if he'd given her the piebald instead?

Numb, she watched Lyle gently lift Carleton's arm.

"How many over a hundred?" Carleton grated. "Dammit, Lyle, that hurts!"

"'Bout thirty head," Ben replied.

Serena stared at him. How many of her precious steers had survived? She opened her mouth to inquire, but found she could not utter a sound.

"Most likely you'll be needin' a sling," Cora offered. "I brought a clean dish towel."

"And some whiskey, I hope," Carleton said in a tight voice.

"And some whiskey."

Lyle straightened. "Not broken. Dislocated, I think."

"You *think?* Jehosaphat, man, aren't you sure?"

"Makes no difference, boss. Treatment's the same—hang it in a sling and eat left-handed."

"Left-handed," Carleton muttered.

"Got apple cake bakin'," Cora quipped. "An' biscuits and beans and bacon. Lots of bacon." She sent him a hopeful look.

"Bacon," the trail boss breathed. "We got a hundred and thirty dead beeves out there and we're eating bacon. Where's the whiskey, Cora? God help me, I need a drink."

Chapter Nineteen

"You gotta tell her, Carl." Ben spoke in low tones to avoid being overheard. "Serena's a ranch owner like the rest of us. She has a right to know."

"That's over eighty percent of her herd." Carleton winced as he shifted his slinged right arm. "A loss like that will wipe her out."

"Maybe. Maybe not." Ben unrolled his bedroll next to his brother's, pulled off his boots and stretched out full length. "Gotta tell her anyway."

Carleton groaned inwardly. It was three o'clock in the morning by the position of the stars. Another half hour and Cora's alarm clock would go off. At least Thorny wouldn't bluster about shooting it, as he had every morning since they'd left the valley. Thorny was riding night guard, along with Eli and both the young Bartel boys. The cows were still restless after their run, so he'd doubled the shifts.

Another hour and he'd have to tell Serena about the thirteen dead steers the boys had found with her Lazy A brand. That meant she had only two left to sell at the railhead. Instead of the three hundred dollars she expected—the money she desperately needed to build that house of hers—she'd get fifty or seventy-five at the most. She'd have to borrow to buy winter feed.

He turned painfully onto his good shoulder, cradling his right elbow with his palm. Silas had lost twenty-nine beeves, Eli close to forty. The Double K losses ran to over fifty cows. All of them would feel the pinch on market day. Not only would such losses cut into profits, but the remaining animals had run off some weight and would no longer bring top price.

But eighty percent of Serena's herd? Hell, she'd barely make expenses.

Carleton crossed his good arm behind his head, pillowing his neck against his palm. Something bothered him. Serena's losses seemed disproportionately high.

"Ben, you awake?"

"You kidding? I can hear your brain churning clear over here. What's eatin' you?"

"Did the boys find anything unusual during the loss count?"

Ben thought for a moment. "Nothin' much. Hog found some dead steers piled up at the bottom of a draw. He figured they'd run off the edge of a gully. Most of Serena's stock was in that bunch."

Carleton drew in a long breath. "Seem kinda odd to you?"

"Not really. You know how cows tend to tie up together on a drive. They must have followed the leader right off the cliff."

Carleton made no response. What's done was done. Now he had to tell Serena. Lord almighty, he'd rather have *both* arms in a sling than face her in the morning.

"Get up, you sorry sleepers!" Cora's voice rolled over the blanketed lumps around the burned-out campfire. "Get it while it's hot! Angel-wing biscuits, green chiles in yer scrambled hen fruit. Pile out and grab a plate!''

Voices grumbled and coughed. Some swore. But, one by one, the trail hands rose, clapped on their hats and boots, and rolled up their pallets.

Carleton opened his eyes and immediately wished he hadn't. After more whiskey than he should have drunk last night, his head felt like a wagon wheel with the iron band around it shrunk too tight. Standing up made his temples throb, and his stiff, swollen shoulder ached like the devil.

Gritting his teeth, he made his way to the chuck wagon in his stockinged feet. With only one arm, he couldn't even pull on his boots.

''Mornin', Mr. Kearney.'' Cora gave him a solicitous once-over. ''My stars, you look awful.''

''Sure appreciate your encouragement,'' he replied dryly. ''Where's Serena?''

Cora thrust a cup of hot coffee into his left hand. ''Around the front of the wagon, I expect. Thad wanted to talk to her 'bout somethin'.''

Without a word, Carleton moved out of the breakfast lineup and made his way to where Jem was hitching up the mules.

''How far we goin' today, Uncle Carl? Ruby's okay, but Pandora's got a rock in her foot or somethin'.'' Jem's green eyes widened at the sight of the trail boss's bootless feet.

''Not too far. I figure we're three or four miles from Captain Jack's Spring. We'll water the herd and let 'em rest. It'll be a slack day.''

''Oh, boy!'' Jem chortled. ''Can I try out one of the cow ponies? Maybe I could ride drag, just to—you know—try a bit of real cow herding?''

Carleton gazed into the moss-colored eyes of his nephew. The boy was pushing hard toward manhood, anxious to prove his worth to the other men and to himself, much as he himself had done years ago, an eager, green youth marching off to war in a gray uniform that hung off his shoulders. Real life grew a boy into a man real fast, he reflected.

And real life out here made old men out of young ones even faster.

"Talk to your pa about it, Jem. If Ben says it's all right with him, tell Snap to give you the gray pony in my string. And ask him to look at Pandora's foot."

"Gee, thanks, Uncle Carl." With trembling fingers Jem slipped the harness over Ruby's head. "Didja wanna see Thad? He's over behind those juniper bushes talking with Serena."

Carleton followed the direction of Jem's gesture. He'd taken three steps forward before he remembered his boots.

"I'll get 'em, Uncle Carl. Wait right here!"

Jem dashed around the corner of the wagon, returning in a few moments with a dusty black leather boot in each hand. "I rolled up your bedroll and stashed it in the wagon with the others. Better sit down while I get these on."

"No time. Just hold 'em steady and yank when I tell you."

While Jem pulled the boots on for him, Carleton searched his mind for the words he'd need for Serena. He spotted her twenty yards away, deep in conversation with Thad. As he strode toward them, he heard his nephew's voice.

"I'm just awful sorry, Serena. Maybe next year..."

Serena spun away from her foreman. Crossing both arms over her middle, she stared up at the sky, her lips pressed together.

Thad tipped his hat back with his forefinger and watched her in silence.

"What am I going to do?"

"I dunno," Thad said gently. "You still got half a herd left back at the ranch. At least half of them will calve come spring, so..."

Carleton watched her struggle for control. Closing her eyes, she began to rock her body back and forth. "Come spring," she choked out. "My sisters...my sisters won't—" Her voice broke.

A shard of anguish cut into his chest. Worse than any dislocated shoulder or bullet he'd taken in the war was the pain of watching her suffer. *Lord in heaven, he wished the losses had been his.*

In the next instant, an idea came to him and the sick feeling in his gut eased away. It was the perfect solution. The only solution.

After breakfast, when the men had finished dumping their plates and cups into Cora's bucket of hot wash water and were getting ready to mount up, Carleton stepped his horse over to the knot of hands at the remuda gate and spoke from the saddle.

"Drive 'em easy through Firewater Gulch to Captain Jack's Spring. Let 'em water in the flat, then graze in Smoke Creek Valley. We'll camp there tonight, so if you're needin' a haircut or a bath—" his gaze rested on Hog for a split second, then flicked to Thorny "—this'd be a good time. Captain Jack's Spring bubbles out hot water like a teakettle on a stovetop."

"A bath!" Thorny yelled, his face screwed up in distaste. "Why would I wanna do a thing like that!"

"To smell pretty," someone volunteered. "For the calico skirts in Winnemucca."

"I'm gonna have me a manicure, not no bath! Gotta have soft hands for lonesome ladies in a cow town with no excitement 'cept when trail crews roll in."

"What about the rest of yore poor ol' worn-out body?" one of the men called out.

Thorny's whiskered face took on a hurt look. "Nuthin' wrong with the rest o'me!"

"He's dead right, boys," Silas offered. "Most of him hasn't seen sunlight since his short-pants days. It's prob'ly soft as silk beneath his underwear."

Serena listened to the ribald joshing with only half an ear, her thoughts caught up in the disastrous loss of all but two of her fifteen steers. Somehow in all the planning and dreaming she'd done since she rode out of Wildwood Valley at the rear of the Double K trail drive, she never anticipated failure. Hardship, maybe. The discomfort of long hours on horseback, the hard, often rocky ground beneath her bedroll at night. But never defeat.

Numb with shock, she stumbled through the daily routine, downing Cora's sourdough biscuits and thick, black coffee, getting her trail assignment from Carleton's crude buckaroo geography scratched in the dirt with a fork handle, and saddling her horse.

Not see Jessie and Mary Irene in the spring? She didn't know whether she could stand it.

By midday, the horizontal rock formations they'd been skirting narrowed into a broad, flat gully through which the cattle churned like a black-and-white tide.

"They smell water ahead," Eli shouted.

Serena nodded. She could almost smell it, too. She couldn't wait to strip off her filthy garments and soak them—and herself—in one of the pools of hot water Eli said dotted the strange, pockmarked mountain ahead. Shaped like a huge, flat table, the stone beckoned.

"Chili Rock," Eli called out. "Hot springs and cool breezes. Sound good?"

In answer, Serena tried to smile. Another hour and she could soothe her body and focus her tumbling thoughts. Something deep inside her brain questioned whether she could even make it to next spring without her beloved

Jessie and Mary Irene to sustain her. Heartsick down to her toes, she raised her head, settled her gaze on Chili Rock and kicked the mare into a trot.

By the time they watered the herd at Smoke Creek and turned them out to graze, Cora had beef roasts baking in her Dutch ovens hung over the fire pit Jem and Snap had dug earlier. The aroma was tantalizing.

"It's my special rub that does it, honey," the cook confided to Serena. "Red pepper, paprika and oregano."

The roasting meat smelled good, but Serena doubted she could eat a bite of it. Hog and some of the other men had done the butchering on the trail last night, after the stampede. For all she knew, just twenty-four hours before, one of those roasts had been a healthy Lost Acres steer.

"I think I'll take a bath while the men eat, Cora. I'll have more privacy."

Cora regarded her with sharp blue eyes. "They done washed up already—those that are so inclined, anyway. Nobody'll bother you up there, not with my sizzlin' roast fer supper. And—" the cook's plump cheeks flushed with pride "—for dessert I made raisin pies. No cowhand's ever walked away from my raisin pie. Got brandy in it."

"Maybe I'll have some later, Cora." Serena headed toward the curtained wagon for the soap and towel the cook kept for her on a special shelf inside.

"Sure, honey. I'll save a couple of pieces."

Thad sat back on his haunches and regarded the other men. "The way I see it, Serena lost more than any one of us. Hell, she only started with fifteen steers."

Carleton had arranged a private meeting between himself and other ranch owners on the cattle drive, Eli Harker and Silas Appleby. Thad and Lyle had also been invited to attend.

"I say we chip in and replenish her stock," Thad finished.

"And I say we don't," Lyle snapped. "Let her learn about ranchin' the way all of us have—hard knocks and the luck of the draw."

Carleton massaged his neck where the sling rubbed against the skin. "Some of us have had good luck, too," he remarked quietly. "Good weather, good stock, easy trail drives. Just plain serendipity. Why shouldn't Miss Hull get a leg up on that ladder she's trying to climb?"

Silas and Eli nodded their assent. "No fault of hers them cows stampeded," Eli offered.

Lyle's mouth tightened. "A woman oughtn't be runnin' a ranch in the first place. Oughtta be home bakin' bread and gatherin' eggs, not prancin' along on a cattle drive. Country's goin' to hell."

Carleton clenched his fists and opened his mouth to tell his foreman just what he thought about his remarks, but his brother beat him to it.

"Hold on a minute, LB," Ben boomed. "The issue isn't whether a woman *ought* to be runnin' cattle—Serena *is* runnin' cattle. The point is, are we willing to absorb her losses this once? Say, four beeves each from the Mariah Two and the Bar H, and five from the Double K. How 'bout it?"

"We can rebrand them while she's up at the hot springs takin' her bath," Thad offered.

"I'm not goin' along with it," Lyle said slowly.

Ben pinned the foreman with a penetrating look. "We all know your feelings, LB. But you don't own the herds in question. Carl, Eli, Silas and I own those beeves."

For an instant, Lyle's eyes blazed.

"Sure, I can spare four cows." Eli broke the thick silence. "I already lost forty head—what difference is another four gonna make?"

"Me, too," Silas added.

"Then, with our five, that totals thirteen." Carleton met Lyle's gaze.

His foreman swore under his breath. "It's an unlucky number, that's for sure."

"It's a good move," Carleton countered. "She needs help. Out here, neighbors help neighbors. Who knows, we might need her to pull us out of a hole one day."

Lyle snorted in disgust. "Sure! When you're all herdin' chickens instead of beeves."

The lanky foreman stood up and ground the stub of his cigarette under his boot. "Count me out. But you're right about one thing—neighbors can help neighbors. Serena might turn out to be a real pleasant neighbor to have."

Lyle sauntered away toward the chuck wagon, his spurs chinking at every slow, deliberate step.

Eli lifted his cigar from his lips and blew a casual smoke ring. "I'd watch that one, if I was you," he said to no one in particular. "He's hankerin' after something, and I don't think it's hens and roosters."

"Land," Silas said. "We all hunger after land. That's why we came out to this country in the first place." A faraway look came into his tired hazel eyes. "Lyle's right, in one way, I guess. The West's hard on a woman."

"It's hard on a man, too," Carleton said quietly. He rubbed his shoulder. "Thad, you and Silas take care of branding Serena's cows. We won't say anything about it 'til we get to the railhead. Think you can keep your mouth shut that long, Si?"

"Sure." The sandy-haired rancher grinned. "I'll just keep my jaws flappin' over Cora's roast beef and raisin pie. Sure helps havin' a cookie like her along on a ramble."

Carleton rose. "If you boys'll excuse me, my shoulder's hurting some. I'm going to get some of Cora's liniment."

"Why don't you go soak it in one of them hot springs, Uncle Carl?" Thad queried.

Carleton thought his nephew's green eyes had a definite glint to them, but in the fading twilight, he couldn't be sure. "One of *those* hot springs, you mean."

Eli stood up. "Yeah, Carl. Try to keep Serena up there 'til we're done branding."

He had a point. Someone did need to keep Serena occupied for a couple of hours while the men cut out the beeves and rebranded them. He didn't fancy the idea of Lyle chancing on her alone up on Chili Rock.

Besides, his shoulder *did* need a hot-water soak.

Chapter Twenty

With slow, weary steps Serena climbed the steep path up to the hot springs. In the fading light she could barely see the trail, but she didn't care. The moon would soon rise to illuminate her way back.

Even though she was dispirited over the loss of her steers, she stopped long enough to sniff the warm, sage-scented air and gaze off in the distance as the waning sunset glowed against the hills.

Below her, the camp spread out, silhouetting black shapes against the firelight. The chuck wagon, the horses, even the men looked so small from up here, like toy figures cut from black paper. From her vantage point high above them, it made quite a pretty picture. Mary Irene would surely want to paint the scene.

A painful lump closed her throat. Preoccupied by thoughts of her sisters and how much she missed them, she dragged her tired body up the last switchback and stopped short. The vista was spectacular. A huge magenta sun dipped toward the horizon, washing the sky with crimson and violet light. The darkening plain below her sprawled for hundreds of miles, broken only by clumps of green-gray trees and hillocks swathed with bunchgrass and wild wheat rippled by a warm wind.

Two night thrushes called to each other. Serena listened to the sweet, entreating melodies and felt something swell in her chest. It was so quiet. So beautiful, and somehow lonely.

She rounded the last switchback in the trail and heard a low male voice rise from the shadows.

"Better strip and climb in, Sis. Pretty soon it'll be too dark to see."

Serena sucked in her breath. "Mr. Kearney?"

"Yep."

"W-what are you doing up here?"

"Soaking my shoulder," he said quietly. "Don't let me bother you, Serena. There's two pools—another hot spring bubbles out of this rock. Better pick one or the other before it gets dark."

"Yes, all right, I will." She could just make out his dark head lolling against the rock lip of a steaming body of water. One or the other? Well, he was in one, so her choice was obvious.

"I expected you'd already be here," he remarked casually.

"I rested for a while in Cora's wagon. She made me some tea." Serena strode to the small pool some feet away from him, making sure she oriented herself so they faced away from each other. Fingering the top button of her shirt, she hesitated. "You won't look, will you?"

"Sis, I'm so sore I can hardly move, let alone swivel my head to spy on a pretty girl. Besides, it's so dim I couldn't see much anyway."

It wasn't true, Carleton admitted to himself. His eyes had adjusted gradually to the fading light, and he could see quite clearly. He just couldn't move his head, or any part of his body, without needles of pain stabbing through his shoulder and down his spine. But there was no harm in covertly watching her as she disrobed for her bath. He posed no possible danger.

She dropped her work shirt onto the smooth, flat rock at her feet, and his pulse began to hammer. On second thought, maybe there was a danger—one he hadn't foreseen. That danger was to himself.

With quick, economical motions, she pulled off her boots, then stood and unbuttoned her denim trousers and stepped out of them. Turning her back, she raised both arms to draw her chemise over her head. Her slim, straight back gleamed in the half light, and Carleton stopped breathing. Last, she bent and stripped off her lacy drawers.

Her backside was smooth and softly rounded. He tried not to stare as she gathered up her garments and tossed them into the steaming water to soak, then lowered her perfectly proportioned body into the pool.

Blood pounded in his ears. She edged around the perimeter to position her back toward him, moving out of his line of sight. As she did so, Carleton realized he'd clenched both hands into hard fists. Deliberately he flexed his fingers, lifted his good arm to spread his hand over the rock ledge behind his head.

The sound of splashing water floated on the still air.

"Serena, what are you doing?" The words were out before he could check them.

The answer came after a prolonged silence. "Thinking."

He had to smile. For a moment he'd thought she might be industriously washing out her clothes and missing the glorious sunset. For some reason, he wanted her to just be still and enjoy it with him. Not only that, he acknowledged, any sound of movement conjured images in his mind of her slim, naked body, and his own responded accordingly. Already his groin was beginning to ache.

Her voice was so soft he could barely hear it. "I'm remembering things my mother taught me when I was growing up in Stark County."

"About being a woman in a man's world?" he guessed out loud.

"About…not giving up. There has to be a place in the West for all of us—women, the Indians, everyone. God quit making land—but He's still making people. We have to get along."

Carleton chuckled. "Nothing's easy out here. You know that by now."

"Mr. Kearney?"

Unaccountably, he felt his entire body tense. "Yeah?"

"How do you cope with setbacks? I mean things like a stampede, for instance. Or a failed harvest. Or…" She paused. "Losing your wife."

Jehosaphat! Serena never wasted words making idle conversation. But then talk was cheap. It was ideas that were dear. Her question planted a hard kick in his solar plexus.

"Oh, hell, Sis. You just pull up your socks and keep going the best you can."

"It's a small thing, isn't it—losing thirteen steers. Not like losing someone you love."

"No," he said in a quiet voice. "It's not so small. I know what those steers meant to you—the house for your sisters."

Silence.

Carleton drew in a double-deep breath. "One thing I've learned in fifteen years of ranching is that troubles can make or break a man." Carleton caught the scent of flowers. Her soap, maybe. He closed his eyes and drew in a lungful of rose-perfumed air. It had been a long, long time since he'd smelled anything as sweet. A tight feeling squeezed his chest. For a moment he couldn't speak his longing was so overpowering.

"I think," he said after a long pause, "it's better to get home with a light load than be stuck out on the trail with a heavy one."

"Mr. Kearney? Are you telling me something?"

"Yep. Life's always risky. But if you get caught out, cut your losses and start over."

"Is that what you did? After your wife died, I mean?"

Another question to the solar plexus. She had a talent, all right. He didn't answer.

"Mr. Kearney, are you all right?"

"Yeah," he said, his voice hoarse. "I'm fine."

Liar. A crack split his heart right down the middle. His gut wrenched. His groin ached. "Shoulder hurts a bit is all."

She was silent so long he wondered if she'd drifted off to sleep. When he heard her uneven breathing, he realized she was crying. She tried to stifle her sobs, but little hiccups of sound escaped.

His throat closed. "It's okay, Sis. Let it all out." He wished like anything he could put his arms around her. He waited a good ten minutes, watching the last peach-and-gold light fade into gray and then black. In an hour, the moon would rise.

In an hour, they'd dry off and put on their clothes and go back to camp as if nothing had happened.

Nothing has *happened, you old fool.*

Oh, yes it had! Something had definitely happened—not to her, maybe, but to him. It wasn't anything obvious, or even very surprising. All it amounted to was two people—a man and a woman—talking honestly to one another about the things that mattered most to them. It seemed natural, being unguarded with each other.

A finger of fear curled around his heart. He didn't want

to care about Serena. He didn't mind thinking about her, admiring her stubborn courage. He didn't even mind the heat she aroused in him when he caught her scent or when he'd tasted her lips that one time.

Want her? Yes. But care about her? Run the risk of having her matter to him, the way Ella had mattered? Letting her become part of him, part of his bone and muscle and soul?

Never. But the more he fought it, the more he wondered if it was too late.

"Serena, you still feel uneasy around men?"

"Yes," came her quiet voice from behind him. "Especially around Lyle Bartel."

"You think you'll ever get over it?"

"N-no. Not with Lyle. But Rosy and Hog and Eli and the others—even Snap—don't frighten me like they did at first."

Carleton found himself grinning. "That's because they're not young and predatory, like Lyle."

"Rosy's young."

"Rosy's got a wife down in Mexico."

Silence, then the water rippled. "Mr. Kearney, what will happen when we get to Winnemucca?"

Winnemucca? What did she mean? he wondered.

"Well, the buyer will run the cows through a chute to tally them as they load the railcars. Then he'll settle up with me and I'll pay off the hands. You'll have your money in four days."

"And then what?" Her voice sounded small. Expectant.

"Well, let's see. Rosy will write a letter to his wife with his pay in it. Eli'll probably buy a new pair of boots for himself and a fancy saddle for his new daughter-in-law. Silas and Hog and the other hands will hurrah the town one night and spend the next day sleeping it off and the next year embroidering their stories. Thad and Lyle will likely visit the barber and then play poker and flirt with the waitresses at the hotel.''

"What will *you* do?''

Carleton thought for a moment. Last year in Winnemucca he'd ordered a carved headstone for Ella's grave. And he'd gone to church for the first time in twenty years. He wasn't going to tell that to Serena.

"I'm going to turn around and head for home. I left Marsh doing chores at the ranch—your spread, too, if you remember. I haven't seen Alice or my baby daughter in almost a month.''

To his relief, she laughed softly. "You're homesick.''

"Some. Lyle can take over for me. The hands will ride back with the chuck wagon—should take them another two weeks. Ben's anxious to get back, too. And Thad. What about you, Serena?''

She gave another low, throaty laugh. "I'm going to build a house! I won't have much money from the drive, but Attila and Red Wing are laying well and maybe I can sew some for Miss Addie in town to make ends meet.''

"You're homesick, too.''

"I must be crazy to want to stay on the ranch, but I do. It was Papa's and now it's mine and my sisters'.''

"You're not crazy, Serena. You've been bit by the ranching bug. When you get to heaven, if the Lord hasn't any rusty old patched-up wire fences or ornery steers, you'll never feel at home.''

"Mr. Kearney?''

The sound of her low, controlled voice sent a tremor through his frame. "Yeah?''

"I don't want to stay in Winnemucca one minute longer than necessary. When you head back to Wildwood Valley, may I ride with you?''

Carleton's heart floated into his throat. Before he could answer, she posed another question.

"Would you avert your eyes while I scrub my clothes and dress myself?"

"Sure, Sis." Despite his assurance, he shifted quietly so he could watch her.

She soused her shirt and jeans up and down in the steaming water and wrung them out. Then she splashed out of the pool and dried herself off, keeping her back to him. Only when she began to draw on clean underclothes did he turn his gaze away.

Rolling the damp garments in her towel, she turned toward him. "Mr. Kearney, you have to get out of that pool sometime. Your skin will get wrinkled!"

"Yeah, I guess."

"If you like, I'll rub Cora's liniment on your shoulder and retie your sling."

"You're not afraid to get that close to me?"

She gave a soft laugh. "You kissed me three nights ago. I felt no fear, only pleasure. I think I am getting over what happened years ago."

Beneath the surface of the water, Carleton felt his body harden. *No fear, only pleasure.* He'd thought of little else since that night. He didn't trust himself to be near her on this soft, wind-whispery evening. But she was right—he had to get out of the pool. The skin on the ends of his fingers looked corroded.

But the rest of him, from his waist down, swelled with sweet, aching need. With his good arm, he pulled himself upright and turned to face her.

Chapter Twenty-One

"**Y**ou gonna turn your back when I climb out of this pool?"

Serena gave him a level look. "No, I'm not. You didn't."

The hot spring water sloshed waist-high. Behind her, a swollen gold moon slipped from behind the darkened hills. Moonlight spilled over the slick stone of Chili Rock.

Carleton took a step toward the shallow end of the pool, watching her eyes as the water receded to his navel. She flicked a glance at his face and he chuckled at her effort to keep from blanching. He moved forward another foot and felt the warm water lap his hipbone.

Her gaze wavered. Any second now she'd turn her back. He wondered how long it would take her.

Her eyes held his as he advanced another step. To his surprise, she squared her shoulders as if to brave the challenge.

Which, he realized, was her intent. In some way only she understood, she was trying to overcome her fear of men. Or man. Deliberately he brought his knee up, breaking the surface of the water with a splash.

She jerked at the noise. Her eyes widening in alarm, she sucked air into her lungs in shallow, uneven gulps.

"Turn around, Sis," he said. His voice sounded gravelly, the way it did when he'd been on the trail too long and his throat was dry. "Otherwise, you might see something you're not prepared for." He stepped forward.

Quick as a startled bird, Serena spun away from him to face the moon.

Carleton laughed softly and splashed his way out of the pool. Still chuckling, he dried his trunk and legs with his shirt and, working only his one good arm, awkwardly pulled on his jeans. She resolutely turned away as he struggled to button his fly one-handed. He'd had a helluva time shedding the garment—getting dressed was even more of an ordeal.

"Serena," he said after a long interval had passed with little success. "Think you could ignore the fact that my pants aren't buttoned? I can't do it with only one hand."

Her answer came in a surprisingly matter-of-fact voice. "I can do it."

His eyebrows rose.

"Leave your shirt off," she added. "I'll rub Cora's liniment on your shoulder."

"You don't have to. Jem can do it, or Cora, or—"

"I...want to." He heard her breath pull in and out twice before she spoke again. "It would be good for me. Educational."

Carleton bit off a laugh. She might be small and delicate, and a greenhorn on a trail drive, but she had guts. He could guess her terror at being anywhere near a half-naked male.

After her ordeal back in Ohio when she was just a kid, he marveled that she'd even want to try confronting her fear. He'd seen her edge into the background when the trail hands gathered about the campfire after supper, noted how she stiffened when more than two men at a time paused to speak to her. Even Thad was careful not to crowd her, always announcing his presence with his voice instead of casually clapping a hand on her arm. She'd managed to overcome her anxiety about dancing with a man at the social last summer, but only because he'd helped her toward it.

But this—being alone with him up here, with nowhere to escape but down a precipitous trail in the dark, buttoning his trousers for him—this might shake her resolve.

It sure was shaking his, he admitted. His physical response to her was embarrassingly obvious, if she only knew where to look. His jeans bulged over his engorged member.

You're not what she needs, he reminded himself. *Tonight or any other night.* She needed someone with a future, someone young enough to give her children. He could give her pleasure. He could not give her a life.

She walked toward him with small, hesitant steps. Her small hands fluttered at his waist. Gently he directed them to the top button of his fly.

Her fingers brushed against the denim and a fire kindled in his groin. Carefully she slipped the metal disk through the loop, her head bent over the task.

He caught her wrist, lifted her hand away. If she touched him once more, he'd explode. Gritting his teeth at the hunger that raged through him, he worked to keep his voice steady.

"No more," he said, his tone hoarse. "I can manage."

"If you'll sit down on that rock behind you, I can reach your shoulder more easily. Where's the liniment?"

"In my jacket pocket." He settled himself on the flat stone surface she'd indicated, trying to slow his pounding heart.

"This?" She withdrew a tin of Beeman's salve and

twisted off the top. When she got close enough to touch him, she laid her small, warm hand lightly against his shoulder. His heartbeat skyrocketed. She hesitated, then smoothed a bit of the ointment on his flesh, tentatively at first, then more deliberately. As soon as she massaged it in, a glow of comforting heat spread over the surface of his skin. Her fingers worked another dab of the aromatic concoction into the bruised areas of his back and shoulder.

Carleton's entire body throbbed to life. He closed his eyes and let her work over him, listening to the two night thrushes call to each other in the silence.

He liked the quiet intimacy of the situation. He realized suddenly he had not been this close to a woman for over a year. And Serena... Hell, she'd never been this close to a man, by choice anyway, except for that night he'd kissed her.

She'd let him kiss her, though. In fact, he recalled, she had clung to him instead of pulling away. He wondered if she would again.

Damp strands of her silky dark hair brushed his chest. Afraid to move for fear she would stop her ministrations, he held his breath and opened his eyes.

A spill of golden moonlight shot fire through her thick waves. He reached up his hand to touch them just as she tossed the tumbled mass over her shoulder with a twist of her head.

"This must hurt," she said. "Your muscles are drawn up tight."

Carleton chuckled. That wasn't what hurt.

Her hand stilled. "What's funny?"

"Nothing. Life. Hell, everything, I guess."

He wanted to hold her, but he couldn't lift his right arm. He wanted to kiss her, taste her, but she'd fly right off this mountain if he so much as made a move toward her. *He wanted her to touch him, but he couldn't ask.*

She repositioned herself in front of him, bent to rub on more salve. "I can't get close enough," she announced.

He opened his knees, and she stepped between his thighs.

His groin began to ache all over again.

Her breath wafted over his bare skin as she worked the liniment into his shoulder, rubbing in gentle circles, her thumb grazing his chin. He suppressed a wild urge to open his mouth and capture a finger, lave it with his tongue.

What the hell was the matter with him? He'd popped out his shoulder, not his brain! Had he gone loco from the homemade hooch Cora had secretly poured into his coffee? The soft, sage-scented air, the luminous golden light from the moon drifting above them like a round, fat lantern— none of it was helping him keep his wits.

He wondered whether Serena was aware of anything unusual. What was she thinking as she worked her fingers methodically back and forth on his burning flesh? She stood so near his swollen manhood, pinned between his thighs, if he reached out...

"Mr. Kearney?" she breathed.

Carleton grunted.

"You can put your shirt on now." She took a step backward.

Carleton unwadded the damp garment, shook it out and gingerly drew one sleeve over his stiff right arm. Angling his left hand behind his neck, he pulled the garment across his back. By the time he got to the buttons down the front, his hand was shaking.

Serena moved forward again. "Lean forward. I'll retie the sling around your neck."

Carleton shut his eyes. The need to touch her was overpowering. He felt the square of huck toweling slide around his right elbow, felt her hands fumble behind his neck, tying a loose knot with the pointed ends of the triangular-shaped material. The smell of her, the heat of her breasts so near his face as she bent over his shoulder made him light-headed.

Almost of its own accord, his left hand reached for her.

She froze, sucked in a shaky breath. Motionless, her hands resting at the back of his neck, she seemed to wait. Her warm, soft flesh beneath the thin cotton shirt she wore burned his palm.

"Serena," he said in a quiet voice. "Don't be frightened."

"I'm not," she said after a moment. "At least I think I'm not. My heart's beating so fast I can barely think."

Carleton laughed softly. "Then don't. God knows my own heart feels like it's on a stampede."

"Mr. Kearney?"

"Sis, we've been sleeping ten feet from each other for almost a month. Don't you think it's time you used my given name?"

"You're the trail boss. All the men call you Mister."

"Maybe. But up here, alone on a night that feels like it's just waiting for something, I think you might use my name. You gonna call me Mister after I kiss you?"

She looked at him, the moonlight glinting off her dark hair. Shadows hid the expression in her eyes. "Maybe," she said again. "It depends on whether I like it or not."

He could hear the smile in her voice, and his heart lifted. Maybe she wasn't as frightened of him as he'd thought. Just other men. At the thought, his chest swelled.

"Serena, I can't figure you out sometimes. I never know what you're thinking."

"I was thinking this is another one of those lovely moments when you...realize how beautiful things are. For a moment, I almost forgot about losing my herd."

Surprised, Carleton chuckled. She often said—or did— the unexpected. Maybe that's why he'd felt off balance around her ever since the day she rode out to the Double K and claimed her father's ranch. She'd pumped life into the run-down old spread.

She'd pumped life into him, too, whether he wanted to admit it or not. Just the same, he wanted her to think about what was happening now, between them. Male jealousy, he supposed. He wanted her to focus on him, not her herd of cattle.

He rose and stepped in close, pulling her forward until he could smell her hair and hear her soft, uneven breathing. One of her hands came to rest on his upper arm, whether to draw him closer or push him away he couldn't determine. His slinged arm lay between them.

"Serena?"

"I don't want to hurt you," she whispered. "Your arm."

"I don't want to hurt you, either."

She raised her face. "You won't." She reached her other hand toward his shoulder. "Kiss me, Mr. Kearney."

"Gladly, Miss Hull." He bent his head and found her mouth. Her lips were cool under his, and trembling slightly. She felt small-boned and fragile beneath his fingers, her mouth soft, her body pliant. A fierce longing tore at his gut. *He was so hungry for life. For love.* With a groan he caught her to him and deepened the kiss.

Her muscles tensed under his hand, and then her rigid frame began to relax. Her lips parted, her mouth opening to him, warm and achingly sweet. Her tongue grazed his for a fleeting instant, then retreated.

His body heated with desire, his blood singing in his veins like wind moaning through trees. He struggled to keep from drowning, fought against the pull of her against his senses, but when she moaned softly, he felt himself go under.

He broke contact. Her forehead rested against his chin.

He wished he'd shaved, but it was too difficult to manage left-handed.

"You all right?"

She nodded her head against his jaw. "I think so, Mr. Kearney. This time I liked it quite a bit."

His heart somersaulted between his belly and his throat a few times before he could speak. "You did?"

She sighed, blowing a puff of warm air against his chest. "Yes, Mr. Kearney, I did."

"Must not have been too good—you're still calling me Mister."

She gave a soft laugh and shook her head. "It was...very good. I'm just getting used to the idea of you kissing me. Used to the idea that I wanted you to."

Carleton blinked. A rush of sheer animal pleasure tightened his groin. *She wanted him to.* If she had any idea how much he ached to scoop her up in his arms and find someplace soft and private, she'd flee like a scared rabbit. Thank God they were standing on a block of granite and there was no place to go but down the mountainside and back to camp.

She tipped her face up to his. Gently he brought his hand to the back of her neck, feeling the soft curls brush his knuckles. *Take it easy, old man,* he admonished himself. *You're in real danger of getting carried away.*

"We can't head back yet," he said. "Won't be able to see the trail until the moon climbs higher."

"I don't want to go back yet," she whispered.

He kissed her again, a long, long kiss that had him teetering on the brink of losing control. He flicked his tongue across her bottom lip and his senses went haywire.

"Serena," he breathed against her cheek. He felt her lips brush his neck where the top button gaped open, heard her whisper something.

"Carleton," she said.

His breath stopped at the sound of his name on her tongue. "Sounds nice. Say it again."

He covered her mouth as she opened her lips. Her body began to tremble. She clung to him, wound both hands behind his neck.

"Am I hurting your shoulder?" she murmured when he pulled away for breath.

Not his shoulder. But everything else was either on fire or swollen and aching. "I'm hurting," he admitted in a hoarse voice. "But it's nothing either one of us can fix."

He looked into her eyes for some sign of withdrawal. She looked back at him for a long minute, and then suddenly she smiled. "Perhaps one of us can fix it later, when we get to Winnemucca."

Carleton's heart flip-flopped. "I don't think so, Sis. Some things are best left alone. Bum shoulders and...other things."

Serena gave him a long, steady look, her dark eyes a maddening mix of innocence and feminine wisdom. "If you say so."

Carleton groaned inwardly. He liked her. Wanted her. And she was beginning to trust him. He didn't want to stop holding her, kissing her, but their feelings could add up to a dangerous combination.

"Come on, Sis. We'd better pick our way down to the dusty old world again. Dawn comes early on a trail drive."

Deliberately he lifted her hand from behind his neck and laced his fingers with hers. Turning her toward the trail, he gave her a little push. "You'd best hold on to me. Follow behind in case you stumble."

Leading her by the hand, the shaken ranch owner headed for the trail that led back to camp.

Chapter Twenty-Two

Serena took small, careful steps along the trail cut into the side of Chili Rock, grateful for Carleton's steadying hand clasping hers. The moon climbed into the velvety night sky, illuminating the twisting path, but still the trail boss seemed in no hurry. His slow, steady pace did not alter as he led her down the mountainside.

For that she was grateful. Their gradual descent gave her a chance to calm the tumult of emotion inside. Her heart thudded so hard inside her rib cage she was sure he could hear it. When she thought about the wondrous feelings evoked by his hard, muscular frame pressed against breasts, his mouth gently exploring hers, her body flushed with heat. She was so giddy with sensation she felt she could fly.

What had started out as a tentative exploration of intimacy with a man had led to an unnerving discovery about herself. She liked the way he made her feel, reveled in the sweet, aching tension that built below her belly when he kissed her, traced her lips with his smooth, warm tongue. When Carleton touched her, something deep inside fluttered to life.

She wondered if her mother had felt such things with

her father. Was that why she gave up her life with Black Eagle's tribe and went away with a white man? Was it just such an unexpected ecstasy blooming hot in her veins that her mother had experienced?

Her mother's words rang in her memory. *You cannot know how deep the river is until you step in it.*

Serena tightened her fingers in Carleton's grip. This man was not to be feared, but rather respected. Trusted. Even, she thought with surprise, enjoyed. She had dipped her toe in the water and now she knew. Her entire being wanted him. She gasped at the audacity of her thought, stumbled over a rock, and swore under her breath.

Carleton's low laughter rolled over her. "Careful," he cautioned. "Takes more than two left feet to walk down Chili Rock and get to night guard duty in one piece."

"I'm doing my best," she retorted. Her nerves were strung tight as barbed wire.

He chuckled and tightened his grasp on her hand. "Some days," he remarked without looking back, "no matter which way you spit, it's upwind."

Serena stomped a few yards in silence before she recovered her equilibrium. Infuriating man. Brusque, single-minded. Practical. Cows before people, she reminded herself. She wasn't angry at him, exactly. She was unnerved by her physical reaction to him. Her thoughts were in such disarray she could barely concentrate.

When they reached camp, laid out at the base of the mountain, Hog's light tenor voice rose to meet them, accompanied by Thorny's mournful-sounding harmonica.

"'Oh Shenendoah, I love your daughter…away, you rolling river….'"

The song made her want to cry.

Carleton did not release her hand until they reached the rear of the chuck wagon. With a gentle squeeze, he unlaced his fingers from hers and strode into the firelit circle of men.

"Where ya been, Carl?" Eli spoke through a blue haze of pipe smoke. "Hardly any of Cora's raisin pie left."

"Soaking my shoulder. Any problems with the herd?" He shot Eli a penetrating look.

"Nope. 'Less you count square-dancin' a bunch of clumsy steers around a branding fire." He sent the trail boss a surreptitious wink.

"Serena!" Jem motioned to her from the wagon. "I saved you some pie, and guess what? Uncle Carl let me ride his gray pony and help—" He stopped abruptly and stared at her.

"Gosh, Serena, you look like you've been poleaxed or somethin'."

"Jem!" Cora commanded. "Come help me with the...um, biscuits."

"Biscuits! Aw, Cora, I don't know nuthin' about makin' biscuits."

"Bacon, then," the cook huffed. "Help me...er, slice it up for the mornin' meal."

Serena stepped out of the shadows. "Carleton let you help with what, Jem?"

"N-nothin', Serena. Just...a bit of cattle scrambling, like Mr. Appleby says."

Still dazed from the hour she'd spent with the trail boss up on Chili Rock, Serena barely listened to the boy's reply. All she wanted to do was stretch out on her bedroll, close her eyes, and remember how her breasts had throbbed when Carleton had held her tight against him.

"You all right, Serena?" Cora peered at her over the coffeepot. "Land sakes, you look like you been bush-whacked by lightnin' bugs! Yer hair's down and—"

She snipped off the sentence with a grin. "Jem saved

you some pie, honey," she said in a gentle voice. "But I don't think you need it."

"Thanks, Cora," Serena managed to reply, her thoughts elsewhere. "I'll eat it in the morning."

She moved past the grinning cook, lifted her bedroll out of the wagon, and spread it in her usual spot next to the rear wheel. Ten feet away from Carleton, she thought.

Ten feet. Dear Lord, she wondered if she could stand it.

Two weeks later, on a cold, rainy afternoon the Double K cattle boiled down the main street of Winnemucca. Hail the size of grapeshot pelted them, and the men were wet and tired and cross as hibernating bears.

The cursing hands drove the herd into a holding pen next to the railroad yard, secured the remuda into another, and then surged toward the Cattlemen's Hotel. Cora and Jem drove the chuck wagon over to the livery stable for the night. Nothing Serena could say would convince the stubborn woman to share her hotel room.

"I stayed there once," the cook said. "Fourth floor it was. Climbed so many stairs it made me dizzy. Sheets weren't half as clean as mine!"

Cold and weary, Serena finally gave up. She was too tired to eat supper; all she wanted was a hot bath and a mattress that didn't have rocks under it. Tomorrow the trail boss would meet with the buyer from Chicago, Clive Sawyer, dispose of the herd, and pay off the hands.

Tomorrow, Serena reflected as she massaged her aching neck, she'd be no richer, except in experience. She'd have her trail pay, but she knew almost all of her profits had been lost in the stampede. She'd barely have enough to pay Thad his back wages.

She pressed her lips together to keep them from trembling. Forty dollars wasn't enough to build a house. When she got back to Lost Acres she'd have to write Jessie and Mary Irene and tell them....

Her throat tightened. How could she tell her sisters they couldn't join her for another whole year?

Heartsick, she propelled her tired legs up the front steps of the hotel. Thad and Jem and the other men straggled after her.

Her chest constricted as she watched Carleton and Ben ride down the wide, muddy street past the hotel and the comforts of civilization. The two brothers would take the first shift guarding the penned herd. Both men wore rain ponchos, hunching their shoulders against the cutting wind. As she watched, Carleton turned down the brim of his dark Stetson. Water sheeted off the edge.

Serena lugged her small satchel containing her personal belongings and a change of clothes up the stairs to the second floor and into a small but tidy room at the end of the long hallway. Below her men's voices and laughter boomed, punctuated by a tinny piano playing "Clementine."

With a sigh of relief, Serena closed the door behind her and thanked her lucky stars she would be blessedly alone for the entire evening. She hadn't been assigned a night guard shift, so there was no need to go out.

She surmised Carleton would seek a doctor to treat his dislocated shoulder as soon as he came in. She knew there was a trick to popping the joint back in place; she'd seen her mama do it to her father once.

With chilled fingers, Serena lit the kerosene lamp on the night table and began to prepare for her bath. Within twenty minutes, a copper tub and two steaming teakettles of hot water had been set on the floor in the center of the room by a pudgy, smiling hotel clerk. He wished her good evening and pulled the door shut behind him.

Serena emptied the kettles into the tub, added two pitchers of cold water, and stepped in. She lowered herself into the hot water, drew her knees up and leaned her head back against the curved metal edge. Closing her eyes, she resolved not to move a single muscle for at least an hour.

Her thoughts drifted to Carleton. Ever since that night on Chili Rock, his behavior toward her had changed. She'd watched him covertly without really being aware of it, noticing that now he paid her no attention whatsoever. He still assigned her night guard duty and an occasional turn at riding drag, just like the other hands.

But occasionally she caught him looking at her from across the campfire at night, his shadowed eyes inscrutable, his fine mouth unsmiling. At night he took pains to lay his pallet as far from hers as possible, though she noticed he always waited until Lyle had dropped his saddle onto a spot before he settled down. She noted, too, that, without drawing attention to his doing so, the trail boss always positioned himself between Lyle and her.

She didn't know what to think about the short-spoken owner of the Double K. Ever since he'd kissed her, made her heart pound and her loins ache with wanting him, he'd appeared disinterested. He didn't seek her out, never rode night duty with her, even sent Thad to talk to her about trail matters instead of coming himself.

Maybe she didn't matter to him? Maybe to him she was just a girl to dally with when there was nothing better to do?

But when he had touched her, held her close with his pulse beating irregularly in his neck—surely that wasn't just a cowboy's casual dalliance?

Maybe he wanted to avoid calling attention to his feelings among the men, a voice suggested. She sighed and slid deeper into the deliciously warm water.

She'd think the matter over on the long ride back to Wildwood Valley. There would be days and days on the trail with just Ben and Thad and Carleton. The others would travel slower, bringing in the remuda and accompanying Cora and the chuck wagon. And days and days on the trail meant nights and...

A rap at the door jerked her back to the present. "Yes? Who is it?"

Behind her, the door creaked open. "S'rena?"

Jem's voice sounded high and a bit unsteady. "You in there, S'rena?"

"I'm here, Jem," she said without turning her head. "In the tub. What is it?"

"S'rena, I got a l'il problem. Thad and Lyle were drinkin' somethin' an' I asked what it was, an' I guess I drank too much of whatever it was, cuz I'm feelin' kinda dizzy."

"Jem, for heaven's sake! That's the second time this year you've gotten drunk."

"Kin I jus' lie down a while in your room so's I can recover some? Maybe I can sober up 'fore Pa gets off guard duty."

"Go on out to the livery stable," Serena ordered. "Cora's there with the chuck wagon. You can rest out there and stay out of sight."

Jem lurched forward. "Can't. I'm too fuddled to make it that far. Might end up in the horse trough."

In spite of herself, Serena had to laugh. Young Jem was learning about moderation the hard way.

"Shut the door, Jem. There's a cold breeze blowing on my back."

"Sure, S'rena." He stumbled to the door and back-handed it closed with a thump.

"Take off your boots," Serena said gently. "Lie down on the bed for a while until you feel better."

"Thanks, S'rena. You're awful nice."

The bedsprings creaked and two loud bumps told her his boots had hit the floor.

"Jus' don' want Pa to find me. You unnerstan, don'tcha, S'rena? He'll tell Ma and she'll make me clean her printing press for a month."

His voice drifted off. Serena waited until she heard his light snoring and then she rose, stepped out of the tub and dried herself off with a towel.

She'd dress and go down to the hotel dining room. Jem would need lots of strong, black coffee when he woke up.

She was halfway up the stairs, a tray of coffee and two sandwiches in her hands, when Carleton appeared on the landing above her.

"What the hell are you doing traipsing about this hotel alone? I thought I told Thorny to keep—"

Serena gritted her teeth. "I'm not 'traipsing.' I'm sobering up your nephew!"

Carleton lifted the tray from her grasp. She noted he used both hands and the sling was gone. The doctor must have fixed his shoulder.

"Not again," he groaned. "Where is he?"

"Asleep in my room."

"Ben's looking for him."

"I know. That's why he's asleep in my room," Serena replied. She tried not to smile, but lost the battle when Carleton chuckled.

"The little devil's trying my patience," he said.

"He's trying to be a man."

"Yeah," Carleton agreed. "Guess so. Sometimes I wonder if he knows what he's in for."

Serena inserted the key in the lock. "Would you care to hear a woman's opinion?"

Carleton balanced the tray in one hand and snaked his other onto the brass doorknob. "I would." He held the door shut, waiting.

Serena looked into the dark blue eyes of the man facing her. "My mother taught me it is the way of all things to mature. Foals grow into stallions. Male calves become bulls. Boys become men."

"You telling me something I don't already know, Sis?"

Serena resisted an impulse to punch him. "I'm not finished yet.

"His father shouldn't punish him for being young, and for getting drunk. Instead, Ben should teach him how to grow up. Teach him how to handle liquor. When a man is young, he must invent the way. When a man is older, as you are, he knows the way."

Carleton's dark eyebrows rose. "You think I know the way, Serena?"

"I think you wouldn't whip your son if he made a mistake."

"I haven't got a son."

"We're all your sons—all the trail hands, Hog, Rosy, Thorny, the twins—everybody. You lead well because you help us grow. That's why you're the trail boss, Mr. Kearney. You know where you're going and how to get there."

Dumbfounded, Carleton stared at her. "Now just how does a little banty hen from Ohio know so much about men, old *or* young?"

Serena flashed him a smile. "Just observant, I guess. Something I learned from you. Now, about Jem..."

Carleton opened his mouth to speak, then shut it with a snap.

Serena took the tray, pushed open the door, and marched inside. Carleton rolled his eyes toward the ceiling and followed. "Damned unpredictable, out of the ordinary, upsetting female," he muttered under his breath.

He couldn't wait until they hit the trail for home. Without the audience of trail hands and cook, he'd show her a thing or two about men. Or about *this* man, at any rate.

No outspoken, know-it-all little bundle of soft curves was going to tie *him* up in knots.

Chapter Twenty-Three

The bawling mass of cows surged against the wooden slats of the holding pen as Hog and Rosy, on horseback, prodded them onto the chute. One by one, the animals stumbled up the inclined plank walkway and onto the waiting railroad car while the tally man counted and marked his pad.

In a way, Serena was sorry to see them go. After almost five weeks on the trail with them day and night, she knew some of the cows by name. She turned away when the last steer was loaded and watched Carleton and the buyer shake hands on their bargain. By suppertime, the hands would have their trail pay in cash, and the ranch owners would be planning how to spend their profits.

She guessed she'd have about eighty-four dollars. Her two remaining steers would have sold at the late-season price of twenty-seven dollars a head, and she expected another thirty dollars in wages. Still not enough to build a house. Not even enough to buy winter feed from the Double K to last until spring.

Discouraged and tired to the bone, Serena plodded back to the hotel, climbed the steep wood steps and entered the dining room. Thad and Jem sat at a corner table, each nursing a cup of hot coffee. She took the empty chair next to Jem.

"How's your headache?" she inquired. She reached for the sugar bowl, twirled the spoon in the granules to keep her mind off her sisters and the home she wouldn't be able to build for them.

Jem sent her a bleary-eyed look. "Better'n my stomach," he mumbled.

Thad clapped his younger brother on the shoulder. "He's doin' okay, Serena. Considering he spent most of the night visitin' with the owls roosting on the privvy roof."

"Was he sick? Is he—?"

"I ain't sick," Jem interjected. "Wish I had been, though." He hung his head over the steaming cup.

"Uncle Carl had a man-to-man talk with him last night," Thad volunteered in a subdued voice. "And then Ben found 'em and harangued ol' Carl about stepping into his territory. By the time they sorted it all out, it was gettin' light outside."

Jem lifted his head and surveyed her with dull green eyes. "You get your pay yet, Serena? And your steer money?"

Serena spilled sugar on the table. "Not yet, Jem. Won't be much of either, I'm afraid."

"Why, sure there w— Ow! Whadja do that for, Thad?" He reached below the table to rub his shin.

Concentrating on the mess she'd made on the table, Serena swept the grains of sugar into a napkin and folded it into a neat square. "I guess I've had enough of cattle driving for one season. I can't wait to get home."

Thad nodded. "Dad and Uncle Carl are leaving tomorrow at sunup—if they're speakin' to each other, that is. Carl always heads back to the valley in a hurry—specially when Ella was expectin' the baby. And Dad gets to missing Ma so bad he's like a caged bear. You goin' with them?''

"Yes, I plan to."

Jem eyed her. "What do you miss the most, Serena?"

What did she miss? The question caught at her heart. "I miss my sisters," she said over the tight feeling in her throat. "I've missed them since the day I rode away from Stark County."

"Gee, Serena, I'm real sorry. Think you'll ever go back there?"

Serena hesitated. "No, Jem," she said quietly. "I'm never going back. Jessie and Mary Irene will come out here. Eventually." She took a deep breath to control her trembling voice.

"I also miss my favorite hens, Red Wing and Attila," she added. She managed a smile for Jem. "And my sunflower bed out front. The seeds were just starting to sprout when I left and..."

Her voice died as the Double K trail hands straggled into the dining room in twos and threes, followed by Carleton and Ben. Ben carried a locked metal cash box. Serena recognized it as the one Cora guarded in the chuck wagon. No one had access to it except the trail boss, who carried the key on his person.

"Well, boys," Carleton said in his quiet voice. "Pick up your wages."

Hog and Thorny scrambled to be the first man paid. "Get outa the way, ya big galoot," Thorny yelled. "You ain't at the head of this line."

"Hell I ain't!" Hog brushed the burly cowhand aside and took his place. "I got as much right to my renunciation as you do."

Serena bit her lip to keep from laughing at another of Hog's malaprops.

"Haw-haw!" Thorny brayed. "That's re—" He paused

and looked thoughtful for a moment. "Re-num... Renu-meration. That's it. It means gettin' paid."

"And gettin' laid," Silas Appleby murmured from a back table. "Oh, sorry, Serena. Forgot you were present."

One by one, the men stepped forward and took their pay. Serena watched Silas withdraw cigarette makings from his shirt pocket, roll three lumpy smokes and give one to Thorny and one to Hog. The last he kept for himself.

Smoking, thought Serena, would be the next male activity on Jem's list.

And after that would be...

She felt warm all of a sudden. *After that would be girls. Physical attraction, then longing, then—*

"Señorita," Rosy whispered. "You are spilling out the sugar!"

Serena blinked and stared at the wooden tabletop. The entire surface sparkled with white crystals. She brushed her palms toward the center, forming a small mountain of sugar. As she tried to locate another napkin, the line of men waiting to receive their wages got shorter.

Thad and Lyle invited Jem to join them for another round of five-card stud and some "hair of the dog," as they put it, but Jem shook his head. Busy counting the crisp green bills in his pay packet, he barely looked up as the two foremen left.

Serena smiled at Jem's bent head. Maybe for him there would be an interlude between smoking and young ladies. Maybe he'd want a man's job, and a man's pay before he got interested in...other things.

Last to be paid were Silas, Eli and Serena—the ranch owners. Carleton laid a tan envelope in her hand.

"Your wages and your share of the profits," he said, then turned his attention to the two men.

Serena opened the envelope surreptitiously and counted

the bills. Two hundred...three hundred... "Four hundred and thirty-five dollars!" she blurted. "Why, that can't be right!"

Carleton sent her an enigmatic look. "Are you questioning my integrity, Miss Hull?"

"Oh, no, I—I mean yes. Where did all this money come from?"

"From the sale of your herd," he replied calmly. "That's what we came for, Sis."

"But most of my herd was lost in the stampede!"

Carleton's face remained impassive. "Guess you miscounted."

"Oh, but I didn't! Thad told me—"

"Thad can subtract eight pieces from one of Alice's chocolate cakes and still come up figuring he's got four more comin.' I wouldn't trust him with subtraction."

"Subtraction! Excuse me, Mr. Kearney—this appears more like *addition*."

"Well, he's not too good at that, either," Carleton hedged. He raised an eyebrow in the direction of the cattle buyer's table. "What about it, Clive? Your tally man know what he's doing?"

"What's the brand, little lady?" came the rich voice from the other side of the room.

"Lazy A," Serena answered.

All three men studied the tally pad laid out on the buyer's table. After a short consultation, Sawyer spoke.

"Fifteen head's the count."

Fifteen head? She got paid for all fifteen steers in her herd? That could only be possible if...

She looked from Silas's ruddy face to Eli's leathery, bearded one, to Ben and finally to Carleton. The innocent look in his blue eyes told her everything. The three ranchers had donated cows to replenish her lost herd.

Tears stung under her eyelids. She was more than grateful. She was profoundly moved.

"I can't accept your charity," she said, working to keep her voice steady. "It is very kind of you—all of you. But, I cannot let you do this." With shaking fingers, she began counting out the money to be returned.

"Hold on a minute, Missy." Eli blew a smoke ring into the hazy air above him. "Each of us contributed only three or four cows. Hardly noticeable in herds the size of ours."

Silas nodded in agreement. "We want you to have it, Miss Serena. We don't want to see you go under."

Unable to speak, she turned to Carleton and his brother.

"Look at it this way, honey," Ben offered in a gentle voice. "It's the way we do things out here in the West."

Carleton inclined his chin.

Serena stared at him. He couldn't be serious!

But he was, she could see it in the set of his jaw, the uncompromising look in his eyes.

Dumbstruck, she watched him walk toward her, gather the bills she'd counted, and slip them back into the envelope. Then he leaned over and tucked the packet in her left breast pocket. "Ought to be about enough for a lot of winter feed, or a little house. Maybe both."

"Mr. Kearney, I—"

"Thought you were going to call me Carleton," he murmured near her ear. "Now shut up and take the money, Sis. Out here it isn't mannerly to question a favor."

Dressed and ready to ride by five the following morning, Serena walked to the livery stable to say goodbye to Cora. The crisp, cold morning air burned in her lungs, driving away all doubt about her course of action. She'd accept the money and pay it back when she could. Right now, the most important thing was the house for her sisters. When she reached Wildwood Valley, the first thing she'd do was pen a letter to Jessie and Mary Irene. The second thing would be to hire Mr. Svenson to build her house. And then she'd pet her hens, visit with Amanda Frieder when she wasn't working at the mercantile in town, and tend to her sunflowers. Oh, she could hardly wait to get home!

She rounded the corner of the hotel and ran headlong into Ben Kearney, saddlebags slung over one shoulder, saddle under his arm. They walked in silence to the livery yard where Serena headed for Cora and the chuck wagon inside the stable.

"Make it snappy," Ben called after her. "Carl's an hour or two ahead of us."

"He is? I thought we were all riding together?"

"Me, too. Got some burr under his saddle 'bout three in the morning. Said he'd meet us at Smith Flat at dusk."

"What about Thad?"

"Changed his mind. Or I changed it for him. He's gonna stay and keep his eye on Jem. He said to give you this."

He fumbled in his pocket and handed her a one-hundred-dollar bill.

Thad's back wages as the Lost Acres foreman. She'd paid him last night out of her earnings. "But—"

"He said you'd back-talk him some. He won't take it, Serena. He wants you to build that house you're hankerin' for and buy some more cows. Pregnant ones," he added with a twinkle in his eye.

Serena's eyes stung. Her heart full from the generosity of her neighbors, she reached up and kissed Ben's cool, whiskery cheek.

The tall man blushed. "You think I'm gonna pass that on to Thad, you're wrong," he teased. "Pretty girl hasn't kissed me since...we left Wildwood.

"Jessamyn," he murmured under his breath. "Damndest woman I ever met. Can't live without her."

Afraid her tears would spill over, Serena turned away.

Outlined in the dim light inside the stable, the chuck wagon sat tucked into a corner. Light glowed through the thin canvas curtain separating the cook's private quarters from the chuck box and its clutter of pots and skillets, coffee mill and water barrel. Serena moved toward it while Ben saddled their horses.

"Cora? Are you awake?"

"No!" came the raspy reply. "But I'm up, if that's what you mean. Leastways my body is." The curtains flapped open and the older woman levered her torso down onto the straw-littered plank floor.

Serena tried to smile. "I came to say goodbye. We're leaving as soon as Ben saddles our horses."

"Land sakes, honey, Carleton left hours ago. You'll hafta ride like the wind to catch him. What's eatin' him, anyway? Wait here a minute. I got somethin' I want you to take along, just in case."

"Just in case what?"

But the cook had disappeared into the wagon interior. When she reemerged, she thrust a flat parcel wrapped in brown paper into Serena's sheepskin jacket pocket.

"Take care o' yourself, child. I'm lookin' forward to meetin' your two sisters when they come."

"Oh, Cora, I'll miss you. And your sassafras tea."

"Trouble tea, I call it. Don't waste yer energy missin' this old lady—I'll be along with the rest of the trail crew in a coupla weeks, more or less. We'll have a big whing-ding come Christmas at the Dixon House ballroom."

Cora paused and a thoughtful look passed over her face. "Might need a new dress, now, mightn't we?" she muttered to herself. "In the meantime, Serena girl, don't let Ben run that mare's legs off. Ride hard but careful."

"I will, Cora. I promise." She hugged the soft bulk of

the cook's body. A blade of loneliness sliced into her chest. Cora reminded her of her mother.

Ben led her mare forward and tied her trail satchel behind the cantle along with her bedroll and rain slicker. "Time to mount up, Serena."

She hugged Cora again and led the mare outside. Through the wide doorway she watched Ben smack a kiss on both the older woman's cheeks and ruffle the short, gray curls on her forehead. In the next instant, the tall man joined her and swung into the saddle with a groan. "Sure will miss that woman's grub."

"You *can* cook, can't you?" Serena teased. She hated goodbyes. She needed to keep her mind occupied and off Cora's tear-shiny blue eyes.

"Sure. Beans 'n hardtack in my saddlebags just in case we can't catch that hell-for-leather brother of mine before supper. Or, if you prefer, hardtack 'n beans."

Serena flashed a look at him as they walked their mounts through the livery yard. "What does it matter if we catch up to Carle—Mr. Kearney?"

"No matter," Ben said evenly. "Except he's got the rest of the food in his saddle pack."

Just as they turned the corner at the hotel, Serena glimpsed Cora framed in the stable doorway. The older woman flopped a tiny white hanky up and down in farewell, then stopped suddenly and blew her nose into it.

An unseen hand squeezed Serena's heart. She raised one arm, made a fist and waved it once over her head. Then she dug her heels into Sandy's sides and flew down the trail after Ben.

Chapter Twenty-Four

After four days on the trail home, Serena had seen Carleton only at night, across the campfire she and Ben built each evening. Carleton had avoided her ever since that night on Chili Rock, and during the long days of riding through miles of wild rye grass and juniper scrub, Serena racked her brain to puzzle out why.

On the fifth day, she and Ben arrived at the rendezvous campsite to find Carleton absent again.

"Well, he's been here, sure enough," Ben muttered. "Those tracks are his. Can't help wonderin' what the hell's eatin' him. He could at least stick around long enough to help with supper!"

He gave Serena's face a quick look as they dismounted to make camp, grabbed a bucket and tramped off to get water from Fern Creek.

She guessed her building anger toward Carleton showed. Following her mother's training, she had worked hard to keep her emotions in check, making her face impassive and her voice calm. As an Indian, she sighed, she must be a failure.

Well, so be it. An Indian woman would hide her feelings under an expressionless mask and never talk back to her man. A white woman would rage, inside and out. She guessed she was a white woman from the way she felt right now. Carleton hadn't spoken more than three sentences to her since they left Winnemucca.

At that moment, Carleton stepped his gray pony into the clearing and dismounted. He turned away from her to unload his saddlebags and bedroll from behind the saddle, and she directed a hard look at his ramrod-straight back. She hoped he could feel the daggers in his spine.

He must have felt something, because he slowly pivoted his lean, taut body to face her. "Something on your mind, Sis?"

That did it. "Don't call me Sis!" she yelled. "My name is Serena Elizabeth Hull, and don't you forget it!"

Carleton blinked. Serena stalked toward him, all fluffed up like a little banty rooster. With her dark eyes blazing fire like that, her chin stuck defiantly in the chill evening air, she was a sight. Sparks practically jumped off her skin.

"Well, Serena Elizabeth Hull, is something wrong?"

Frowning, she opened her mouth, closed it with an exhaled puff of air, opened it again. Tears glittered in the corners of her eyes.

"I— No. Yes! How can you even ask?"

He'd never seen her so angry that her control wavered. What in the hell had set her off?

Without realizing what he was doing, Carleton moved a step nearer. "I'm asking because there's no other way to find out what's—"

"Don't come any closer!"

As if his boots moved of their own accord, he advanced anyway. She stood her ground, fists propped on her hips, her unwavering gaze beneath the brim of her black Stetson pinning him with an unnamed accusation.

The closer he got, the more delicious she looked, her cheeks flushed, her dark eyes sparkling. He studied her as he'd wanted to for the past week—up close and at his leisure.

And wished he hadn't. Nope, she hadn't changed a bit. She still turned his body inside out, teased his senses until he sweat even on the cold, windy days they'd endured the past week. God in heaven, he wanted to knock that hat off her head, loose her shiny, dark hair, and bury his face in the silky mass.

He was steady enough as long as he didn't see her, didn't watch her body moving with her horse or see the subtle, enticing sway of her hips as she moved around the campfire or walked down to the creek to wash.

But when he *could* see her, hell reigned in his groin. After that night on Chili Rock when he'd kissed her until he ached, he knew it was safer not to look at her. As long as he kept an hour's riding distance between them, he was in no danger of losing his head.

Nights, however, were a different story. Now that the doctor in Winnemucca had fixed his shoulder, he had two good arms. He wanted nothing more than to lock his hands behind her slim back and never let go.

And that, you burned-out old fool, is more frightening than looking down the barrel of a hundred cannon.

He couldn't afford to lose his heart. He'd lose himself. If he couldn't live without seeing her, hearing her low, quiet voice sweet-talking her horse or laughing with Jem and Thad, he was finished. She'd marry eventually—probably some ambitious, up-and-coming young foreman or rancher, and then she'd be lost to him forever.

He wanted her. And the solution was obvious. *Don't* want her!

"Did you hear what I said, Mr. Kearney?" Her trembling voice rose an octave. *"Did you?"*

Had he said "low and quiet?" Whatever gave him a cockeyed notion like that?

The hair on his bare forearms prickled. Not only was she scaring the good sense out of him by looking more female than any woman had a right to, now she was getting under his skin.

"Hellfire, Serena, what's got under your butt?"

Instantly he called back the words, but too late. She'd goaded him beyond reason, and now she needed a lesson in...something.

"You!" She shouted the word in his face. "*You're* what's gotten under my—" She broke off with a gasp. "Oh! I mean under my...whatever."

Carleton bit back an irrational urge to laugh. "Okay, Sis, have it your way. What's gotten under your 'whatever?'"

She puffed herself up again. Toe-to-toe, she jabbed her forefinger in his chest. "Not 'Sis'! Serena! You can't even remember my name! You don't know who I am!"

"I sure as hell know who you are, Si—Serena," he amended. "You're that spunky little thorn in my side makin' my life miserable!"

He didn't know where those words came from either, but they sure felt good clearing his throat. "*More* than miserable. Now get your soft little backside out of my sight!"

Stunned, she stared at him.

The air between them seemed to heat up and hang, heavy and still, waiting for something to happen.

"Serena," he said, louder than he intended, "what is it you want?"

"You," she blurted. "I mean, I want you to talk to me. You've been like a sphinx for days. We see you only at night and then you're surly as a wounded bear."

Carleton shook his head. He couldn't think of a single thing to say.

"*Say* something!" she demanded. "*Do* something!"

Say something? his brain screamed. Like hell he would. Why invite trouble? *Do something?* Another matter entirely. He grabbed her shoulders, pulled her into his arms and kissed her, hard and deep.

Something inside him snapped. "Serena," he groaned, his voice ragged. He yanked her hat off and sailed it away somewhere, then brushed his lips across her temple.

"Serena, kiss me, dammit. Kiss me!"

He felt her body tremble against his, her uneven breath gust past his ear. "Kiss me," he whispered. He tipped her chin up with his thumb and her mouth met his.

Her arms came up, fluttered near his shoulders, but did not touch him. At last her hands settled behind his head and she rose on tiptoe to meet him.

She broke the kiss. "You are a very quiet man," she said shakily. "I never know what you're thinking. What to expect."

"My number one rule," he told her in a hoarse whisper. "Talk little."

They stared at each other for a full minute, and then Ben crashed noisily through the underbrush and strode into camp, a tin bucket in his hand.

"Water," he announced unnecessarily. "For cooking. Hey, where's the fire you two were s'posed to build?"

A soft laugh escaped Serena's lips.

"Right here, you big oaf." Carleton struggled to keep a straight face. "You just can't see it." He moved away from Serena.

"Hell I can't," Ben muttered to himself. "Raging like a prairie scorcher."

That night Carleton spread his pallet a good distance from camp, shucked his boots and lay staring up at the stars until his eyes burned.

Next to the campfire, a sleepless Serena tossed and

turned on the hard ground. After an hour of listening to her thrash beside him, Ben began to sing in an amused, sleep-drowsy voice.

"If a body meet a body, comin' through the rye... If a body kiss a body, need a body cry...."

Serena whapped him on the rump with her hat.

"Don't blame me, honey," he murmured. "You're the one in love."

"That's preposterous!" She hit him again.

"Just like settling down edgy steers," he mused aloud. *"Every lassie has her laddie, none they say have I..."*

Serena rolled over and pulled the blanket up to cover her ears.

At the first sight of Wildwood Valley's dusty main street, Serena's entire body tensed with anticipation. Four more miles and she would be home.

Ben dismounted at the edge of town and, with a jaunty wave goodbye, strode into the newspaper office. Through the front window, Serena glimpsed the sheriff's tall frame bent over a blue-aproned figure. A thread of longing encircled her heart.

She was lonely. Lonely for Jessie's clear voice and girlish laughter, for Mary Irene's soft, cool cheek pressed against her own. Lonely for a man's strong arms.

Side by side, she and Carleton rode to the Double K gate in thick, uneasy silence. The Double K owner reined in the gray pony and turned in his saddle. "Guess this is it, Sis."

Serena sighed in frustration at his continued use of the nickname. Never in a million years would she admit he'd come close to divining a Hull family tradition; Mama and both her sisters called her Sissy.

"So much has happened I feel as if I've been around

the world, not just to Winnemucca. In a way, I'm sorry it's over."

"There's always next year," Carleton reminded. "Your herd ought to be twice the size by then."

She nodded. "Next year," she repeated.

There was nothing more to say. Carleton had his responsibilities as owner of the Double K and father to Alice and baby Sarah. And she had hers—Lost Acres Ranch. She snapped the reins and the mare stepped forward. When she drew near, she tipped her hat. "Mr. Kearney."

"Miss Hull." He gave her a sober two-finger salute.

She walked her mount past the tall man in the saddle, sensing his eyes on her back. Each yard that separated them reminded her of the chasm that lay between them. Every bone in her body wanted to turn the horse around and...

And what? Just what do you expect him to do? Invite you home to supper with Alice and his baby daughter?

She closed her eyes. She felt his gaze follow her all the way up the road to the Lost Acres gate.

"Miss Serena!" A deep voice called out from the porch of the Double K ranch house. "Hold up a spell."

Marsh, the hired man, lumbered across the road toward her. She drew rein and waited for him.

"Got a letter for you! Jes' come yesterday."

Serena's spirits soared. A letter! She moved to meet the stocky black man. Dismounting, she tore open the envelope with shaking fingers and scanned the few lines.

"...Jessie...pneumonia...early November...buried next to..."

Her mind went numb. Somewhere an animal began to scream, a horse maybe...such an odd sound, like a dried-out bellows pulling in and out, and so far away. Where was it? she wondered. It sounded close, but where?

And then Carleton was beside her, holding her. She

pounded her fists against his hard chest, hit him and hit him while he struggled to pin her arms. Marsh's big, dark eyes were round as saucers.

"Bring her horse," Carleton ordered. He picked her up in his arms and headed for the shortcut through his mowed rye field.

Someone was crying and choking at the same time. Not Marsh or Carleton—a woman's high-pitched wailing. Her throat burned. Carleton's long strides rocked her body against his.

Her mind felt muddled. Something had happened. Something about Jessie.

Oh, dear God, no! No!

Carleton's low voice came to her through a swirling gray fog.

"You're all right, Serena. Take a deep breath."

"Marsh." He spoke over his shoulder. "Go on ahead and light a fire in her stove."

"Already done it, Mr. Kearney. Fetched up a bucket of water and wound her little clock, too. Anythin' else?"

"Unsaddle her horse and put her things on her front step. Then go tell Alice I won't be home for a while."

At the edge of the rye field, Carleton paused while Marsh opened the gate. Silent now, the woman in his arms curled against him. The screaming was over, he guessed. Thank God. The sound cut into his belly like a saber.

He kneed open the front door of the tiny barn house where Serena lived and stepped inside. The stillness in the single room was broken only by the ticking of the clock on the wooden desk. Two worn armchairs and a battered pine table filled the small space. No bed, though.

"Where do you sleep, Serena?"

"In the loft," she said in a dull voice. "Up the ladder."

He set her on her feet, caught her when her legs buckled.

Slowly he walked her to one of the chairs and pushed her down onto the cushion.

She sat unmoving, staring at the floor, her head bent to one side, her legs splayed in front of her. Carleton's eyes swam. She looked like a broken doll.

Quickly he added wood to the fire Marsh had lit in the woodstove, filled the teakettle from the bucket of fresh water on the wooden sideboard and set it over the flames.

"Come on, Serena. Got to get you upstairs."

He scooped her out of the chair and walked to the ladder with her in his arms. Setting her on her feet, he placed both her hands on the rail. "Climb," he said. He closed her fingers over the wood. "I'm right behind you."

Without a word she put one foot on the bottom rung. His hands at her waist, he lifted her up. Another step, another lift. Her rounded backside bumped his chin. Seven more steps and then she stumbled off the ladder and onto the floor of her loft on all fours.

Carleton drew in a careful breath and followed her. The roof was too low to stand up, so he crawled after her.

He didn't remember the barn having a loft. Thad must have built it for her last summer. It made a cozy sleeping area, with the mattress positioned under the single window. Last time he'd seen that window it was just a square opening in the wall; now it had paned glass and lace curtains.

Serena curled up on the bed hugging her belly. She rocked her body rhythmically back and forth, but she made no sound. He wished she'd cry or shout or something. He couldn't stand to see her in such agony.

By the time he got her boots off, the teakettle was sighing on the stove downstairs. He climbed back down the ladder, found a cup and her stash of tea. When the brew looked about strong enough, he slipped a flask from his hip pocket and splashed in a generous shot of whiskey.

Before he climbed back up the ladder, he lit all three

kerosene lamps and carefully replaced the globes. When Ella had died, nothing was worse than that hour of fading daylight between dusk and sunset.

Back in the loft, he set the steaming cup on the braided rug beside the mattress and leaned over Serena's still form. She was awake. Her dark eyes looked stunned. Tired. He'd seen animals look that way when hit hard between the eyes. His throat closed and a jagged pain ripped his heart open.

He smoothed the hair off her forehead and she caught his hand. "Don't leave me," she said in a low, clear voice.

He lay down beside her and gathered her close.

"Stay with me. Please."

"Serena, I—"

"Please," she repeated. "Don't go."

He closed his eyes as she pressed her body against his. "Your heart is beating," she said.

"Good. Keeps me alive."

"My heart is beating, too." Her voice sounded slow, and she had difficulty pronouncing words. "Does that mean I'm alive?"

"You're alive, Serena. You've been kicked pretty hard, but you're alive."

She drew in a shuddery breath. "Feel dead. Numb all over, as if I'm frozen inside."

Carleton stroked her hair. "It will pass. Just hold on."

She moved one hand to his top shirt button and slipped it free. Then she slid her fingers downward. When she had all seven buttons undone, she spread the material wide and laid her cheek against his bare chest.

"Stay with me," she murmured. "Until I can feel something again."

He wanted to stay, wanted to so desperately he wondered if he dared. She was numb with shock and grief, reaching out to him for warmth, for something to hold on to during the racking waves of anguish. In the face of death, the human heart desperately, instinctively, sought life. Later, he knew she would mourn and heal. Right now, she needed to be held.

Her hand tugged at his belt. "I'm cold," she murmured. "Be close to me."

He undid the buckle, pulled off his jeans and laid them beside his boots. Her fingers fumbled with the buttons of her shirt, and Carleton caught her hand and gently moved it aside. Working slowly, he slipped the buttons free.

She sat up to shrug out of the garment and then raised her arms as he pulled the lacy chemise over her head. Her jeans and the soft muslin drawers she wore underneath joined the pile beside the mattress.

His breath stopped at the sight of her slim, naked form. Very deliberately, he reached for her shoulders, eased her trembling body down next to his, and wrapped her in his arms.

Her heart thudded erratically against his. His breath ruffled the loose tendrils of hair at her temple. He longed to smooth his hands over her torso, stroke her skin until it heated under his palm. He ached to touch her intimately, but now was not the time. Now she needed to be reminded only that she was alive and safe.

She nestled tight against him, drove her head into the hollow of his shoulder and keened like an injured animal. Carleton clenched his jaw at her pain and held her, rocking her gently while she wept.

When the paroxysms of grief eased, he held the cup of whiskey-laced tea to her lips. She gulped a mouthful, coughed, gulped another.

He smiled as she settled against him and closed her eyes. She was fighting. She'd be all right.

He guessed he would be, too, despite the difficult night he foresaw ahead. He wouldn't leave her. And he wouldn't take her, either. She needed him, but not that way. At least not tonight.

Sometime after midnight, he rose and descended the ladder to her tiny kitchen where he stoked up the fire and brewed another cup of tea. On an impulse, he checked outside the front door for her things.

Marsh had laid her satchel on top of her saddle. Beside it was a wicker basket containing a loaf of fresh bread, a small crock of butter and some cheese. Alice must have sent it over.

He sliced thick slabs of bread, slathered them with butter and cut the cheese into squares. Wasn't much of a supper, but it was better than nothing. He loaded it onto a plate, set a fresh cup of hot tea in the center and blew out the lamps he'd left burning. Balancing the plate in one hand, he climbed up to the loft.

She was still asleep, her face mottled and swollen from crying, her delicate, gently curving form curled into the warm hollow he'd left. She didn't waken when he slid onto the mattress next to her and pulled the quilt over them.

He left the bread and cheese untouched. When she woke up, she'd need to eat, and anyway he wasn't hungry. His heart ached watching her struggle with her sister's death, seeing the cycle of acknowledgement and anguish fade into periods of almost unnatural calm.

He'd reacted the same way when Ella had died, had doggedly waded through the periods of agonizing grief, rested in the heavy black numbness that followed. That first night was a living hell, he remembered. He didn't want Serena to face it alone.

He must have fallen asleep, because when he opened his eyes, she was awake, lying close to him, looking into his face with hugely dilated dark eyes. She had unbraided her hair, and it flowed about her shoulders like a waterfall of heavy silk.

Oh, God, he wanted her.

Her next words shook him to the core.

"Touch me," she said in a low, steady voice. She laid her palm on his belly, and he sucked in his breath.

"Serena..." He was going to say he couldn't risk it. She would move under his hands, and he'd be a goner. He didn't dare touch her.

"Touch me," she repeated. She looked straight into his eyes. "All over."

"I can't. Not like that." His voice was hoarse with desire. "I'll want to take you, Serena, and that's not what you need right now."

"It is what I need," she said in that same low, controlled tone. "I need to feel alive."

She smoothed her hand over his chest, stroking slowly up and down, lingering over his nipples. His skin burned under her fingers.

He lifted her hand away. "You've got to stop, Serena. I want you too much to be sensible much longer."

She smiled at him, eluded his grasp and replaced her palm on his belly. "Do it," she whispered. "All of it."

"I can't, not without hurting you."

"You will not hurt me," she replied softly. "I want it as much as you."

Her soft mouth sought his, and at the touch of her lips he was lost. Her flesh heated under his hands. She moaned with pleasure, and the sound drove him on until he thought he couldn't stand not being inside her, and then she whispered something, the words breathed into his mouth as he lifted his head for breath.

"Be with me."

Something within him clenched. "Serena, are you sure?"

In answer, she pulled him on top of her. Through the haze of need surging within him he realized something.

He was a man, and she was not afraid of him. At least with him, she had conquered her inner demons. He felt humbled that she had chosen him.

With a groan he positioned himself and entered her. She was tight and sweet. Her body moved hungrily with his, urging him deeper.

She cried out at the moment of her climax, clung to him, sobbing with pleasure as the spasms shook her. He thrust into her one last time and felt his spirit soar out of his body and float free.

He knew that for her their coupling was an instinctive, desperate reaching out for life. For him, it was the rich culmination of his hunger for her, body and soul.

And he also knew it could have no future.

Chapter Twenty-Five

Christmas Eve, 1887

Dearest Mary Irene,

You have been very brave these past weeks, my darling one, and I am proud of you. Just a few more months and we will be together.

I have a good cry each day about Jessie. I can barely speak her name without choking. People here have been very kind—Cora has been out twice and Amanda comes whenever she can get away from her duties at the mercantile.

Each day I drag myself out of bed to help Thad with the chores. Now that Mr. Svenson is finally starting on the house—our very own house!—I am feeling somewhat better. He says it will go up quickly once the worst of the winter weather is over. My sunflowers have so far withstood the frosts, all but three, which I found uprooted yesterday morning. Probably that dog Snap keeps in the Double K bunkhouse. Lately I've been too dispirited to care much what happens around the place, except for our new house and my sunflowers. Both are a symbol of hope for me.

With the cold weather the hens have stopped laying, so my trips to town are few. Tonight everyone in the valley is gathering for the big Christmas Eve social at the Dixon House Hotel. I don't feel much like going, but Thad insists. He says it will do me good.

I hope you are keeping up with your schoolwork. The schoolmistress out here is very strict. When the house is finished, you will have a desk all your own in your bedroom. I enclose a sketch of the floor plan as Mr. Svenson envisions it. He has included a special loft for my sleeping room. When I got the letter about Jessie, I spent four days just looking at the sky out my upstairs window. The view of the clouds in the daytime, the stars at night, is quite calming.

Mr. Kearney was very kind during the worst part of my mourning. Alice, though, is as tart and unfriendly as ever. She did send food over, though, so I cannot think but that she means well underneath.

All the hands are finally back from the trail drive. An early blizzard detained them in Nevada for an extra week, and when they rode in, they were all hungry and cold and bad-tempered. Thorny's nose was frostbitten.

Tell Aunt Letty you will need two trunks for your trip out in the spring. I'd like some of Jessie's clothes to remember her by, and your clothes and books and paints should fill another.

I love you dearly. I cannot wait to bake cookies together again.

Your Sissy

She laid down the pen and gazed at the ladder leading up to the loft. She had not seen Carleton since the night they'd spent together. Every afternoon the rancher sent Marsh over to check on her, but Carleton himself hadn't set foot inside her door since that day.

She understood why. They had come together in desperate hunger and need, and while they might be drawn together—even privately hold each other dear—she knew he had his obligations to Alice and baby Sarah and to the Double K. And she had hers.

But all the same, she missed the sight of his long, lean frame moving with easy grace across the rye field, missed the sound of his low voice. And, she acknowledged, she missed lying safe and warm in his arms.

It had helped to get Mr. Svenson started on her new house, situated on a little rise a half mile away from her made-over barn. It hadn't helped to have the string of events she now recognized as harassments continue. She found the henhouse door left open, or sections of fence pushed over. One night she even had the eerie sensation that someone was stalking outside her little home.

Each evening as the sun went down and the rich, warm twilight flooded her tiny room, she longed to be with Carleton. Just hearing his voice on the cattle drive had sent a thrill through her belly. Now, her body ached for his touch. She had waited impatiently for the Christmas Eve social when she would see him again.

She closed her eyes. Oh, God, the scent of him, the feel of his hard muscled body against hers. No matter what she did, she couldn't stop thinking about him. Wanting him.

The social was held on a clear, bitter cold evening just three weeks after Cora and the trail crew returned from Nevada. Serena didn't feel much like dancing, but she hoped the talk and the supper provided by the valley ladies would help take her mind off the ache in her heart.

As she entered the hotel ballroom, she searched unconsciously for Carleton. The sight of his tall frame across the warm, music-filled room sent her heart skittering. Unsmiling, he started toward her.

At her side, Amanda squeezed her arm. "Dance with

him, Serena. You look truly beautiful in that new dress, and Mr. Kearney's been lonely since his wife died.''

Amanda whirled off in the arms of Jason Bartel, who sent her a very grown-up nod. His twin brother, Eldon— or Hadit, as he was now called—hung at the edge of the crowd waiting to cut in. The change in both boys since the trail drive was remarkable.

The change in herself was even more remarkable, she realized.

Her new dress *was* lovely. Cora had insisted on it, giving her the fabric as a Christmas gift and hounding her for days to go into town for fittings with Addie Rice, the seamstress. Made of pale green silk, it had puffed sleeves and a flounce around the low scooped neckline, edged with lace. The swirling skirt had a double lace flounce near the hem. Addie had made the skirt so full Serena couldn't walk past anything without feeling the need to turn sideways.

But the change she felt inside was what gave her existence new meaning, made her breath catch at the thought of being near Carleton Kearney. She didn't know how she had come to hunger for this man the way she did, but Lord knew she did. She just didn't know what to do about it.

Carleton reached her and without a word pulled her into his arms. In silence, except for the pounding of her heart, they danced the slow waltz scraped out on Eli Harker's fiddle and Thorny's harmonica. When he spoke at last, his voice was low and oddly strained.

''How are you, Serena?''

''Well, thank you. And you?''

He groaned softly. ''Got the damnedest yen for bread and cheese lately.'' He looked into her eyes. '''Round about midnight.''

Heat surged below her belly. ''Th-thank you for sending Marsh over,'' she stammered. ''For thinking of me.''

''Haven't thought of much else,'' he said quietly. He guided her expertly away from Lyle Bartel, poised to stride onto the floor to claim her.

"Carleton," she said when they were safely past the rangy foreman and she had summoned the courage to speak. "Thank you also for…that night."

She paused, unsure whether she could go on with emotion choking her voice. "I needed it. You. You'll never know how much."

He tightened his arm about her waist. "I know," he said. "I needed you, too." He held her gaze, his eyes smoke blue in the light shed by the candle-studded chandelier. "I hope you don't regret it," he added. "I don't."

Her breath quickened. *Regret it?* She'd lived on the memory of that night in his arms through the worst weeks of her life. It had kept her going.

The music droned to a close. She opened her mouth to speak, but Lyle imposed his tall frame between them.

Carleton hesitated. Under her hand she felt the muscles of his forearm tighten. Then with a frown, he withdrew. The instant he released her, she felt cold all over.

Lyle pulled her tight against him. "You look good enough for a man to eat, honey," the Double K foreman rasped in her ear. "Much too pretty to spend days out fixin' fence."

Serena stiffened. "How do you know what I do during the day?"

His eyes glittered. "Oh, I been watchin' you, pretty lady. Thinkin' maybe you oughtn't be running that spread of yours by yourself."

"I'm not running it by myself. I have Thad to help me."

"Thad!" he drawled in derision. "Thad's not dry behind the ears yet."

She ignored his comment. "Thad is an excellent foreman," Serena retorted. Something in Lyle's lazy tone made her uneasy.

Lyle tugged her uncomfortably close, pressing his chin against her temple. "What you need is a real man, honey. A partner."

Amanda flashed past in the arms of Silas Appleby. Serena noted the puzzled look her friend sent her over Silas's shoulder. At the social last summer, Amanda and Lyle had been all-evening partners. Tonight he stood on the sidelines, watching Serena, while Amanda was partnered by others. She wondered why.

As if reading her thoughts, Lyle gestured at the petite blonde. "Mandy's pretty, all right. But she doesn't own one square foot of land."

Land? That said it all. Lyle's interest followed where his mercenary calculations led—straight to her ranch.

"Would you excuse me? I'd prefer to sit down for a while."

"Sure, Serena. Come on outside with me—got something to show you."

"Some other time, Lyle." She moved away from him toward the punch bowl where Cora sat with Jessamyn Kearney and baby Sarah. In the next instant, Lyle grabbed her arm and propelled her past the ladies and out the hotel entrance.

"Let me go," she commanded.

"In a minute." He dragged her out onto the empty porch and backed her up against the railing. Pinning her hands behind her, he yanked her into his arms and settled his mouth on hers. His tongue plunged past her teeth.

She twisted violently, but he continued his invasion, a wet, sloppy exploration of her mouth.

She broke free, and when he released her hands to grab her head, holding it still so he could kiss her again, she brought her knee up and slammed it into his crotch. She fled into the hotel.

Just inside the doorway, she met Carleton heading toward her, his mouth pressed into a grim line.

"Did he hurt you?" he demanded. "I saw him take you outside. I waited 'til I couldn't stand it any longer and—"

"N-no, he didn't hurt me. I think I might have hurt him, though. When we were on the drive, Eli showed me what to do. He had a feeling Lyle might—"

She stopped to catch her breath. Carleton stepped in close and put his hands on her shoulders. "That damn fool. Lyle's always been impulsive. Sometimes goes off half-cocked. Try not to let it frighten you, Serena."

"I'm not frightened. I'm mad as a wet hen, but I'm not afraid of him."

"You want to sit down? Have some lemonade?"

She shook her head. "I want to dance," she said with conviction. "But just with you. Can you fix it so no one cuts in?"

Carleton raised his dark eyebrows. "All evening?" he inquired.

She nodded.

"Maybe. Maybe not. Depends on how much talk you want to start."

The joy she felt at the prospect of being held in his arms drained away. "Oh, of course. I hadn't thought—"

He cut her off. Encircling her waist, he drew her forward. "Don't think, Serena. Just dance with me." His voice sounded unsteady.

The music slowed. Over the next hour they spoke no words to each other outside of what their bodies said as they moved in unison. Serena matched her motions with Carleton's, inhaled the scent of his skin, felt his soft mustache brush her temple, and knew she would always remember this night held close in his arms. This, and the night they'd spent in her loft. Each event would be treasured among those special, magical times she was single-mindedly gathering into her memory.

Such moments would have to last her a lifetime.

Christmas morning brought snow to the valley. From her bed in the loft, she watched through the window as the white flakes drifted down in silence. How beautiful it was, so slow and quiet. Peaceful. She stretched her arms over her head. It would be cold out— Good gracious! Her sunflowers!

She rolled off the mattress and threw her blue flannel wrapper over her nightgown. Stepping quickly into a pair of goatskin slippers, a gift from Amanda and her parents, she flew down the ladder and out the front door. Clutching the robe together at the front, she bent over her flower bed.

The protective lath cover Thad had contrived to shield her plants through the winter was covered with snow-laden hay. Bless her foreman for thinking up the insulating scheme! With luck, and Snap's annoying dog restrained in the bunkhouse where he belonged, the plants would survive until spring. And then next summer...

Her spirits rose. Next summer Mary Irene would be here with her, and her flowers would bloom and she would be happy again.

Buoyed by the prospect of the coming new year, she turned to dash back inside and stopped short. Carleton strode toward her across the snow-covered rye field, white flakes dusting his hat and the shoulders of his sheepskin jacket. Her breath caught, and an unreasoning joy swept over her as she watched his easy, long-legged gait.

"Merry Christmas!" she called.

He raised one hand to tip the brim of his Stetson. "Morning, Serena. Alice sent a basket of..." His voice faltered as he took in her attire.

Serena hugged the wrapper about her shivering frame. "I was just checking on my sunflowers."

A grin split his tanned features. "...scones," he finished. "And an invitation to Christmas dinner at the ranch house. Ben's coming out from town with his family."

"Oh, I don't think—"

"And Cora." He added an unspoken entreaty in his deep blue eyes. "Your sunflowers won't miss you."

Serena returned the rancher's steady gaze. She understood the message in his gaze, acknowledged it and sent him one of her own. *Don't ask me to your house unless you really want me there. You, not Cora.*

"I'm f-freezing, Carleton. Come inside."

He cleared his throat. "The trail crew got together and…well, they got a present for you." From inside his jacket, he produced a paper packet.

Serena stared at it, then at him. His shadowed eyes gave no hint of anything, but she read in his stance an odd hesitancy. "Come inside," she said gently, "where it's warm."

She led the way into her cozy room, tried to keep her eyes off the ladder up to the loft. Adding more wood to the stove, she reached for the coffeepot.

"I won't stay, Serena," he said in a hoarse voice. "I want to, but I can't. Alice needs help. I just stopped by to bring this."

He set the basket on the pine table and folded her fingers around the packet. "Open it. The boys are so anxious about your reaction they can't concentrate on their poker game."

Serena peeked inside the envelope and gasped. "A railroad ticket! But—"

"It's for your sister. In the spring. Or as soon as the stage roads are passable."

Tears stung into her eyes. "Oh, I couldn't accept—" Her voice broke.

"'Fraid you don't have a choice," he said gently. "You can thank the boys when you come for dinner. They'll be joining us."

He drew another package from his jacket and handed it to her. "This is from me."

The brown wrapping paper unfolded to reveal a small, shiny twenty-two caliber revolver. Serena looked from the gun to Carleton.

"Thought it might come in handy," he remarked casually. "Fits in an apron pocket."

Her heart overflowing, she moved toward him. "Thank you," she said in a trembling voice.

"Merry Christmas, Serena."

He turned to go, then suddenly pivoted back to her and

caught her hard against him. "I'll show you how to fire it tomorrow," he said, his voice gravelly. He kissed her until her thoughts swam. She closed her eyes and let herself float under his mouth, felt her knees turn to jelly.

"Would you...would you like...some coffee?" she said when she could speak.

"Nope." He gave her a slow, lopsided smile and held her away from him. "To tell you the truth, Serena, I don't trust myself."

He kissed her again, held her close for a long moment, and then was gone.

Shaking, Serena walked to the open doorway and watched the tall man retreat across his rye field. She thought about how much her life—her self—had changed since last summer when she'd come out West from Stark County. She had known heady triumph, defeat, agonizing loss, even love. Threaded through all of it was the enigmatic owner of the Double K.

At dusk she arrived at the Double K, half-frozen from the clear, cold air, a proper dress and petticoats packed in the satchel tied to her saddle.

Cora helped her change in the upstairs bedroom—Alice's room, she guessed from the ruffled gingham bedspread—and then both women joined Alice and Jessamyn Kearney in the kitchen.

From the stove, Alice sent her a sour look. Serena smiled at her and offered to take over the care of baby Sarah.

The kitchen table had been expanded to double its size, large enough to seat twelve—the six Kearneys, plus Cora and herself, and the hands—Rosy, Snap and Lyle, as well as Marsh. It was the only time all year, Ben explained, when the entire ranch population ate a meal at the same table.

When Alice finally announced dinner, it was a tight squeeze but they all fit after a fashion. Thad and Jem volunteered to sit at the corners, providing they got third helpings of dessert. Alice had baked two double-layer chocolate cakes—Thad's favorite—and Cora brought four pies, two apple and two mince, the latter flavored with brandy.

Serena took a seat across from Carleton and held Sarah on her lap. All through the meal she sensed the ranch owner's eyes on her, but she didn't dare meet his gaze. She knew her face would flame, her hands tremble if he smiled at her. She didn't want to add to Alice's pique. Instead, she concentrated on feeding baby Sarah bits of mashed vegetables and turkey dressing, listening to the lighthearted banter around her.

When Cora rose to clear for dessert, Thad swooped into the kitchen, lifted Alice's hair off the back of her neck, and planted a kiss on her nape as she bent over the sink.

"Double chocolate cake!" He sighed dramatically. "The way to a man's heart."

Alice turned scarlet with pleasure. Serena watched the two of them in the kitchen and made a silent resolution to have a talk with her young foreman the very next morning. Thad had no idea how his teasing affected his cousin.

Seated next to her, Lyle Bartel began to behave with disturbing familiarity. Under the babble of voices and the clink of plates and silver, his remarks to Serena went unheard by all but her.

"A baby suits you," he intoned as she offered Sarah bits of apple pie filling. "You oughtta have one of your own to worry over instead of a bunch of cows."

Serena ignored him.

"And to get a baby," he breathed near her ear, "you need a man." He pressed her arm suggestively.

She looked up. Across the table, Carleton's steady gaze held hers. The unfathomable expression in his eyes sent a chill up her spine. She edged away from Lyle.

To her relief, the meal ended. Carleton took the baby from her, and Serena lost no time joining the other three women in the kitchen, attacking the mountain of dishes while the men smoked and talked ranching and sipped brandy in the parlor. Jem cycled back and forth between that room and the kitchen, and Serena felt a pang of sympathy for his indecision. Caught between childhood and adulthood, Jem was unsure whether he wanted a boy's third piece of cake or a man's brandy-laced coffee.

She had been caught the same way, she reflected as she dried plates and stacked them on a shelf. Somehow during the cattle drive she had stumbled, or been pulled, into womanhood. And it had culminated that night in her loft.

Her body heated at the memory. She was in love with Carleton Kearney.

In a strange way, she was thankful she'd spent the evening with Carleton and his household. Seeing the rancher with his family had not tempered her longing, but it had definitely steadied her thinking.

Carleton already had heavy family responsibilities, obligations so pressing and so all-involving there was no room in his life for another. As desperately as she wanted him, Serena realized she could never marry him.

She glanced with envy at Jem, choosing another piece of cake instead of joining the men in the parlor. In a way she, too, wished she could be young instead of a grown woman with desires that would never be filled.

Chapter Twenty-Six

January passed into February, and under Mr. Svenson's skilled direction, her house grew from a rough sketch on the back of a scrap of wallpaper into a framed structure with spaces for doors and windows, a staircase and even a laundry porch. Each day Serena rode over to take the carpenter and Thad some lunch and a quart jar of hot coffee wrapped in a thick towel and stayed to inspect their progress. Some days she begged the use of a hammer and worked along with them nailing studs and measuring planks for flooring.

Every night Serena gave thanks for the two men laboring so hard on the far hill. She knew they were pressing hard for completion—or at least enclosure under a roof—by spring.

On this late February morning she watched the sun rise through her tiny upstairs window, then dressed and climbed down the ladder to check for eggs and inspect her protected bed of sunflowers before she visited the privy. Just outside her front door, she stumbled into Lyle Bartel.

He was not mounted, but on foot, and for a split second Serena's neck prickled. A ranch hand avoided walking at all costs.

"Thad around?" the lanky foreman inquired.

"I thought he was at the bunkhouse, eating breakfast with the hands," she replied. A shiver crawled up her spine. "Is something wrong?"

Lyle grinned at her. "Nuthin' that can't be put to rights. You're up kinda early, aren't you?"

"I always inspect the— I thought I'd ride into town to see Amanda," she invented hurriedly. She wasn't about to let Lyle follow her into the henhouse.

The foreman nodded. "I'll check back later." He wheeled and ambled away, bypassing the road in favor of the shortcut across Carleton's rye field.

Serena stared at his retreating figure. Not for one minute did she believe he'd come looking for Thad. She fingered the pistol she now routinely carried in her apron pocket. She hoped she never had to use it, but lately the tall Double K foreman had been hanging around her place at odd hours. It made her uneasy. Today, she resolved, she'd practice loading it the way Carleton had shown her at Christmas.

A week later, on the first morning in March, Serena rolled over in bed and sat bolt upright. Her house would be finished soon, ready to nail the shakes on the roof and paint the walls. She couldn't wait! Tomorrow she'd ride into town and mail the railroad ticket and all her extra egg money to Mary Irene for her trip out west. Her sister would arrive in just a few weeks.

Her heart soaring, she gazed out the window at the graying dawn sky. But it wasn't gray, it was deep rose, and the light flickered oddly, as if a candle—

Fire! Something was on fire! She leaped to the window.

On the far hill, smoke poured out of the unfinished roof of her house. Flames licked at the walls, blackening the wood into a gaunt skeleton of beams and framing. Her stomach lurched.

She threw on jeans and a shirt, jammed her feet into her boots and scrambled down the ladder and out the door. She'd be damned if she'd let her house burn down! She'd fight for every timber with every ounce of strength she could muster.

As she raced to get gunnysacks from the hay barn to fight the blaze, she heard someone at the Double K ring the dinner gong. It rang and kept on ringing it—the signal for trouble.

She set off across the meadow on foot, her breath coming in jerky gasps. Behind her horses thundered and men yelled. Thad, Rosy and Carleton pounded past her, shovels and gunnysacks slung across their saddles. Lyle and Snap followed at a slower pace.

By the time she arrived, the entire building was an inferno. Dazed, she wrapped both arms about her middle and fought for control. Unconsciously, she moved toward the blazing structure.

Carleton blocked her path. "It's too late!" he shouted. "We can't beat it out, and we don't have enough water. I'm sorry, Serena. Really sorry."

"Too late?" she screamed. "It can't be too late, it can't be. It's the house for Mary Irene…all my money…all my…"

Dumbstruck, she stared past him at the blackened structure. *All my hopes and dreams, gone.* She sagged forward, let Carleton steady her while she watched the building slowly disintegrate. She wanted to throw up.

The men stood next to their horses, watching helplessly. *"Faena del diablo,"* Rosy muttered. "Work of the devil."

Dazed, Serena turned away. It was all she could do to take a single step. She couldn't face telling Mary Irene. But she knew she had to. She'd go back to her tiny room, try to stop shaking. Then she'd sit down at the kitchen table and write to her sister, explain to her…

No! She couldn't do it. Wouldn't do it. Instead, she decided, she would ride into town and borrow money. She would rebuild the house, every foot of it. And, she vowed, she'd dig a well. Maybe if she'd had a closer water supply they could have saved it.

* * *

The bank turned her down. "You've already borrowed to build your house, Miss Hull," Mr. Sullivan, the bank manager, reminded her in a kind but firm voice. "And to pay your foreman's back wages," he added. "I can't very well advance you any more until you've paid off your outstanding loan."

Sick at heart, she rose and turned away from the wiry gray-bearded man seated behind the desk. She had only one hope left. She'd have to ask Carleton Kearney for help.

Every bone in her body rebelled at the idea. She was already indebted to him for Big Red, his prize bull, and for replenishing her herd after the stampede. She couldn't ask him for more.

Not only that, she reminded herself, she'd made a bargain with Carleton last summer. *If I can't make enough money ranching by spring to build a house and bring my sisters out, I'll sell out to you and go back to Stark County.* The owner of the Double K would remember the bargain, too.

So weary her body ached from her head down to her ankles, she mounted her mare and rode back to Lost Acres. She trudged unseeing past her sunflower bed and into her tiny residence, climbed the ladder to the loft and fell on the mattress without even taking off her boots.

Did she have the strength to last even one more day? Closing her eyes, she let the tears seep from under her lids.

When the first wave of despair had eased, she blew her nose and began to weigh her options.

If I can't make enough money by spring…

By evening, she knew what she had to do. She rose and went downstairs, splashed cool water on her tear-swollen face and slowly opened her front door.

Now was as good a time as any.

In response to the message Thad brought from Serena at dusk, Carleton rode over to Lost Acres, taking the shortcut through the field. All day long he'd wanted to go to her, but one of his mares had difficulty foaling, and he couldn't get away. An hour ago he'd delivered the wobbly colt, washed up and grabbed a bite of supper. Now he wanted desperately to be with Serena.

She was outside at the front of her place, staring at the patch of sunflowers which had miraculously survived the winter. She'd planted the seeds in October, he remembered, and nurtured the tiny sprouted plants through the winter under mounds of insulating hay. He knew sunflowers were annuals; they should have blackened and died, but by some stroke of luck and because of her daily care, they hadn't. Now, she had a head start on an early summer bloom. Carleton shook his head in a combination of disbelief and admiration. Just as he dismounted, Serena leaned over and suddenly pulled a plant up by its roots.

"Serena."

She halted for a moment, her back to him. Then she bent low over the flower bed. Her shoulders heaved, and he knew she was crying.

"Serena, listen."

She turned toward him. Her eyes looked dull and unfocused, the way they had when her sister died.

"I can't go on," she said in a lifeless voice. "I'm going to sell out to you and go back to Stark County."

He caught her shoulders. "No, you're not."

"Yes," she countered. "I am. I'm tired. Exhausted. It's…hopeless."

He shook her gently, forced her to look at him. "You're discouraged. Any rancher would be after what you've been through. But what you've got to do is what we all do— pull up your socks and go on."

She stared at him, tears shimmering in her dark eyes. Deliberately she pulled out of his grasp and planted her hands on her hips.

"For an intelligent man, Carl, you are the biggest fool. I'll never be a rancher. I'm a woman, and I'm alone. I'm trying to do it one-handed!"

Carleton longed to pull her into his arms and sweet-talk her. Instead, he reasoned, what she needed right now was not love words, but a little sass.

"For an intelligent woman, Sis, you are surprisingly pigheaded. You're already a rancher. You've just taken another setback, but losing that house has nothing to do with ranching. It has to do with your pride."

She bristled. "What's my pride got to do with it?"

Carleton's heart contracted. He didn't want to hurt her, just help her face facts. "You've made some sort of pledge to yourself about getting your sisters—sorry, your sister—out here, and in your mind that requires building them a house."

"Well? What of it? It's plain as pancakes Mary Irene needs a proper place to live."

"Come down off your high horse, Serena. When Ben and I first came out here after the war, we spent the first year living in a tent."

"That's you and Ben," she snapped. "My sister..." Her voice faltered. "Mary Irene is not a soldier. She's a young girl."

"I didn't say we were alone," he returned quietly. "Ella, my wife, was with me, and Alice, too. Alice was just a baby."

"So?" She stared at him with eyes that sparked fire.

"So, maybe it's about time to follow the bend in the road."

"It's no use," she blazed. "I've made up my mind."

He reached out for her, but she broke away and yanked another sunflower plant out of the ground, tossed it at his feet. "You see these?" She pulled up another.

"I see 'em."

"I've struggled over them, prayed over them for months, just like I did over that house. It cost me every penny I had and more." She stopped to catch her breath. "And just when I thought my dream would come true," she continued in a low, tired voice, "life came along and kicked me in the teeth. It's not worth it."

"Sure seems that way sometimes," Carleton said in a quiet voice. "But if you want guarantees in life, you don't want life. Real life, that is. Sometimes—"

"Sometimes!" Serena exploded. She pulled up two more sunflowers and threw them at him. "Let me tell you about 'sometimes.' I need more than 'sometimes.' I need my sister, my family. I need something to hold on to besides 'sometimes.'"

Carleton gripped her shoulders so hard his knuckles whitened. "Hold on to the land, Serena. It's the only thing you can count on besides the fact that it takes a bull and a cow to make a calf. Land is what brought us out West in the first place. It's what sustains us, makes the hardship and the losses worthwhile."

"I need more than that!" She tried to pull away, but he held her fast.

"God knows I need more than that, too. We all do. But in the end, death takes everything else. Only the land survives."

She gave up struggling against his grasp and stared at him, a light dawning in her eyes.

"Don't give it up, Serena. Not to me, not to anyone. Hold on to it."

She stared up into his face, her eyes hot and challenging. "Lyle wants to marry me," she said after a moment.

"I figured that. What do *you* want?"

"I don't want Lyle." She hesitated, then raised her head and looked him straight in the eyes. "I want you."

"Thank God," Carleton said, exhaling. "For a minute I thought you were going to talk me out of another fifteen head of cattle!"

A sputter of laughter erupted from Serena's throat. How could he make light of her situation? On the other hand, how could he not? If you didn't laugh at times, you died of sorrow.

"And a bull," she added.

He caught her hand and brought it to his cheek. "Hell's half acre, I'm glad you can still see the humor of it."

"Some of it," she amended.

He turned his lips into her palm. "You know I want you, Serena. I just can't—"

"I know," she said, her voice quiet.

He pinned her hands in his. "Come inside, Serena. I've got some things on my mind—one about your sister's coming out here, and two—" He broke off. "Two can wait. Come inside and…make me some coffee."

Coffee wasn't what he wanted, but he had to do something to get his mind off how soft she was, how good she smelled. His groin ached from wanting her. He longed to touch her, hear her voice cry out for him.

Neither of them spoke until the coffee was ready. Then he sipped the hot brew slowly and chose his words with care.

"Send for your sister now." Carleton absently stirred more sugar into the cup at his elbow, gauging the effect his suggestion had on her. "She can live here with you for the time being, until you recoup your losses and rebuild on the hill. By next fall, after the drive, you'll have another four hundred dollars."

"This old barn is too small. I don't want to cram Mary Irene into a place like this—she's better off in Stark County, in a real house with Aunt Letty."

"She's better off with you, and you know it. This place might be big enough for two. The loft is, as I remember."

Serena stared at him. The memory of that night in her loft was always with her. She was shaken that it had stayed with him, too.

"Send for Mary Irene," Carleton repeated. "If you need money—"

"No," she said, her voice uneven. "I have enough for that." She thought for a moment. "Carleton, do you really think—"

His steady gaze held hers. "I really think." He rose from the pine table. "How about going into town with me tomorrow morning? Alice needs some things at the mercantile and Marsh is down with his rheumatism. We could ride on to Deer Creek and wire—"

Serena leaped up from the table and threw her arms around his neck. She began to weep, and Carleton pulled her into his arms and let her cry it out. Only when she stopped her hiccupping sobs did he tip her chin up and cover her soft, wet mouth.

"Tomorrow morning," she murmured, when he released her. "How early?"

"Sunup." He kissed her again.

"Carleton?" she managed despite the buzzing in her head.

"Yeah, Sis?"

"Tell me the rest. The other thing you had on your mind."

"The other thing's about you. I want you to stay away from Lyle."

"I do stay away from him."

"I think he might have set your house on fire."

She jerked upright. "What? You can't be serious!" Fury boiled up inside her. "But why?"

"To drive you into marrying him. He wants the ranch. And you. He figures if he can bring you to your knees, you'll have him, just to save your skin."

Working to control her rage, she took three deep gulps of air. "And what do you figure?"

Carleton inhaled a long, long breath and released gradually. "I figure you deserve better than that."

"I already have better than that," she whispered against his cheek.

"Serena," he began, his voice gravelly. "I've said what I came to say, and if I stay…"

He sucked in a breath and stared up at the beams over his head. Above, in the loft, lay heaven. Forcing himself to step away from her warm, pliant body would be a kind of hell. He wondered which she would choose.

"Tell me to go," he whispered.

As if in answer, she moved in his arms. When he looked at her, she raised her arms and began to unbraid her hair.

"I don't want you to go," she breathed. She turned toward the ladder. "I want you to come upstairs."

It was hot and sweet, and he took his time. She arched her body under his, writhing as he moved his hands and tongue on her skin. She moved instinctively, abandoning herself to her inner needs with a primitive exultation she'd never dreamed possible. His fingers eased and probed, his tongue circled her nipples, then moved below her belly. It was ecstasy and torture when he touched her that way.

She reached for him, heard him gasp as her hand closed around him.

"Wait," he rasped.

She waited, motionless herself until his tongue began a deliberate, feathery flicking back and forth across her heated flesh. She moaned and then he was inside her, calling out her name while he thrust and withdrew and slowly thrust again.

She wanted it never to end. "Don't stop," she whispered. "Don't ever stop."

He slowed his motions. She felt his arms tremble as they supported his weight. She wound her legs around his back and tipped her hips to meet him. "Carleton," she moaned. *"Carleton!"*

Something within her broke free, pushed her over the edge into mindless pleasure. She clung to him, sobbing, until it was over, and then he drove deep inside her, stiffened for a split second, and convulsed with a hoarse cry. They lay together, their limbs entwined, until their breathing quieted.

"Did you plan this?" she asked after a time.

"No. I've thought about it a lot, but...no."

"Did you want it?"

He chuckled and tightened his arms around her. "Hell, Sis, I think that's pretty obvious, don't you?"

Serena smiled lazily. "Yes. Pretty obvious."

"Damnedest cup of coffee I ever had," he said dryly.

Serena rolled on top of him, pinned his body between her thighs and took a very gratifying revenge.

Chapter Twenty-Seven

Carleton was right, Serena thought as she made her way to the henhouse to gather the eggs. She should have sent for Mary Irene months ago, after the news came about Jessie. Now, faced with waiting until next year, when she could afford to rebuild her house, she could see how wrong she'd been to delay.

Do not waste the gifts of life, her mother had said. *Take what is offered and enjoy it before the season passes.*

Dressed for town in her split riding skirt and boots, she rounded the corner of the shed Thad had built to house her chickens. It was an hour before dawn, when she would ride into town with Carleton and wire the railway ticket to her sister—too early for Thad or anyone else to be stirring.

But why was the henhouse door unlatched? In her rush of joy at Carleton's suggested plan yesterday evening, had she forgotten to secure it?

She slowed her pace. The chickens clucked nervously from inside the structure, and all at once the door sagged open.

Her breath caught. Something, a predator, had gotten in. With caution, she tiptoed forward and reached for the latch.

A hand snaked out and fastened around her wrist like a

band of steel. "Thought you'd never get here, pretty lady."

"Lyle! What are you doing out here?"

"Waitin' for you." He shook his long blond hair out of his eyes and scanned her from head to toe with a calculating look. "Took your time gettin' here, but you sure do look nice."

Panic rose at his lazy, suggestive tone. "I'm on my way to town," she said quickly.

"No, you ain't. You're here in the henhouse. With me."

"Lyle, listen—"

"I don't want to listen, Serena. Or talk, neither." He shoved her against the rough board wall and pinned her body with his. "What I want is a lot quieter."

Serena fought to stay calm. She had the pistol in her skirt pocket. If she could just work her hand down—

"Don't move, honey," he muttered. "Just stand still and let me…"

Serena froze. He slid his hand under the bandanna knotted about her neck, then circled his forefinger around the top button of her shirt.

"Let me go, Lyle," she said, keeping her voice controlled. "This is wrong."

"Not if we get married after. What about that, Serena? You an' me?"

"No. Get out of my chicken house."

"Not yet, honey." He thrust his groin against her thigh. "Not yet."

She inched her right hand into her skirt pocket, touched the small revolver. How to cock it without letting him know?

Lyle shifted his weight and she brought the gun up inside her skirt, pulled back the hammer and jammed the barrel against his rib cage. "Back away from me, Lyle. Do it now, or I'll pull the trigger."

His light brown eyes widened, but he didn't move.

"Did you hear me?" She jabbed the revolver into his flesh. "Move away!"

"I hear you, honey." He grazed her cheek with the back of his knuckles. "You're bluffin'."

"Lyle, I'm warning you...."

He gave a soft laugh and dropped one hand onto her breast.

She squeezed the trigger.

The bullet struck him under the shoulder, in the fleshy part of his upper arm. Lyle reared backward and caught at the wound with his hand. Blood covered his fingers.

"Why, you damned little—" He flung himself on her, ripped her shirt open to expose her chemise.

Serena tried to fight him off, but he was too heavy. Even wounded, he was stronger than she, and he was quick. He rammed his fist down the front of her undergarment and closed his hand around her breast.

She cried out, struggled to twist out of his grasp. His breathing labored, he kicked her legs out from under her. When she landed on the straw-covered floor he fell on top of her. He rolled her over, loosening his belt.

"No!" she screamed. "Lyle, don't!"

He gave an ugly laugh. "Yes!" he hissed. "You're gonna be mine, now. This ranch and this chicken house and you—all gonna belong to me."

Pinning her between his legs, he tore open his fly. "Even that burned-out house on the hill you were buildin' is mine, now. I'm sorry I had to do that, but—like that bunch of your steers—it was the only way." He forced one knee between her thighs. "So just be good and let me—"

"Take your hands off her," a quiet, authoritative voice spoke from the doorway. "Get up," Carleton ordered.

Lyle didn't move. Serena clawed her way out from under him and rose on unsteady legs.

"Pick up your wages, Bartel, and clear out. You ever

set foot near her place again, or lay a hand on her anywhere in the state of Oregon, I'll kill you.''

Lyle stood up, buttoning his pants. Carleton pointed the gun barrel at the wall. ''Over there.'' The cowhand shambled to the spot indicated.

''You want to press charges, Serena?''

''N-no. The last thing I want is to ever see him again.''

The Double K owner gave a brisk nod. ''You heard her. Now get out.''

Shaking, Serena watched the lanky foreman plunge toward the door and disappear. His footsteps crunched away over the hard ground and suddenly her knees wobbled.

Carleton holstered his weapon and took a step toward her. ''Did he— Are you hurt?''

''No,'' she breathed. ''I'm all right. How did you know—?''

''Heard the chickens making a ruckus.''

''You're early for our trip to town—the sun's not up yet.''

''Actually, I'd say I was right on time.'' He glanced at the open henhouse door. ''I did some checking last night. Lyle had an empty kerosene tin stashed under his bunk.''

''He did burn my house down. He admitted it.''

''I heard.''

''And the…other things he said?'' She hesitated. ''Did you hear them?''

''I heard most of it. Put it out of your mind, Serena. Go inside and get warm. I'll clean up here.''

While Carleton swept up the blood-spattered straw, Serena went inside to wash up and change clothes. Within an hour Carleton was finished, and she was mounted and ready.

''Let's go,'' he said, his voice calm. ''Your sister's waiting for that railroad ticket.''

Calmer now, Serena stepped her mare after his gelding through the rye field.

"Think Mary Irene would like a pony this summer? That foal I brought yesterday is a little beauty."

"Carleton, I can't afford it."

"When's her birthday?"

"November." Unconsciously she scanned the road ahead for any sign of Lyle. Nothing met her gaze but a hawk swooping in the crisp morning air.

"You can afford it. You can pay me after the drive next fall." He flicked a look at her face, then opened the gate for her.

Serena knew he was making conversation to keep her mind off Lyle's assault. She stepped the mare through, watched him swing the gate to her ranch shut. "I owe you too much already. I'll never get out of debt."

"There is one way," he said quietly. "I've been meaning to bring it up, but the time never seemed just right."

"You advised me to avoid Lyle," she said with a wry smile. "I'm not sure I want to hear any more of your ideas."

Carleton rode beside her at the same slow pace for a full minute before he spoke. "My idea is for you to marry me."

Dumbstruck, Serena stared at him. "You can't marry me! You've already got your hands so full of responsibilities you don't take time to eat properly. On the trail drive, Cora told me—"

He snapped his reins. "Cora should mind her own damn business."

"Carleton, Alice doesn't like me. She's your stepdaughter, and she resents me."

"True, she does," he remarked, his tone noncommittal. "But that won't last."

Serena kneed her mount to keep pace with him. "Whatever makes you think so? Alice has hated me since the day I knocked on your front door. She's not going to change."

"Maybe. Maybe not."

Exasperated, Serena kicked the mare into a canter.

"She might be too busy to care," Carleton called after her.

"She's already too busy," Serena shouted over her shoulder. "The poor girl has her hands full with the baby and cooking for the hired hands. How can you suggest—"

"Thad's going to marry her."

She pulled the mare up short. "What? Thad? He is? How do you know?"

"He asked my permission."

A slow warmth crept over her. So after she'd talked with him at Christmas, Thad had finally wakened up to the situation. "Does Alice know about this?"

Carleton chuckled. "Alice has known since she was twelve years old."

"I mean has he asked her?"

"Dunno. I left them in the kitchen together. We'll see when we get back. Now, about you and me, Serena. We can live in the ranch house—all of us, Mary Irene and Sarah and you and me. And the cook I'm going to hire."

"And Alice?"

"Alice and Thad will build their own place. Thad's got a spot all picked out."

"I hadn't planned on ever—"

He reined to a halt, reached out and grabbed the mare's bridle. "I love you, Serena. Does that make a difference?"

Her heart swelled with joy. "Well, yes."

"And you love me. Leastways you did yesterday," he joked. "Don't know about today."

"Yes, I love you," she blurted. "You know I do. But... I must talk to Alice."

"Well, Sis," he said with the slightest rasp in his voice. "Could you do it pretty soon? You're keeping me up nights."

"I am?" The sense of power she felt made her giddy. She wrestled the bridle out of his hands and reined the mare away. "Guess we'd better hurry, then," she called back to him.

Carleton swore and started after her. They raced their mounts all the way to the telegraph office in Deer Creek.

"Alice," Serena began when the worn-looking young woman had poured her a cup of coffee. "We need to talk."

Alice clanked the enamelware pot back on the ranch house kitchen stove. "What about?" she snapped.

"About you and me," Serena said quietly. She sipped the bitter brew and reached for the sugar bowl. "About your father."

"My father! I'd have thought you'd want to speak about Thad, not my father."

"No, not Thad. Despite what you may think, Alice, your cousin is my foreman and nothing more."

"I see," the young woman said. Her tone indicated she didn't believe Serena's words. She circled her forefinger around the edge of her cup, a frown creasing her high forehead.

Serena took another sip of coffee. "What is it I have done that you dislike me so? Is it because I'm half—"

"You came out here," Alice interrupted. "Upset everything. And then Thad..." She clamped her jaw shut.

"Then Thad came to work for me," Serena finished. "He lives in your bunkhouse, though, as he did before. Eats with your hired hands. You must see a great deal of him."

"Not like before," Alice said slowly. "Now his concern is for you instead of—"

Serena nodded. "You're in love with him, aren't you?"

To her amazement, Alice's hazel eyes filled with tears. She stared down at her hands, cradling her cup.

"I've tried not to be," she said, her voice a low whisper. "Ever since I was eleven years old. He kissed me on my birthday that year. He was twelve. I guess I never got over it."

"Some things a woman remembers all her life," Serena said softly. She laid her sun-browned hand on Alice's pale one. The girl refused to meet her eyes, but she made no attempt to slide her fingers away.

"I don't feel much like a woman sometimes."

"It's been hard, hasn't it, since your mother died?" Serena observed, her tone matter-of-fact. "You've cooked and cleaned and cared for Sarah at the expense of your youth. Perhaps your father shouldn't have expected so much of you."

"I don't think Papa even noticed," Alice said wearily. "He was half-crazy after we buried Mama. Walked around in a fog. Oh, he ran the ranch all right, managed the hands and the stock, but…I don't know, inside he just folded into himself. He's better now, since the trail drive. He seems…almost happy sometimes."

Serena nodded. "He was pretty remote, I remember."

"He kept his pain locked inside, but I knew how he hurt. So, I just pitched in to carry us through."

"Thad," Serena ventured, "did the same for me, offered himself as my foreman because I needed help. But that's all he offered, Alice. Believe me."

"I do," Alice said in a small voice. "And I'm sorry I was so—I'm sorry for all of it."

"No lasting harm has been done." Serena smiled at the downcast girl across the table. "How old are you, Alice?"

"Eighteen. But that's not true, about no harm."

Serena's raised eyebrows tightened the skin of her forehead. "Not true? What do you mean?"

"I mean I talked Lyle into doing things—letting your hens out at night, cutting your clothesline after you'd done your wash. Other things." Her lips trembled. "I wanted you to go away. To leave Thad alone."

"Did you ask Lyle to burn down my new house?"

Alice's eyes widened. "No! Of course not! Oh, Serena, please, you must believe me! I asked Lyle to help me...discourage you, but I had no idea— Oh, you must hate me!"

"I don't hate you, Alice. I will admit I regret doing my laundry twice on those occasions, and fixing all that fence...."

Alice hung her head, her usually pale cheeks flaming. "You going to tell Pa?"

Serena shook her head. "No. But your father is the reason I wanted to talk with you. You see, Alice, I wondered if you disliked me because of my heritage. I'm half Modoc, or maybe you knew."

"I didn't know."

"My father was Jeremiah Hull, your Uncle Ben's deputy. Chief Black Eagle was my grandfather. My mother lived in the mountains near here years ago. Her name was Walks Dancing."

"I've heard she was the most beautiful woman in the territory. It doesn't make any difference that you're half Indian, Serena. Not to me, anyway. Why should it?"

"Because," Serena said quietly, "I want to marry your father."

Alice's face was a study. Surprise, confusion and relief warred in her eyes.

"Not Thad?" she whispered. "Papa?"

"Not Thad," Serena assured her. "Your father."

"Oh!" Air whooshed out of the young woman's lungs. *"Oh!"*

And then she smiled, her face lighting up from within. "I thought— Good gracious, I thought you and Lyle..."

"No," Serena said quietly. She replaced her cup on the saucer. "Would you mind?"

"Well, no. There's only three bedrooms upstairs, and I've turned one into a nursery for Sarah. Where will you sleep?" she blurted.

Serena bit back a laugh. "With your father."

Alice blushed scarlet. "Oh, of course. I wasn't thinking."

"You will no doubt marry someday, Alice."

"Oh, no. Not unless Thad— I can't get him to notice me, just my cooking!"

"He notices you. But a man's attention can be so subtle you miss it."

"I wish I could—" Alice broke off. She stared into her cup.

"You wish you could...?" Serena prompted.

"Fix myself up so I was really pretty. Beautiful, even. Like you."

Serena laughed. "You should have seen me on the drive. Beautiful I was not. I wasn't even clean!"

Alice sent her a shy smile. "Could you... I mean, the men—the hands and Mr. Appleby and Mr. Harker—they talk about you like you're a kind of princess."

"Men can be very shortsighted," Serena observed. Except for Carleton, she acknowledged, who searched beneath the surface for the real person underneath.

"Maybe," Alice pursued hesitantly, "you could advise me how to...um...attract Thad?"

Serena squeezed her hand. "Maybe. Now, let me take Sarah for an afternoon while you and Thad go...on a picnic. I think you might not need my help as much as you think."

She rose to leave, but Alice caught her hand. "Thank you, Serena." Tears swam at the edges of her lids. "Thank you for making my father happy, and for...everything else."

Chapter Twenty-Eight

Four weeks later, on the first day of spring, the morning stage pulled up in front of the Dixon House Hotel and a slim, dark-haired girl of thirteen stepped down onto the street.

"Mary Irene!" Serena broke away from Carleton and raced toward her sister.

"Sissy!" The girl threw herself into Serena's arms. "Oh, Sissy, it's been so long! I thought I'd never get here. After the train there was an old, bouncy stagecoach, and then another, and— Are there kittens, yet? Where does Amanda live? Can we visit soon? That must be Mr. Kearney. My heavens, he's so tall! Is he nice? He looks quite fierce, doesn't he? Why are you laughing, Sissy? Is my face smudged?"

"Darling girl," Serena choked. "Your face is perfectly beautiful. It's your busy tongue I'm laughing at."

Mary Irene wrinkled her nose. "What's wrong with it?" She stuck her tongue out as far as it would go and peered at it, her eyes crossing in the process.

Serena hugged her, smoothed her hand over her sister's soft dark curls and hugged her again. "You haven't changed a bit, Mye. Oh, I do love you. How I've missed you!"

A reflective look passed over Mary Irene's gray eyes. "You've changed, though, Serena. I could tell the minute I stepped off the stage and saw you standing there with him—Mr. Kearney. Is he why, Sissy?" She whispered the question and Serena had to smile.

"He looks awfully handsome," her sister continued in an undertone. "Is he nice? Do you kiss him? Does his mustache scratch? May *I* kiss him? I've always wanted—"

Serena laughed until tears choked her voice. Her dear, darling sister was here at last in Wildwood Valley and she wanted to see if Carleton's mustache scratched.

Oh, thank you, God. My cup is again running over!

The day after Alice and Thad spoke their wedding vows before Reverend Lindstrom in Wildwood Valley's tiny whitewashed church, Serena and Carleton were married at the Kearney ranch house. Assembled in the parlor were Ben and Jessamyn Kearney and their son, Jem, and neighboring ranchers Silas Appleby and Eli and Miriam Harker. Ranch hands Thorny, Hog, Snap, Rosy, the new Double K foreman and Marsh also attended.

Cora Boult and Amanda Frieder arranged flowers and made coffee. Serena's sister, Mary Irene, stood up with her. Ben stood up with Carleton, and a beaming Thad Kearney, newly married himself, gave the bride away.

During the ceremony, Cora sniffed audibly, along with Carleton's stepdaughter, Alice, and Jessamyn Kearney. Mary Irene watched it all with discerning dark eyes and smiled at baby Sarah on her lap.

Afterward, Alice and Cora served lemonade and Cora's special Wedding Tower cake—layers of applesauce, chocolate, and lemon cake iced with burnt sugar frosting and topped with pink roses fashioned of loaf sugar.

Thorny honked into his pocket handkerchief while Hog and Rosy kissed the bride, pumped the groom's hand and then kissed the bride again. Snap refused to kiss anyone, but shook Carleton's hand with rough affection, and when

Eli Harker brought out his fiddle, the stocky wrangler asked Cora for a waltz.

Serena caught Carleton's gaze across the crowded parlor as the music, a Scottish reel, soared over the buzz of human voices. His smoky blue eyes held hers with an unspoken message.

From this day forth, we are one family, one flesh.

Yes, her mind echoed. She loved him, this man who had rebuilt her faith in herself and her trust in people, who had pointed the way to her future. She could not imagine a life without him.

She smiled at her husband and thought irrationally of her sister's question. *When you kiss him, does his mustache scratch?*

She'd never noticed.

At Carleton's now-questioning look, she moved toward him, intent on finding out.

And in an unnoticed corner of the room, Jem Kearney took a long, appreciative look at Mary Irene Hull and bolted into manhood.

* * * * *

Author's Note

Heroines depicted in many Hollywood western films erroneously suggest that women in the Old West were delicate, inept and occasionally witless visions in starched ruffles and perfect makeup. Contrary to that image, women in the West were hardy, capable and intelligent. In addition to keeping house, bearing babies and fighting occasional prairie fires alongside their men, a number of women also ran ranches, newspapers and other business enterprises with skill and courage.

The idea for Serena's taking on the Lost Acres Ranch came from an 1894 photograph of the two Becker sisters of San Luis Valley, California. Dressed in long skirts, straw hats and leather gloves, the women are branding cattle on their Rio Grande Ranch. In the photograph, one sister has the calf's front legs secured with her rope; the other sister stands poised with the hot branding iron.

Helen Wiser Stewart was another example of the frontier woman's intrepid spirit. Upon the death of her husband, she kept her Nevada ranch, managing it so well for the next twenty years buying and selling cattle, raising crops and acquiring more land that she became the largest landowner in Lincoln County, Nevada, with holdings of over two thousand acres.

Other women, such as Elinore Pruitt Stewart, homesteaded land in Burnt Fork, Wyoming, alone and under her own name.

There are no doubt thousands of similar instances of women's bravery and courage about which we will never know.

Source: *Women of the West,* by Cathy Luchetti and Carol Olwell, Antelope Island Press, St. George, Utah, 1982.

Three-time
RITA Award winner

Cheryl
Reavis

is back.

HARRIGAN'S
BRIDE

Available in November 1998 from
Harlequin Historicals

Don't miss it.

Available at your favorite retail outlet.

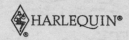

Not The Same Old Story!

Exciting, glamorous romance stories that take readers around the world.

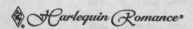

Sparkling, fresh and tender love stories that bring you pure romance.

Bold and adventurous—Temptation is strong women, bad boys, great sex!

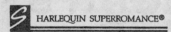

Provocative and realistic stories that celebrate life and love.

Contemporary fairy tales—where anything is possible and where dreams come true.

Heart-stopping, suspenseful adventures that combine the best of romance and mystery.

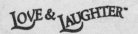

Humorous and romantic stories that capture the lighter side of love.

What do you want for Christmas?

A DADDY FOR CHRISTMAS

'Tis the season for wishes and dreams that come true. This November, follow three handsome but lonely Scrooges as they learn to believe in the magic of the season when they meet the *right* family, in *A Daddy for Christmas*.

MERRY CHRISTMAS, BABY
by Pamela Browning

THE NUTCRACKER PRINCE
by Rebecca Winters

THE BABY AND THE BODYGUARD
by Jule McBride

Available November 1998
wherever Harlequin and Silhouette books are sold.

CHRISTMAS Treats

PENNY JORDAN,

DAY LECLAIRE &
LINDSAY ARMSTRONG

bring you the best of Christmas romance
in this wonderful holiday collection where
friends and family gather to celebrate
the holidays and make romantic wishes
come true.

Christmas Treats is available in November 1998,
at your favorite retail store.

HARLEQUIN®
Makes any time special ™

COMING NEXT MONTH FROM

HARLEQUIN HISTORICALS